A BLACK

HOLE in

NEASDEN

DAVID SUTHERLAND

For Jasper

Scholastic Children's Books,
Commonwealth House, 1-19 New Oxford Street,
London, WC1A 1NU, UK
a division of Scholastic Ltd
London ~ New York ~ Toronto ~ Sydney ~ Auckland
Mexico City ~ New Delhi ~ Hong Kong

First published in the UK by Scholastic Ltd, 2002

Copyright © David Sutherland, 2002

ISBN 0 439 99440 3

Typeset by M Rules
Printed by Cox and Wyman Ltd, Reading, Berks

10 9 8 7 6 5 4 3 2 1

CHAPTER one

Three pearl-white beach balls drifted silently across the lawn. Looking down from above, Jack left off coiling his bungee cord and followed them with his eyes. Gracefully they rose up and over the first line of trees, almost as high as the top of the tower. For a moment they hung there, glowing golden in the early light, then one by one they pushed their way down through the canopy and vanished into the vastness of the jungle.

Why three? Must have been a lot of post.

He continued to gather the cord into big snaky loops. He peered over the edge. He knew the height of the tower and he knew his own height. He knew the length of the cord and he knew just how much it would stretch. Never having been a Boy Scout, he was less sure about the knots involved.

But apart from that there shouldn't have been a problem.

Why don't I ever get any post?

Jutting out from the edge of the roof was a boom that had been used to hoist heavy furniture to the upper floors. On the end of it was a hook where the pulley had hung. The bungee cord was blue and Jack tied a loop in one end. He yanked it tight; it seemed to hold well enough. Lying flat on his stomach, he extended himself out along the boom and hung the loop over the hook. Seven floors below was a grassy garden. The white table and chairs looked like something belonging to a doll's house.

Smiling to himself, he slid backwards off the boom and sat cross-legged while he tied the other end of the cord around his ankle. It took him a while to get the knot right; his first two attempts slipped, but the third held reasonably well.

He stepped up to the edge, shook loose the coiled cord and let it drop. It hung in a long "U" about a third of the way to the ground. Scowling, the boy rubbed his nose. He would have to jump absolutely straight down, so as not to swing in and hit the wall on the way back up. That was very important. He decided to hang from the end of the boom and drop from there. He did a little jogging on the spot to warm up. He stretched his arms and rotated his shoulders. Slowly he edged out on to the boom again with nothing beneath him but air. He checked that the loop was secure on the hook.

OK . . . this is it.

Locking his ankles, he leaned to one side, swung slowly around and hung upside-down like a tree sloth. The beam was I-shaped and he gripped the bottom of the "I" with his fingers. Hanging there, he looked up at the cloudless mauve sky. He tilted his head backwards and scanned the horizon upside down. He felt giddy and dizzy and couldn't help but laugh for the sheer madness of what he was doing. He released his legs and let them dangle below. The loop of blue cord trailed down and then up again, swaying a little in the breeze. He closed his eyes. He was as ready as he would ever be. . .

Just then, a dog barked very nearby. The boy opened his eyes. A brown-and-white head appeared at the edge of the tower.

"Yarf! Yarf!"

The boy groaned.

"Duncan, for heaven's sake, not now! Can't you see I'm busy? What are you doing up here?"

Apparently the dog wanted to ask the same question. "Yarf! Yarf!" he repeated, jumping up and down in a uniquely canine expression of urgency and importance.

3

Jack stared at the dog and adjusted his grip. "Don't distract me! Do you want me to fall and break my neck?"

"Rrrarfrarfrarf! *Yarrf!*"

"Go away!"

Disobediently, the dog sat down to watch. The boy's legs dangled freely beneath him and he altered his grip again to relieve his aching fingers. He looked down at the tiny garden table. It suddenly seemed an awfully long way to fall. He thought about the dodgy knot around his ankle. He knew it was completely crazy. If he had been honest, he would have had to admit that the interruption was not entirely unwelcome. Of course, he couldn't let on that to Duncan.

"Now you've completely ruined my concentration!" he cried indignantly and, swinging his feet forward, he walked a few steps up the wall and got one leg over the top. He clambered back on to the beam, turned to straddle it and sat facing the dog.

"So. What's up then? What is it?"

"Rrarfrarfrarrf yarf!"

He reached out to ruffle the dog's fur.

"Speak! Speak to me!"

"Rarf rarf!"

The dog cocked its head from side to side. His sharp black eyes focused hard. Clearly it had a lot to say. It yapped more plaintively. The boy shrugged and shook his head.

"*Yarrf?*"

"C'mon boy, you can do it!"

"*Rrr* . . . yes, of course I can do it, you pillock," the dog said finally. "I just thought you might have got the hang of Terrier by now. Obviously too much to expect. What are you doing up here?"

"What am *I* doing up here? Bungee jumping: you tie a rope around your leg and it stops you from hitting the ground. It's great. You wouldn't like it."

The dog peered over the edge, then looked at the rope.

"You're right there. How do you get back up? After you jump and you're hanging upside down by one ankle?"

"What do you mean, *how do you get. . .?*"

Jack stared dumbly at the dog. He hadn't actually thought of that. He clambered on to the flat roof and began coiling the cord again.

"OK, clever-clogs," he demanded. "What on Earth did you come to tell me?"

Duncan curled his lip and shook his head. He had never had a very high opinion of humans.

"We're not *on* Earth, rrr-emember?"

Momentarily sidetracked by this delightful thought, Jack paused to scan the sea of rainforest that surrounded the tower on all sides. It was wild and immense and beautifully untouched, slightly surreal under the violet sky. In the west, the sun had just appeared above the horizon, bringing the scene alive with colour: acres of green and gold, splashes of yellow, vermilion, turquoise. . . A dawn chorus of birds and who-knows-what-else racketed from the treetops.

Duncan scratched behind his ear, had a quick gnaw at his hind leg, stood, shook himself down and pronounced curtly: "You have a letter."

"*A letter?* What do you mean? An Earth letter?"

"Not an Earth letter. It's from the Prrr-incess of Tau Ceti. Something about a party. A once-in-a-lifetime, mega-rave sort of party."

Jack was suddenly very interested. He turned to face the dog.

"Princess of who? What party? Since when do you read my mail?"

"I do not *rrread* your mail," Duncan cried. He put his nose in the air and pronounced in a highly affected manner: "I simply happen to have an *acute* sense of smell. And this envelope *smells* like a party invitation. If you're not interested, then clearly I needn't have bothered you."

With that, the dog trotted across to the other side of the roof where a semicircular opening exposed a deep lift shaft. There were no lifts as such but, above the hole, a metal frame supported a pulley system that controlled four thick, vertical ropes about a metre apart. Leaping across the void, the dog latched neatly on to one of them, wrapping tail and legs around it. This trick had taken some practice, but Duncan had never been daunted by the lack of an opposable thumb.

He barked into the abyss, "*Rrarrf!* Henry? You can take me down now."

A hollow voice echoed up out of the depths, "*Right away, Mr Duncan.*"

There was a distant whirring and creaking, a *clunk* and a whistle and all four ropes began moving simultaneously: two up and two down. As the dog disappeared below roof level, Jack shouted, "I'm coming too, Henry!" and, slinging the coil of rope over one shoulder, he made a heroic leap and grabbed the other going-down rope.

This extra weight might have caused Henry some difficulty in regulating their speed of descent, had it not been for Jack's elderly Aunt Agnes, who happened to join one of the going-up ropes at more or less the same time, thus providing a little counter-balance.

"Hello," she called, looking up. "Is that you, Jack? You're up early."

"That's Duncan. I'm Jack over here."

"Oh. So you are. It's only just gone April, you know. Straight back to bed for me."

"Yeah, right . . . April is pretty early. Want me to wake you up in a few months?"

Auntie Agnes passed up between Jack and Duncan, ignoring them both. At the top of the lift shaft the un-oiled pulleys squealed and she could have sworn it was a choir of angels.

"Oh! They're singing again! Can you hear them, Jack? I'm going to heaven this time. *Up up up!* I never liked this planet, you know. But – oh. . ."

She looked down again, perplexed, as if only just realizing something. Her voice fell. "I haven't died yet, have I. Have I? Oh dear . . . *but don't you go looking up my nightie when I'm on the ropes!* I saw you! You'll grow hair on the palms of your hands, you will."

Jack groaned and looked away and the rope carried Agnes aloft, her voice trailing away through the upper floors of the tower. A moment later, boy and dog arrived at the ground floor and the ropes creaked to a halt. They stepped into a vast, round room, over ten metres across, with half the curved wall made of glass. It served as the kitchen, dining, sitting and general-hanging-around-in room. To the left of the lifts, an open-plan cooking area was demarcated by a row of yellow cupboards that arched gently into the centre. To the right, the wall was windowless but contained two heavy doors: one black and one white. Directly across from the

8

white one were double French doors that led down some steps to the garden.

Duncan headed straight for a leather armchair on the far side. He jumped up, turned three circles then parked himself with his head on crossed paws. In a sunny spot opposite, a man sat reading at a large round table.

Jack chucked the bungee rope on the floor and called, "Hello father-person." Rummaging in a cupboard, he came up with a bowl, spoon, cereal and some milk substitute apparently made from celery.

"Did I get a letter or something?"

Professor Cornelius Plant surfaced from his book slowly, like a diver returning from the bottom of the sea. Peering up through Buddy Holly glasses, he mumbled weakly, "Hmm. Morning. Sleep well?"

"Yeah sure. I've been up for ages. Did I get a letter?"

Jack put his breakfast things on the table and sat down. His father pursed his lips and thought at the ceiling. At forty-eight he was really too young to be a professor. In fact, until recently, when he discovered a black hole under his rhododendron and developed a mild obsession about garden tools, he had been a part-time philosophy lecturer at Neasden Polytechnic. He had achieved a certain notoriety there for his controversial work on grommets[1].

"Hmm . . . *a letter*," he pondered. "Now, surely if you had *got* a letter, then you would indeed *have* a letter, would you not? But as you do not seem to *have* a letter, one must conclude that you did not yet *get* a letter. Obvious, when you think about it. Shall we go over that again?"

It is a well-known fact that philosophy lecturers (and grommet experts even more so), often find it impossible to give a straight answer to anything. He smiled rather smugly and turned back to his book, adding, "You must learn to speak precisely. Say what you mean."

Jack leaned his head on one hand with an intensely bored expression and groaned to himself, *Why me? Why this family? Why so difficult?*

"Yeah, so did I get a letter or not?"

Professor Plant went on with his reading. His black hair parted in the centre and hung in long, lank waves beyond his collar. He had some-how never stopped looking like a student — a

1 Grommet: a unique type of rubber washer typically used as an electrical insulator and analysed in depth by Cornelius Plant as profound metaphor of the human condition. His books include his (failed) PhD thesis, *Grommets Throughout History; a Retrospective* (1992); his epistemological treatise, *Why is a Grommet?* (1994) and perhaps most importantly, *The Way of the Grommet* (1998); all available from Neasden Polytechnic Press for surprisingly little money.

somewhat lost student. His skin was pale, as though the only colour he ever got was from the light in the refrigerator. In recent months, he had had no such refrigerator. His lips moved silently as he read. Jack tapped his thumb and waited one full minute.

"*DAD!?*"

Jack's father looked up again, as if seeing his son for the first time that day.

"Hello. *What?* What is it?"

Enunciating very carefully, Jack spoke as if to a complete idiot, which he sometimes felt was the case: "A letter . . . *in an envelope?* Rectangular? About so big with paper inside? My name on it, maybe?"

His father stared at him for five seconds with no expression whatsoever. His small grey eyes had the disturbing faculty of never blinking.

"Oh . . . yes," he said. "I think there was something. Now that you mention it."

He turned back to his book and read a bit more. He reached the bottom of the page. He turned the page. Finally, without looking up, he put his hand in his shirt pocket and produced a small blue envelope. He handed it to his son.

Jack sighed and took it from him. On the front, his name alone was written in elaborate, calligraphic handwriting. Something like a coat of arms was displayed in the top left corner. Jack opened it carefully. Sitting up on the sofa, Duncan sniffed and craned his neck for a better view.

Inside was a card. The card read:

In Celebration of Nothing in Particular
Her Very Royal Highness, Princess of Tau Ceti
Invites You to the Palace for a
Once-in-a-Lifetime, Utterly-Mega-Monster-Rave
From Any Time until Whenever. . .

On the back of the card was a map, supposedly showing how to get to the palace. Under the map was written:

John Wayne Memorial Door Prize: ᛘᚢᚦ

"Well? Was I rrr-ight?"

Jack turned to Duncan in astonishment.

"Almost word for word! How do you do that?"

The dog shrugged and shook his head. "Humans are *so limited*."

"But you missed the bit about the door prize."

"*Rrrf.* Only because I didn't sniff that side."

"The answer is no," Jack's father pronounced calmly, turning another page of his book. He had the irritating habit of paying attention at all the wrong times.

"*What?* Why not? I haven't even asked yet."

"So, ask."

"Can I go to this party later?"

"No."

"But why not?!"

"Show me."

Professor Plant held out his hand. Jack gave him the card. His father studied it for a few moments.

"Absolutely out of the question."

He slipped the card into the back of his book, reached for the cereal (also made from celery) and poured some into his bowl. Jack slumped in his chair and frowned intensely. It was so infuriating . . . *so typical!* The only really exciting thing to have happened for ages and he wasn't allowed to go.

(What he meant, of course, was – if you didn't count travelling through a black hole to another galaxy, living in a tower in the middle of the jungle where the concept of school did not exist and where his dog, for some little-understood reason, had suddenly become capable of speech – if you didn't count any of *that,* then yes, this party could be the biggest thing ever.)

He could not believe he wasn't going. He toyed with his untouched cereal and tapped the heel of his foot in a way that he knew got on his father's nerves. He scowled vigorously. The father-person had given the wrong answer; that's all there was to it. He drummed his fingers, trying to work out how he might expose this error. His father was not immune to reason. He was a philosopher after all. It was just a matter of finding the *right* reason.

"There must have been quite a lot of post. Did Fiz get an invite?" Jack asked, trying to reopen the subject. He knew that if a conversation with his father lapsed for more than thirty seconds, the chance of getting it going again was like jump-starting a fifty-ton lorry.

"Hmm? No. The rest was for me."

The dialogue was about to die again. Jack had to make his bid before his father got his nose stuck back in his book.

Huffing a little, he cleared his throat and launched: "Dad, listen, about this invitation, I mean, I know you think that teenage parties are just a lot of mindless, self-indulgent pleasure-seeking with flashing lights and over-sexed girls in skimpy clothes, wildly gyrating to loud and tuneless music – and from a certain point of view, that is partly true. But it's not always like that, and what I had in mind was to go as a sort of Ambassador for Planet Earth. You know, a chance to do my part to further the cause of peace and goodwill throughout the universe."

Duncan snorted, rolled on to his back and almost exploded with repressed doggy laughter. Jack's father looked up with one eyebrow trying to escape off the top of his face.

"Ambassador for Planet Earth? *You?* Heaven help Planet Earth. Anyway, the universe is at peace. Everywhere except the Earth."

Jack grimaced and continued: "Yeah, OK, but we haven't been here very long and I think there are a lot of misconceptions about our planet that need to be clarified. We're obviously deeply misunderstood. I feel it's my duty to help build some *cross-cultural bridges.* By attending this routine social function – which will probably be really dull and tedious – I would at least be helping to create a sense of community: you know, people coming together, sharing, caring, overcoming their differences and all that. I feel it's my responsibility as a citizen of the universe to go to this party."

Duncan spluttered again and the blank look on his dad's face told Jack he'd better change course.

"Right. Well, the other thing I was thinking," he went on, barely pausing for breath, "was, you know how Royal families are all so hopelessly neurotic and socially de-skilled and everything? Well, I don't think we should hold that against them. It would be really rude and prejudicial of me not to go to this party just because the girl is, you know, a *princess* and a bit *disadvantaged.* I think that coming from a healthy and well-balanced family like our own, I may be able to help her towards a fuller, more normal and rewarding life."

Jack's father finished his cereal and pushed the bowl away. He stared at it, wondering why everything had to taste of celery. He looked at his son: *Fifteen years old . . . dreadful age to be. All those hormones coursing about. Surely Kant must have written something about adolescence? No, probably not. Philosophers always bottle out on the really hard stuff. Ethics, epistemology, the existence of God — such things pale into insignificance compared to a teenager with a party crisis.*

The professor sighed again and brought the tips of his fingers together very lightly, just under his chin. He removed the invitation from the back of his book. He studied it for another five seconds and made a concerted effort to apply himself to the subject.

"We don't know anything about these people. She might not even *be* a people," he said. "Have you thought about that?"

"Of course. That's the whole point. We've been living here for three months and I haven't met a single alien. Not even a little one. You're always saying how there's no crime or violence or anything like that here; it's one of the main reasons you wanted to move!"

"Yes, that's true, but—"

"So what is the problem then? This is the first real contact we've had since we got here!"

The professor paused. He scratched his head and pushed his glasses up on his nose.

Probably harmless enough, he told himself. *Could even be fun, I suppose. Fun with aliens. Good aliens. Nice aliens. Father must be a colleague; some philosopher-king of the old school. What could be the harm in it? Kids need a social life. I went to a party once myself . . . that what's-her-name was there . . . Margaret Something: red hair, stutter, glasses taped up in the middle . . . locked herself in the loo for six hours. I think she may have fancied me . . . wonder what ever became of — ?*

"*DAD!*" cried Jack.

"Eh? What?"

"*The party,*" Jack nudged gently. "Can I go or not?"

"Hmm . . . party . . . well, hmm. You really want to go?"

Jack nodded with careful eagerness. It was a delicate moment. He could faintly smell victory. It was absolutely crucial to say as little as possible. The professor sighed. He looked again at each side of the invitation. He scratched his head.

"Oh, all right, you can go then."

He handed the card back to his son.

YES! Jack shouted to himself.

"But only if your sister says she'll go with you."

NO! The sweet smell of success was instantly tainted by the sour stink of certain failure.

"Dad! You know Fiz never wants to go anywhere or do anything – especially not since we moved!"

Professor Plant picked up the empty bowls and started towards the sink.

"Well, it might be good for her to get out a bit more. Make some new friends."

"*New friends?* She never had any old friends."

"It's my last word on the subject. If Fenella says she'll go with you, then you can go. If not, then not. But that's final."

"Never happen," Jack groaned.

His father began washing up the breakfast things and Duncan stirred on the sofa.

"Shouldn't rrr-eally be a prrr-oblem," he said quietly.

"Oh, glad you think so," Jack snorted. "It'd be easier to get Aunt Aggie into the SAS than to get Fiz to go to a party."

Duncan yawned and licked his lips.

"I think you're missing something. I don't envisage a prrr-oblem," he repeated.

Just then, the rope lifts creaked into life.

"That's probably her now," Jack muttered.

But no sooner had he said this, than a blood-stopping, air-splitting scream shrilled down the lift shaft. Professor Plant froze, listening, his hands dripping wet.

The hysterical shrieking slowly gave way to words that sounded something like: "LET GO OF MY HAND, YOU GHASTLY MACHINE!

HENRY? LET GO, I SAY!! YOU'RE CRUSHING MY FINGERS!"

Jack's father ran to the lift shaft and looked up. Agnes was on the far-left rope with her hand stuck in the pulley at the top.

"HENRY!" he shouted. "*STOP!* Reverse!"

The ropes immediately changed direction and, as they did, the scream of pain and anger became one of terror as poor Agnes lost her grip and plummeted the full length of the lift shaft. A tonsil-wobbling, throat-throbbing, horror-panic burst from her lungs. It grew in an impressive crescendo and as she streaked past the opening to the kitchen, Jack was just able to register a ghostly-white flapping and a blur of red lipstick –

– then a subdued *flump, SPROINNG!* as she hit the safety trampoline. This resulted in her flying back *up* the lift shaft just as far as the kitchen. The professor caught her in both arms without really trying. He turned around and set her down gently on the floor, propping her up against the cupboards. Jack and Duncan rushed over.

Agnes looked up at them. Pencilled eyebrows arched unevenly over thick blue eye shadow. Her hair fell in tired, grey waves and a long Bambi night-dress left only her bare feet and ankles exposed. She had stopped screaming, but her mouth was still moving of its own accord. Her lipstick was badly smudged. Her face was whiter than her nightie. Bambi too looked very shaken. Agnes looked all around, clearly wondering where the kitchen had suddenly come from.

"Is that you, Corny?" she whimpered.

It was hard to tell which of them was more distressed. Grommet experts tend to be less than reliable in a crisis.

"Yes, Agnes, it's me."

"You're not dead, are you?"

"No, I'm not dead."

Agnes looked away, slightly disappointed.

"So I'm not in heaven, then?"

"No, you're not in heaven. Nor the other place either. I think you got on the up rope when you meant to go down. Is that what happened?"

Agnes thought about this carefully and disagreed.

"No, Corny. Heaven is up. I want to go up to heaven. With the angels."

"Yes, well, the rope lift doesn't go that far. Let's take a look at your hand."

It was badly bruised and already swollen. The professor examined it as if it were a beanbag.

"I hope you haven't broken anything," he said. He was actually referring to the pulley system but Duncan pushed his nose forward and sniffed.

"Thrrr-ee minor frrr-actures with internal bleeding," he reported. "Damage to the first and second knuckle, severe swelling and tearrr-ing of the ligaments. Multiple external contusions with—"

The professor turned his eyeball-drying gaze on the dog.

"Thank you for that expert diagnosis, Duncan, but I really think Agnes ought to see a doctor."

Duncan huffed and trotted back to his armchair with his nose in the air.

"Just trrr-ying to be helpful."

"I'll have to take her to Emergency, I guess," Jack's dad muttered, virtually talking to himself. "Can you stand, Agnes?"

His sister's head suddenly retreated and she screwed her face into an expression of utter repugnance.

"Oh, I never could stand Agnes!" she blurted in alarm. "Horrible woman! Always making faces at me. She wears too much make-up and I told her so. Who does she think she is? At her age!"

Jack and his father helped her to get up.

"Are you taking her to hospital in London?" Jack asked.

"Have to. No one told me what to do in an emergency. Agnes, come sit over here for a minute while I get your things ready."

Jack sat at the dining table with his aunt as his father disappeared up the lift shaft.

"Am I going to London?" she asked.

"Looks that way. The doctors are going to fix your hand as good as new."

"*Rrr* . . . doctorr-rrs," Duncan growled. "What do they know? You want to lick that hand, Agnes. Lick it to keep it clean. Best thing for it."

Agnes licked her hand.

"It'll be nice to see London again," she said dreamily. "I never liked this planet, you know. Don't you miss London? Don't you miss the telly and the footie and Mr Carlisle's sticky buns?" A far-away look descended over Agnes. "He puts ever so many raisins in them," she added dreamily.

Sticky buns were not exactly at the top of Jack's list, but he wouldn't have minded knowing how Arsenal were doing. They must be well into the new season. He missed his mates as well, but for the time being, having no school and a talking dog seemed a pretty good trade-off.

"It'll be cold and wet in London I expect," he replied, just to change the subject.

Agnes eyed him curiously then transferred her gaze to the sun-drenched garden. She could never get her mind around the idea that the new planet had totally different seasons and climate. The days were even more confusing. It was light for about forty hours and then dark for only three. Everyone found it hard to know when to sleep. Initially they had stubbornly tried to keep to

London time, but that often meant getting up as the sun was going down or vice versa. At the end of three months each of them had worked out their own waking and sleeping rhythms, which were surprisingly varied. Almost no one slept at the same time and there was always someone up wandering about.

Jack's father reappeared, carrying a small sports bag.

"Come on then," he called. "We'd better get going. Any idea what time it is on Earth?"

"Feels like a Wednesday to me," Agnes offered.

Jack shrugged and helped her over to the door where his father was waiting.

"Are you ready? Better put your coat on just in case. All set? Why are you licking your hand? Never mind. Let's go."

Professor Plant carefully unlocked the black door. It was about fifteen centimetres thick and made of extremely rare and strange *Exotic Matter*, the only material capable of withstanding the colossal gravitational force created by a black hole. He slid it to one side. Instantly the room darkened as all the light was sucked out of the immediate vicinity. There was also a great clattering and crashing as half the breakfast dishes went with it. Jack pressed himself against the door as it slid closed again automatically.

His father and Auntie Agnes were gone.

23

CHAPTER two

Here is a picture of Jack Plant at the age of five; see him playing by himself in the front room of a big Georgian house in Islington? The house belongs to his mother. There she is, coming through the door after a hard day's work, briefcase in hand and visibly knackered, but immaculately turned out in her dark-grey, corporate-lawyer's suit. See Jack's dad at the table in the background, poring over a mountain of papers? He is working on his (failed) doctoral thesis. See Jack's big sister Fenella slouching at the other end of the table, arms folded, bored out of her mind and scowling at the salt cellar?

Jack frequently overhears his parents rowing. Jack's mum thinks his dad is a dreamer. She thinks he's totally unpractical. She cannot believe she has married a man obsessed with little rubber washers.

He never used to be like that, she says. Jack's dad thinks his mum is a workaholic who spends all her time helping rich people to get richer and never has time for the more subtle joys of life. Like her own children, for example. She never used to be like that, he says.

In this next picture we see Jack at the age of eight, lying in bed. It is nine o'clock and he's trying to stay awake until his mother gets home. She leaves the house so early in the morning and gets home so late that he hasn't seen her all week. At last, the front door bangs . . . he hears footsteps on the stairs . . . his door-handle is turning . . . the door opens . . . but when his mother comes in to say goodnight, Jack pretends to be asleep, just to punish her.

His parents hardly seem to talk to each other these days.

This last snap was taken when Jack was ten. He and Fenella are in the garden of a much smaller house in Neasden, north-west London. See Auntie Agnes sitting in the tree behind them? She's singing "I've Got a Lovely Bunch of Coconuts" at the top of her lungs. Jack is smiling. He has always loved his mad auntie. Fenella is mortified and trying to pretend it's not happening. Gran is there too, over on the right, doing her aerobics workout.

The house in Neasden belongs to their father,

but Gran and Auntie Agnes have lived in it for many years. Now they all live there together. Mum has stayed in Islington on her own.

And that's how it was for nearly five years. No one even so much as dreamed of leaving the planet. Moving across London had been traumatic enough. And it wasn't as if life on Earth had been all that bad. There was no more than the usual amount of crime and poverty, pollution, disease, rape, murder, famine, drug abuse, child abuse, disasters (natural and unnatural), wars (civil and uncivil), refugees, homelessness, unemployment, racism, terrorism, global warming, the slaughter of endangered species, destruction of the environment, genetically modified cornflakes, people-being-really-horrible-to-each-other. . .

But as such things tend to affect only a few insignificant billions of people, they mostly faded into the background. Everyone knew there were problems but, generally speaking, they didn't think about it too much. That was only natural. They had *their own* problems to worry about, which were, quite naturally, far more urgent and important.

Jack's father took a part-time job as a philosophy lecturer and was busy researching a new book. Gran commuted back and forth to Hollywood where she had a supporting role in a big Spielberg film. Agnes launched a passionate correspondence with the Swiss Ministry of Food and Agriculture, concerning the declining number of holes in their cheeses. . .

Life went on. After all, it takes a pretty big crisis to start you thinking about leaving the planet. Not something you do for no reason. If it hadn't been for the disappearing garden tools, they would probably all have just stayed in Neasden.

Cornelius Plant had never especially liked gardening. The idea of things growing in the dirty earth was much too practical and concrete for him. It meant going outside. But as his mother travelled a great deal and Agnes wouldn't have known a *Sweet William* if it stood up in her soup, the upkeep of the garden fell to him.

But not even this total lack of interest could account for the astounding number of trowels and forks and secateurs he lost. One minute they were there beside him in the grass – the next minute they were gone. He started buying them in bulk. At first it was more puzzling than alarming. He also began to notice that the lawn never needed raking; all the loose grass and leaves simply disappeared down a little hole under the rhododendron. This was so convenient that he never really questioned it. He even considered that perhaps all gardens were designed like that now . . . some new central disposal system installed by the council. What was more strange, however, was that no matter how sunny the day was, his garden always seemed slightly dim compared to the neighbours' gardens. There simply wasn't as much light.

For years, Cornelius kept these observations to himself. He had other far deeper mysteries to pursue. It was only through a chance conversation with a colleague at the Poly (Fat Bernard in astrophysics), that he began to suspect that the hole beneath his rhododendron might actually be rather *black*.

He had heard of black holes before of course. He knew that anyone falling into one would initially be elongated beyond the wildest dreams of professional basketball, then reduced to something like a squashed bug on the windscreen of eternity. This was due to the phenomenal gravitational force they exert.

What he did not know (and was soon to learn), was that a rotating black hole, consisting of extremely rare and strange *Exotic Matter,* could become what is known as a wormhole: a negotiable open passage which, instead of pulverizing you, could actually fling you back out of a *white hole* on the other side. And because of the way intense gravity *bends space,* such a wormhole would be a sort of short cut through to another part of the universe. Instead of travelling all those tedious light-years the long way around, you make a nip and a tuck in space-time and pull the other side nearer to you. Simple.

All of this was neatly explained by Fat Bernard in astrophysics. He also explained that all prevailing theories tended towards the opinion that black holes were more likely to be found in the extreme depths of space than in the London suburbs.

"So, have they ever found one then?" Cornelius asked innocently.

"One what?"

"A black hole. In the extreme depths of space."

"Er, no. Not really. We're not a hundred per cent sure they exist."

Now, to a man of more flexible intellect, unburdened by the narrow confines of mathematics, this opened up the possibility that the boffins had simply been looking in the wrong place. But when Cornelius suggested as much, his colleague gave a pained look.

"Listen, if you had a black hole in your garden — even a little one — all of north London and then some would have been turned inside out and swallowed up long ago. Still, I wouldn't go near it if I were you. You might ring the council pest control, but no one knows much about these things. Highly theoretical."

Cornelius nodded sensibly. He had no particular

desire to become Spaghetti Bolognese and he resolved to put some good stout planks across the hole that very weekend.

But when the time came to do it, he hesitated. . .

Something bothered him. Chewing his thumbnail, he stood gazing at the mysterious hole. He got down on his hands and knees and peered under the rhododendron. There was certainly a strong *sucking* sensation, as if someone had buried a very big vacuum cleaner and left it running. He looked at the planks he had prepared and a terrible sense of loss came over him. A potentially rewarding avenue of investigation was being left totally unexplored. He stood up and hooked his hair behind his ears. He pushed his glasses up on his nose. He moved his mouth around, test-driving various expressions of dissatisfaction.

Cornelius Plant was not adventurous by nature. His was a world of the intellect; a world of abstractions and concepts. And yet, standing in his garden in Neasden, he felt the pulse-quickening call for dynamic action. This was no naïve curiosity, it was truly *epiphanal;* a moment when one's path becomes clear and they know precisely what they must do. For some it may be the burning star of creative ambition; the chastening bugle-call of heroic duty; the inner glory of spiritual enlightenment. . .

For Cornelius Plant, it was all about garden tools.

He knew the risks involved. The odds of survival were appalling, the outcome unknowable. He might never see his children again . . . but he'd spent an awful lot of money on spades and trowels over the years and he wanted them back. If only he could retrieve one decent pair of shears – those nice stainless steel ones from Homebase – then it would be worth the risk.

His mother and Agnes were away on holiday at the time. It was mid-afternoon and Jack and Fenella were still at school. He went into the house and left a note that read:

Going down a black hole for some garden shears. Shouldn't be long. If I'm not back for dinner, order a pizza. Save me some. Dad.

He marched back to the rhododendron and began scrabbling in the dirt to enlarge the hole. He worked frantically, clearing great mounds of loose rubble with his hands. About half a metre below the surface, he hit upon something very solid. It was large and flat and unlike any material he had ever seen. It was smooth like glass, but it wasn't glass and inside it swirled in a milky dance of liquid colour, intermittently flashing blue and pink and gold. It was like molten opal, but harder and more resistant than diamond. It was rare and strange: a material held under awesome tension, forged in the nuclear furnace of the Big Bang itself – before this world, before the stars and the planets, before even time began. It was. . .

"*Exotic Matter,*" Cornelius whispered to himself. He could scarcely believe it and yet it was exactly as Fat Bernard had described it.

In the middle of the slab was a hole less than a centimetre across: liquorice-black, crow-black, black like a stack of Bibles in that cupboard under the stairs with all the lights off. Howling from the very soul of ultimate darkness came the haunted cry of the universe: an outrageous, maddening roar . . . terrifying, incomprehensible, enticing.

Cornelius reached towards the minute hole. His ring and watch flew off and disappeared . . . then his glasses . . . then his shirt buttons. The last thing he saw were his fingers turning red and stretching out to twice their normal length, as if made of rubber putty. His arm quickly followed and, before he knew what was happening, his entire body had passed right through the tiny aperture.

Hurtling down the inky plughole, he thought his feet would never catch up with his legs. It was like flying through the eye of a cosmic hurricane, twisting and rolling and whizzing across inter-dimensional space too fast for his own consciousness to keep up. The only bit he distinctly remembered was the awful piped-in music: a tacky version of Greensleeves played on a beep-tone pocket calculator.

The entire trip (which through conventional space would have taken a hundred and ninety thousand years at the speed of light) lasted precisely seven seconds.

Before anyone could say, *"Ensure that your table and seat-back are in the upright position and your seatbelt securely fastened,"* he came flying out of the hyperflume and landed abruptly in some tall grass. A garden fork was sticking in one elbow and the keys to a car he'd owned years ago lay on the ground in front of him. Cornelius picked up the keys, marvelling at them.

"So that's where they got to," he cried. "I looked all over for these!"

He got slowly to his feet. He seemed to be a little taller than he had been seven seconds ago but, apart from the lack of shirt buttons, all his bits were in the right places. He looked around. It wasn't at all how he had imagined the other side of the universe to be. If it weren't for having discussed it with Fat Bernard, he might easily have believed he had fetched up in Peru, or Madagascar. The sky was an odd colour, but the air was clean and fresh and, drawing a deep breath, he couldn't resist an inward smile of self-congratulation.

He had taken a risk and ruined a good shirt in the

process but, when all was said and done, it had come off rather well. He had personally confirmed the existence of life on other planets and confounded some of astrophysics's most cherished notions about dark matter. In seven seconds, he had single-handedly pushed back the frontiers of knowledge and exploration further than any other human before him. But more than that, there would be at least one truly worthwhile result: he was going to get his garden tools back.

He put on his watch, his ring and his glasses. Then he gathered up as many forks and trowels, shears and rakes as he could carry. With a satisfied little nod, he turned to head for home and was temporarily blinded by the glaring white hole he had just been flung out of.

"So that's why the garden always seemed so dim," Cornelius pondered. "All the light gets sucked out and beamed down over here."

Holding tight to his hard-won treasure, he walked back a few paces, closed his eyes and ran, flinging himself headlong into the white hole. He disappeared up to his waist before it promptly spat him out again. Perplexed, he sat up in the grass. A dead rhododendron branch flew out and smacked him in the forehead.

That was when he remembered Fat Bernard saying that you could fall *into* a black hole and *out of* a white hole, but not the other way around. It hadn't seemed important at the time. He paused to consider this new problem: how to travel to a distant galaxy when the sum of your available technology consisted of a dozen trowels and a few hose attachments? This was going to be a challenge.

Cornelius Plant got up and began wandering aimlessly. Beyond the grassy clearing, a wall of lush vegetation grew up in chaotic profusion. Giant trees soared above his head trailing rope-like lianas. Deep-throated flowers a half-metre across yawned and belched. Purple vines threw out tendrils along the ground at near walking speed and multi-coloured leaves and petals drifted lazily down through shafts of sunlight. The air was very humid and a silvery-blue mist emanated from the ground in places.

Squelching through the swampy undergrowth, he came across a vast array of wildlife: bright-coloured birds swooped and shrieked, luminous insects flitted and five-legged lizards nodded and blinked. A silver-winged snake slithered through the mist in between the trees. Emerging from behind an enormous trunk with flat, wing-like roots protruding from it, he startled a pair of hairless, legless, round-eyed blobs, hovering in mid-air. They were shaped like overweight skittles and had smooth, sky-blue skin. Their bottom halves stopped about a metre from the ground. As soon as they saw him they sped off, waving their arms and squealing hysterically.

A moment later Cornelius himself was startled by the sound of his own name.

"Plant Professor! Mr Cornelius Plant Professor?"

Instantly there was an eruption of activity as every living creature within hearing distance fled the area. The air was a flurry of wings and the ground rustled with the scuttling of innumerable feet. Cornelius whirled around. Vacated branches waved and bowed. The silvery mist swirled and rose up all around him. Then everything was still: no sound, no movement. Nothing. Poised like a nervous statue, he strained to listen.

"Plant Professor!"

The voice seemed to emanate from all directions at once . . . an intimate voice, very near to him. Again he looked all around.

"*Who is it?*" he whispered, pulling his shirt closed. "Where are you?"

"Welcome Plant Professor! We are wherever. We are many names known by. In language of you, we would be called DS of UU: The Disembodied Staff of the Universal University. Welcome to our KlΞrM5 Campus, Philosophy Department. It is a bit, way of the out, so you say. So hard to get visiting lecturers. I am sorry there was no one with a body available to meet you. You found the whole-worm?"

Cornelius Plant stood for a moment with his mouth flapping. He turned a full circle, urgently tucking in his shirt and straightening his hair. The voice sounded so near; a warm voice, more female than male although it was impossible to tell.

"Do you mean, the *wormhole*?" he asked.

"Yes. The wholeworm. You found him?"

"Er, yes . . . under my rhododendron. You see I, I lost a few—"

"And your journey was how?"

"Oh, um . . . short, *haha*. But good. I think. Shame about the music, *haha*."

Cornelius laughed an edgy little laugh. He felt very uneasy. He wasn't at all accustomed to conversing with disembodied voices.

"Ah. Sorry so. We wanted to make you at home feel with this popular English Tune-Folk. You have travelled before I don't think?"

"Only to Majorca. You know, two weeks in the summer, that sort of thing."

There was a brief silence while the DS of UU did some quick research into where or what a Majorca was.

"*Interplanetary travel*, we mean."

"Oh! Good heavens, no. I've never left the Earth."

"How awful you for. Is it really as bad as they say?"

"What is?"

"Your Earth planet."

"Oh . . . well, the summer's been pretty poor this year – you know, cloudy and rainy. May was nice. May was—"

"Plant Professor?" the Staff interrupted. An intense seriousness crept into their voice and they seemed to have moved a little nearer. "Are you at all aware of your planet's reputation?"

Cornelius blinked. No, he was not at all aware of his planet's reputation. He'd never even thought about it.

"Our reports tell us you are having fifty-four different wars right now. *Fifty-four!* Why so many wars you have? Why are you so much killing each other? So much suffering . . . so much poverty . . . so much hunger. This Earth planet is the most dangerous place in the universe. Did you know that? Very dangerous for being a pig, example for. Three months and you're a pork chop. Not even so good for being a human: such inequality . . . such bad pollution . . . such bad television. Why are these '*Game Show Hosts*' not on trial for crimes against humanity? Did you never wonder why no one much the Earth visits?"

Cornelius bristled. He wanted to leap to his planet's defence but he couldn't think of one.

"Well, Cheltenham's a nice town," he muttered. "And there's Bournemouth . . . and what about *Noel's House Party*? Eh? That's a classic!"

But he hadn't known that there were fifty-four wars going on. He couldn't even have named fifty-four countries to have wars in. As he thought about it, he realized that the DS of UU were right; the Earth was a pretty violent place.

His invisible companions continued; "Here on planet KlΞrM5 in the Small Cloud of Magellan, we have no crime, no pollution, no taxes, no politicians, no used-car dealers. Everything coexists in symbiotic harmony. Even our mosquitoes are vegetarian.

"Here on KlΞrM5 we only philosophers have. We have philosophers from every planet in every galaxy. But never we had one from the Earth planet. A pity, we said, but so much dangerous. A risk too great. Then we across came your remark-able work; so far-sighted, so revolutionary in scope! We realized that without our support, your efforts may go unappreciated. The Earth people have sadly failed to grasp *The Way of the Grommet*. This will be their terrible falldown. But I need not tell this to you, Plant Professor."

"Er, no," he mumbled. "Why not?"

It was all a bit of a shock. For years he had struggled for recognition within the academic community. His articles were rejected, his ideas ridiculed. He felt barely tolerated at Neasden Poly where he worked. But now, out of the blue, *universal acclaim!* It was a lot to take in. He only wished he had buttons on his shirt.

"We are hoping will you accept our offer of staying to work with us, Plant Professor."

"*Come again?*" This was even less expected. Cornelius coughed nervously and began to jabber. "*Ahem,* well, I only dropped by to pick up my secateurs, you know, *haha.* Not really thinking of changing planets just yet. Perhaps in the spring. It's a big decision, you know, the kids and everything. I mean, thanks all the same. I'm honoured, really. Perhaps we could do lunch?"

He straightened his glasses and tried in vain to face the non-person he was babbling to.

"By the way," he added, "is there any way of getting back to Earth from here?"

"You want back to Earth go? Soon so? We have you been waiting for. We have you this wholeworm built for you inviting. We have English been practising. Five years, only trowels and nozzles. You want back to go? You don't like our campus, Plant Professor?"

Cornelius pushed back his hair, still holding his shirt closed with his other hand. He looked around at the soaring trees and the creeping vines and wondered where exactly the campus was.

"Oh, you mean all this jungle and stuff. Yes, it's lovely. Really. It's just, I mean, listen — I'm not a professor you know. I even failed my doctorate."

The voice came in even closer, almost whispering in his ear.

"We are making you professor right now! Why do you want to Earth go back? Tell us."

Cornelius opened his mouth to speak and immediately got stuck. *Why did he want to go back to Earth?* He'd split up with his wife. He had no social life to speak of. He only had one friend, if you counted Fat Bernard in astrophysics.

"I have two children, you see. And they're . . . well, they're going to save me some pizza." This was the best he could do.

"But your family will here come to live! All them of. We have built another wholeworm to go collecting them by. We connect the two wholeworms to a house for you, so you may go and come. Everything will be provided you for — except pizza delivery. That does not come so far."

The professor sat down on a craggy root to contemplate. Gazing up at the glorious, dappled canopy overhead, he felt dizzied by the sheer beauty of it all . . . not a Coke can or a crisp packet in sight. A pristine planet dedicated to philosophy — with staff who really understood and appreciated his work! It could only be described as an extraordinary opportunity.

He had long dreamed of getting out of London. Perhaps not this far. What would the kids think? Jack would go for it, no question there. It would probably be the best thing for Fenella . . . but she could be so touchy. A professorship was hardly a thing to be sneezed at. *A tax-free professorship.* . . He stood and cleared his throat, shifting nervously from one foot to the other.

"You haven't, er, mentioned anything about my, you know . . . my salary."

"Your what?"

This caught the DS of UU completely off guard and they took an invisible step back. Someone quickly consulted an invisible dictionary to make sure there was no misunderstanding. They did not want to offend an important candidate for the sake of some trifling request.

"Oh," the voice recovered. "Of course. We should have clarified this most important detail. Celery is never a problem. We are giving you as much celery as you like. All year round. Here on Planet KlΞrM5 we get some very big celeries."

Cornelius found this answer most satisfactory and he made up his mind right there and then. His new employers were thrilled. They guided him back to the clearing where he had left his garden tools and showed him the entrance to the return wormhole that would take him straight back to Albemarle Gardens.

Cornelius was at the point of leaving when the DS of UU asked, "One thing more, Plant Professor. What kind of house you would like?"

He shrugged and replied casually, "Oh, an ordinary bungalow will be fine. We'll need five bedrooms, plus kitchen and bath. The usual."

"It will be in one month ready! Pleased to be seeing you soon!"

And so, Professor Cornelius Plant whizzed back to London, told Jack and Fenella about the move, ate some cold pizza, resigned from Neasden Poly, sold his car, told his mother and sister when they got back from holiday, packed and marched them down to the rhododendron where he pushed them all (including Duncan, Gran's drum kit, Agnes's teapot collection and ninety other boxes), into a teeny little hole in the ground. Agnes resisted to the last and virtually had to be wrestled into submission, but it was for her own good. She could never have coped on her own. . .

That had been three months previous. They hadn't heard a word from the neighbours until the day Jack got his party invitation.

CHAPTER three

The amplifier, a Fender Super-Twin reverb, only barely missed his head.

Jack and Duncan had been sitting on the steps overlooking the garden when, behind them, the white door zipped open ejecting an enormous guitar amplifier. This was followed quickly by a guitar case and two smaller boxes. Duncan yelped and ran for the safety of his armchair. Jack ducked and shifted to one side to dodge any further bits of cosmic jetsam. A moment later his sister and his grandmother hurtled across the room, went out through the garden doors and landed in a heap on the grass. The door slid closed.

"I *hate* using that worm thing!" Fiz shrieked, stamping her foot as she got up. "It's worse than the Northern line. Just look! I've broken a nail."

Fenella Isabel Plant glared furiously at her broken fingernail.

"What if the garden doors had been closed?" she ranted. "Someone's going to get killed one of these days. My hair's probably gone all flat."

Her bright-green hair, on the contrary, was perfectly erect, done up in fetching ten-centimetre spikes. White powder blanched her face, offset by heavy black eyeliner and black lipstick. The total of her earrings made up the mystic number seventeen. Dumb-bell studs pierced each eyebrow, as well as her tongue. She was dressed completely in black with luminous orange platform trainers.

"Are you OK, Gran?"

"Fine. I'm fine. Don't worry about me. You'd better check the gear."

Jack stood at the top of the steps. He had somehow assumed that his sister and his grandmother were still in bed. He hadn't realized they'd gone to London. Why hadn't his dad mentioned it? Perhaps he hadn't known either. Looking down, he noticed the end of an extension lead next to his foot. He was about to pick it up when Fiz came up the steps with the guitar case and the two boxes.

"MOVE!" she grunted.

"Hello sister-person. Have you been to—?"

"Mars. Took a wrong turn."

"What's in that case?"

"A sewing machine."

"No, seriously, what's all this about? Hi, Gran."

Jack's gran came up the steps with the amp on one shoulder. It was nearly as big as she was. Petite and sprightly, at seventy-eight Delia Plant looked half the age of her own daughter and had done more with her years than most people could do with seventy-eight lifetimes. Sometimes Jack wondered if there was anything his gran *hadn't* done.

"Hello," she called in a deep, gentle voice. "Didn't Fiz tell you? We're starting a band. You know, I've been doing session work as a rock drummer for years now, but I've always wanted to tour with a live band. Fiz is going to sing and play guitar. She's written some lovely songs, haven'tcha, Fizzy."

"Well, one or two," Fiz replied modestly. She adored her gran. In fact, Gran was the only person with whom she did not behave like a chainsaw with migraine.

Duncan grumbled from the sofa, "*Rrr* . . . even I could sing better than herrrr."

"Shut your gob, you talking mop. Where's the father-person?"

"Who? Oh, you missed the drama. Aggie was trying to get to heaven and got her hand stuck in the pulley. Dad had to take her to hospital. They just left, like, fifteen minutes ago."

Gran set the huge amp down.

"Oh, poor Agnes," she said, wincing at the thought. "Was she hurt badly?"

"It looked pretty bad. Duncan thinks it's fractured. She fell the full length of the lift shaft."

"You're not serious!"

"At least we know the trampoline works."

"Poor Agnes," Gran repeated, shaking her head. "She's not getting on very well here, is she? She hardly got out of bed last month, and now this."

Jack shrugged. "I think it was more of a shock than anything else."

Fiz smirked. "It's too bad about her hand, but at least we can get some practice in before Dad gets back. He's going to have kittens about the noise. You can help us get this gear upstairs if you want to be useful."

If there was to be any hope of getting his sister to the party, Jack had no choice but to be amenable. He picked up the amp.

"Yeah, sure. What about this though?" he asked, pointing to the extension lead with his foot.

"What about it?"

"We don't have electricity. How are you going to—?"

"*Duh* – get with the program! It's plugged into the mains at the house. I just trailed it with me through the worm."

With widening eyes Jack noticed that the flex

was indeed emerging from the crack under the white door.

"*It's plugged in in London?*" he repeated incredulously.

"I just said that. Didn't I just say that?"

"Yeah but, like, a hundred and ninety thousand light-years away? All the electrical cable ever made in all of history would never reach that far!"

"So? It stretched a bit. It's here isn't it?"

Fiz stooped to pick up the flex. She handed it to Gran and started towards the lifts.

Jack shook his head. "Fiz, listen, do you really think this is a good idea?"

"It sure beats standing around talking about it. We're just going to try it and see if it works, all right ickle-baby-boy? If it doesn't work, it doesn't work. Don't be such a mimsy."

"What do you think, Gran?" he appealed.

"Oh, Jack, you know me. I'll try anything once. If you want to have a life, you have to accept that there are no guarantees and no insurance policies. Just go for it; that's my philosophy! It's not as if we haven't taken precautions."

"Yeah? Like what?"

"I removed the fuse and hot-wired the plug. That way we shouldn't get any power cuts in the middle of a number."

This was not reassuring. DIY bungee jumping

was one thing; running an electric current through a black hole was something else.

"It just sounds really dangerous," he muttered. "You know what Fat Bernard said."

"Fat Bernard can go flush himself," Fiz proclaimed defiantly. "I can't have a rock band without power and that's all there is to it."

What Fat Bernard had said, and what was making Jack so nervous, was that anything passing through a black hole would be altered in some way. The change could be very subtle (as it had been for Jack and his family), or utterly radical (as with Duncan, whose brain and vocal chords were so thoroughly reconstituted that he was suddenly capable of speech). It was impossible to predict the effect it would have on 240 volts.

Fiz hollered down the lift shaft, "Henry, we need to take some stuff up to my room, OK?"

"*Certainly, Ms Fiz,*" Henry replied.

The ropes creaked into action and first Fiz with the guitar case, then Gran with the extension lead and the other boxes, then Jack with the big amp, latched on to the going-up ropes.

When planning the Plants' house, the University Technical Staff had had numerous debates regarding the precise meaning of the word "bungalow"; they miserably failed to agree. So, in accordance with architectural practice everywhere, they built something completely different instead; in this case, a seven-storey tower. Each floor had one huge room, linked only by the lift shaft. The ropes themselves were added as an afterthought when it was discovered that Earthlings were not very good at going up and down unaided.

Fiz's room was third from the top and Gran's drum kit had already been installed. Jack put the amp in the middle of the room. His sister unpacked the other boxes, producing a microphone and a stand.

"Where did you get the money for all this stuff anyway?" Jack asked.

"From the mother-person."

She plugged in the amp and switched it on. It *krakkked* loudly before settling into a low, hollow hum.

"Seems to be working," she said, looking up at Gran.

"Mum gave you money to buy an electric guitar and amplifier?"

"No, I mugged her, what do you think? What should I set this at?"

"Try it somewhere in the middle for a start," Gran answered from behind a massive array of drums and gongs and exotic noise-makers.

"But this must have cost hundreds of pounds!" Jack complained. "How come she never gives me money like that?"

"Go figure. She loves me more than you. Don't be a mimsy whinger."

"But, you didn't tell her, did you? About the——"

"*No, I didn't tell her!* Stop fretting. You get more sad by the day."

Their mother still didn't know about the move. It would have been much too hard to explain. Harder for Jack was the fact that she didn't much seem to care what planet they were on. He sulked over to the big window to the right of the drums, folded his arms and leaned back against the sill.

Lovingly, Fiz lifted her new guitar from its case. She manoeuvred the strap across her shoulders, twiddled the dials and flicked the pick-up switches. She plugged it into the amp along with the mike and the leads hissed and crackled like a pair of angry snakes. Sparks flew and a squeal of feedback screamed from the speaker. Gran reached for a pair of industrial earmuffs and Fiz moved the microphone a little further away. The squeal subsided.

"OK. Let's start with, '*I Wanna be Miserable*'," she suggested.

Gran nodded. She made a slight adjustment to her stool and pushed back her cropped, grey-blonde hair. She rucked up her shirtsleeves and gave her bass drum a few preliminary thumps.

She counted them in: "– two, three, four——"

KERRRANNNGGG!!!

A nuclear-powered *G-major* exploded in the room. The air throbbed and mushroomed. All the glass in the windows blew out and when the shock wave hit Jack it was like being punched in the chest by a gorilla on steroids. His legs flipped up and he flew out of the window backwards, along with half of Gran's cymbals.

CHAPTER four

In the emergency waiting room of Central Middlesex Hospital, Agnes and Cornelius Plant looked up as the lights suddenly dimmed, then winked out as the entire ward was plunged into darkness.

Hmm . . . grommet failure, no doubt, the professor assumed. *One perished grommet and the whole world is thrown into chaos and uncertainty. The grommet of light and truth and order, routed by the infernal power of darkness. Hmm . . . that's good.* Taking out his notepad, he began scribbling blindly.

CHAPTER five

At the Central Electricity Board all the telephones started ringing, and Cynthia Howells, a trainee monitoring reserves in the national grid, looked up at her supervisor and said, "I can't understand it. There's been a massive power surge in the Neasden area. In three seconds it's drawn off more electricity than the Thames Valley uses in a year. All of north-west London is blacking out!"

The supervisor, Herbert Dribbling, leaned over his trainee's shoulder and narrowed his eyes at the computer screen in front of them. He was particularly fond of this trainee and he liked to take every opportunity he could to lean over her shoulder.

Snaking his arms around her, he tapped a series of keys to change the display. He could hear her breathing. His professional eye studied the complex graph on the screen, but the other one could not help but notice the rise and fall of her curvaceous pink jumper. His right hand came to rest on Miss Howells's shoulder.

"A power surge," he whispered slowly. "A massively powerful surge . . . *of power!*"

His nostrils flared and he took a deep breath. A crisis was an arousing experience, further heightened by the intoxication of Miss Howells' perfume. He turned his head and looked straight into his trainee's dilating pupils. He squeezed her shoulder, ever so gently.

"Do you know what this means, Miss Howells?" He spoke very slowly, his every word imparting the gravity of the situation.

At that moment, Cynthia Howells could not have cared less what it meant. Dreamily she gazed at her supervisor's face: the ape-like slope of his forehead, the tiny black eyes that resembled two currants stuck in a lump of uncooked dough, the waxy pallor of his skin, the moustache that curled ever-so-delicately over the lipless scrawl of his mouth . . . Cynthia stared at this mouth and felt it beckoning to her, begging to be kissed.

What is it about this man? she asked herself. *Why do I find him so, so. . .?*

Cynthia Howells nodded slowly and tried to remember what her supervisor was talking about.

Their faces were very close . . . *intimately* close . . . close enough to know what he had had for lunch.

"This is an *emergency*," he was saying, gazing directly into her eyes. "Imagine, if you will, the terrible, black, velvety darkness . . . the wild, unbridled panic . . . the crying of little children . . . all of London thrown into chaos. Can you imagine that, Miss Howells?"

Cynthia's manicured fingertips reached up to touch the pearl necklace she had bought on sale at Dickens and Jones. Her rose-blush fingernails perfectly matched her angora jumper. The jumper rose and fell with the excitement of her breath.

"Oh yes, Mr Dribbling," she sighed.

"Call me Herb."

"Herb . . . it really is quite frightening, Herb . . . isn't it. What are we going to do?"

Herbert Dribbling stood erect, buttoning the grey polyester jacket he had had specially tailored to accommodate his manly belly. He threw back his perfectly round shoulders and straightened his tie. Cynthia Howells shifted in her seat.

"I know how to handle a *power surge,* Miss—"

Miss Howells swept back her immaculately trimmed, shoulder-length blonde hair that had no split ends whatsoever. Her lip-gloss glistened under the computer room strip lights.

"Cynthia. . ." she replied breathily.

"I want you to get on to every power station in the country, Cynthia. Tell them to give you all they've got. Understand? I'm going after this one alone."

Until recently, the Central Electricity Board had employed some 5000 people. Then it was privatized and they sacked 4998 of them in a cost-cutting productivity drive. This left Cynthia to answer the phone, monitor the reserves, deal with suppliers, do the accounts and the billing and make the tea. Herb did anything else.

He strode to the door, pushing his comb-over across the bald spot that women had always found irresistible.

He turned and winked. "I'll be back . . . that's a promise."

Cynthia half rose from her chair, about to run into his arms —

But he was already gone.

CHAPTER six

On the far side of the garden were three low bushes. Two of them had thorny spikes two centimetres long. Jack had the great good fortune of landing in the middle one which was no thornier than your average rose bush. Gasping for breath and feeling like he had just gone twelve rounds with Mike Tyson's cat, he was still trying to extricate himself when Fiz appeared running down the garden steps.

"Are you all right?" she called.

Recently, in unguarded moments, Fiz had found herself behaving very oddly and actually caring whether her brother dropped dead or not. She found this extremely confusing. Was she completely losing her sense of identity? Some fatal softening of the brain, perhaps?

"Yeah. . ." Jack wheezed, trying to pump some air into his lungs. "I'm . . . *(pant, pant)* . . . OK . . . *(pant, pant)* . . . I think."

Having freed himself from the bush, he stood bent at the waist with his hands on his knees. His T-shirt was in shreds and his arms were well raked. Looking down, his view of the grass was going dark around the edges. Fiz went up to him and almost put a comforting hand on his shoulder. Luckily she caught herself in time and the hand recoiled. She went to retrieve Gran's cymbals instead.

Gran herself had ended up against the wall under a mountain of drums. She dug herself out and appeared at the window.

"Is everything OK?" she called down.

"Well, I've found three of them," Fiz called back. "How many are you missing?"

There was a pause. "No, I meant, is Jack OK?"

"Oh, he's fine. Just a bit winded."

Of course he's OK, Fiz confirmed to herself. *All he did was fall out of a window. He just said he was OK, didn't he? Faking it up for a bit of attention.*

Jack stood up straight and rubbed his arms. Fiz winced at the red road map of scratches.

"I think you should . . . turn it . . . down a bit," he said shakily.

The creepy sensation of sympathy for her brother finally passed and Fiz reverted to her normal self.

"*Duh,* what was your first clue, Sherlock? Actually, I was thinking of turning it up to see if I could put you into orbit."

She tucked the cymbals under one arm and turned to go. She was halfway up the steps when her brother, still trying to catch his breath, called to her.

"Hey, Fiz . . . I was meaning to ask you . . . I got this invitation . . . to a party . . . do you want to go? It could be cool."

"What party? Where?"

Jack limped up the steps and showed her the card. Duncan, who had fled into the bushes when the windows blew out, suddenly reappeared.

"Why wasn't I invited?"

Jack shrugged. "I don't even know why *I* was invited. But it'll be cool. You can go with me."

"Why do you want me to go? Go by yourself. It's your invitation."

"Because the father-person said—"

"— that you might like to go too!" Duncan interrupted, discreetly kicking Jack in the leg. "He said it might be fun. For you."

Fiz looked down at Duncan. Both dog and boy tried, unsuccessfully, to smile.

"So Dad said you can't go unless I go with you. Is that it?"

"Don't be ridiculous! Of course not! Why would he say that? I *want* you to come. I do. Honest."

Fiz handed the card back to her brother.

"I can't go anywhere today. I'm staying in to squeeze my spots." She turned and went back inside.

"What, *all day*?" Jack called after her.

"No. All month. Besides, I've got PMS."

Jack followed her into the living room. "What's PMS?"

"Pathetically Moronic Sibling."

Leaving her brother looking dumbfounded, she stopped in the kitchen for a glass of water on her way upstairs. Jack slumped despondently into a chair, tapping the card on the dining table.

Duncan looked at Fiz and then at Jack. He had a quick scratch, then leaped up on to Jack's lap and hissed, *"Psst!"*

He whispered something into Jack's ear. A broad smile began to develop. . .

"Dunc, you are a genius!" Jack exclaimed. Grabbing a pen and a scrap of paper, he quickly scribbled a few words.

"Hey, crater-face," he called across the room. "Would you mind reading this?"

He handed the paper to his sister. She looked at the note. She looked at her brother.

"Why?" she asked blankly.

"No reason. Just read it. Please."

Fiz sighed and looked down again at the scrap of

paper. She knew there was some weird ulterior motive at work, but she couldn't figure out what it was.

Probably he thinks he can do some kind of voodoo . . . like a spell or something . . . that if he can make me say it, then I'll become his zombie slave and it will actually happen.

There was a tense pause. Duncan looked up at her with rapt anticipation. She was strongly tempted to refuse; she was very superstitious that way. But then, she had just blown Jack out of a fourth-floor window. Perhaps she owed him just this much. . .

Taking a deep breath, she exhaled loudly and, as mechanically as possible, read the four words that were written on the paper: "She'll. Go. With. You." She tossed the paper in his face and repeated, "She'll go with you. So what? You are completely barking. Get a life."

Fiz turned towards the lift shaft and summoned Henry. Jack sauntered back to the table wearing a huge grin. Duncan trotted after him.

"You oughta lick those scrrr-atches there, boyo," Duncan advised as he jumped up on the armchair. "Best thing for it."

Jack gave his arm a few tentative licks. He looked over at Duncan and they both burst out laughing. Things were turning out rather better than they might have hoped.

CHAPTER seven

The Universal University was set up about fifteen billion years ago, not long after the Big Bang, with the modest aim of bringing a little order to what was then a very chaotic world. The Physics and Geology departments hammered out a few basic rules for the behaviour of inanimate matter (many of which are routinely flouted). The Biology department, through elaborate field experiments and longitudinal studies, was largely responsible for the development of life. In fact, only a tiny handful of rogue deviants managed to spring up spontaneously. For example, there's the Stalking Horror of Taïs, a sort of parasitic nightmare capable of invading your mind and inducing such ghastly hallucinations that its victims often claw their own eyes out.

But far more vile and dangerous than that is a particularly stupid and nasty breed of hominid who refer to themselves (without the slightest irony), as "*Homo sapiens*"[2].

Luckily for the rest of the universe, *Homo sapiens* (better known to the rest of the cosmos as *Homo televisionicus*) have never managed to spread beyond the confines of their insignificant little rock on the fringes of the Milky Way. The worst of their appalling habits, which include killing and/or eating almost everything they come across (as well as some really dodgy haircuts), have thereby been contained. Nevertheless, the UU continue to put out the following warning to all staff and students which cannot be over-stressed:

"Any encounter with an Earth Human, even a little one, must be handled with *extreme caution*. Be afraid. Be very afraid. Especially if you are a chicken. Stay calm and smile a lot (difficult with a beak, but try). Do nothing to provoke a violent outburst. Avoid eye contact and try to appear inedible. Leave the galaxy immediately."

2 *Homo sapiens*: the official Latin term for the humans of planet Earth. Believe it or not – and try not to fall about laughing – it actually means *Wise man*. We are talking about a species that took 100,000 years of technological trial and error to invent y-fronts. *Wise?* Pull the other one, it's got bells on.

Considering the irredeemable stupidity of the blood-thirsty *Homo sapiens,* the directors of the UU had long ago written off the planet Earth as a dead loss. They decided to wait for the inevitable day when the humans wiped themselves out, leaving their planet free to be recolonized.

And that's the way it would have gone, had it not been for the complaints they began to receive about dire television broadcasts being beamed out from the Earth in all directions. *Eurotrash* alone had numbed and confused the minds of millions, but when *Teletubbies* started to reach Orion the problem could no longer be ignored. The peace-loving Orionese thought it was some perverse form of psychological warfare and they could not understand why they were being singled out for such cruel and degrading treatment. Clearly something had to be done. Intelligent life in the universe would not tolerate such an insult.

The problem for the UU then became, which department was going to take it on? Biology completely disowned the Earth humans and refused to have anything to do with them. Media Studies just laughed. Both History and Anthropology toyed with the idea, but it was obvious that Life on Earth would never be more than the teeniest footnote and they couldn't spare the resources.

Finally, it fell to Philosophy. . .

For years they scoured the planet from a safe distance, hoping to find even one enlightened being with whom they could work. As supreme intelligence was crucial, they initially short-listed a beaver, a border collie and a common clothes moth, all of whom demonstrated the deepest understanding of the issues. But it soon became clear that if the Earth were to be shifted from its path of certain destruction, someone would have to negotiate with the humans directly.

The search began again. Just one person was needed . . . someone of rare depth and integrity . . . someone with the purity of vision to transcend the banal and the compromised . . . someone with the uncommon courage to step up unflinchingly to the very brink, beaming the great beacon of truth into the terrible abyss of human consciousness. . .

It was not long before their diligence was rewarded.

CHAPTER eight

Cornelius Plant sat with his sister in the candlelit examining room, trying to account for a strange sense of *déjà vu* he was having.

"Of course we'll need to take some X-rays, but there seem to be three minor fractures with internal bleeding. The first and second knuckles are damaged and there's severe swelling and tearing of the ligaments. Along with—"

"—multiple external contusions!" Agnes exclaimed. "That's precisely what our Duncan said. His very words!"

The doctor nodded at her slowly. The candle flickered, throwing heavy shadows across his face.

"I see. And this Duncan is a nurse, I suppose? A medical student?"

"Don't be ridiculous. He's a Jack Russell."

Agnes retrieved her hand and started licking it again.

The doctor's mouth fell open temporarily. His tongue explored his teeth, as if he might find the words he needed lurking there somewhere. He cleared his throat and decided to address Cornelius instead.

"Yes, well, with a fall like that, we really ought to keep her in for observation overnight. Do you live nearby?"

"We live on another planet," Agnes chimed. "It's only morning there. Different sun, you see. Rises in the west. It feels like April but the days are too long. I don't like it at all. My brother does. Writes books about grommets. Little rubber washer thingies."

The doctor's expression died completely. He pulled his mouth to one side and scratched his cheek. As if the power cut wasn't bad enough. Now all the night-shift loonies were crawling out of the woodwork to torment him. He sighed and turned a questioning look at Professor Plant.

The professor smiled indulgently.

"Well, you know, calling a grommet a *'rubber washer'* is a bit like saying champagne is a fizzy drink. Besides, it's their symbolic value that really interests me. You see——"

He was about to launch into his favourite subject, but the doctor's glacial glance stopped him dead.

"Er, yes . . . observation," Cornelius mumbled, straightening his glasses. "I think perhaps I should stay in with her, if that's allowed."

Suddenly in a hurry to see his next patient, the doctor scribbled some instructions to the radiographer and replied, "I don't see why not, especially as you have so far to travel. Now, take this form. Go out of the door and turn left. Follow the yellow line all the way to X-ray. Stay on this planet. Give the form to the nice woman there. When she's finished, someone will come to collect you and find you a bed."

Instinctively, he buzzed the intercom before remembering there was no power. He huffed and began excavating the heaps of papers and files and odd pharmaceutical samples littering his desk. Agnes licked her hand like an ice cream. Cornelius thanked the doctor and helped her up.

"I do wish the lights would come on," she said as they left. "Reminds me of during the war . . . Mum was busy spying in Romania and she sent me to the McCreedys in High Holborn where I'd be safe. Remember? Course not. You weren't born. Bombs dropping in the street like pigeon doo. Look, Corny, there's the maternity ward! Do you think I should have a baby? I used to carry you around when you were little. I was ever so careful. I'd be a good Mum. . ."

CHAPTER nine

"Didn't you ever want to get married though?" Fiz asked her gran.

She turned the amp down to its lowest possible setting, which was *"Phenomenally Loud"* as opposed to *"Life Threatening"* or *"Annihilate With Extreme Prejudice"*.

"Well, I *was* married," Gran replied dreamily. "Years ago . . . in Borneo. I was doing some research into endangered orang-utans when I was kidnapped by Moluccan pirates. They were going to sell me into slavery so I poisoned their soup. Had to swim fourteen miles to the nearest island. Lived on centipedes and coconuts for eleven days till a boat came by. And then the strangest thing happened: due to some coincidence with an ancient legend, the locals got it in their heads that I was the fabled

White Goddess of Urabarrú and enthroned me in a bamboo palace with twelve doting husbands to service my every wish. That was . . . busy. But you know, not one of them could put up a shelf?"

Gran fixed her tom-toms to a bracket on the bass drum and wagged a knowing finger.

"That's the true measure of a man, you know. And after I took that DIY course, I just couldn't see the point. I mean, sex is one thing, but waking up with the same man every morning of your life? When he can't even put up a decent shelf? What would be the point? Hire a carpenter, that's what I say."

Fiz fidgeted with her many rings.

"Yeah, but what about *lurve* and all that?"

Fiz was twelve when she changed her name and fifteen when she not exactly *fell* in love, but at least stepped in it. He was called Brian Overthrow and, apart from this odd name, she could hardly have said what it was that attracted her to him. He looked OK, but nothing special. He wasn't thought of as bright or talented or charismatic in any way. They had only ever exchanged a few words, like: "Is this seat taken?" or, "Shove out of the way, you great moron."

But everyone in her class seemed to fancy somebody. Fiz didn't and at first she was rather proud of it. But then she began to think that perhaps she ought to — that there might be something wrong with her. She began to cast about for a suitable candidate. As Brian Overthrow was neither hideous nor spoken for, he was granted this dubious honour.

She thought about him constantly. She acquired a picture of him from a friend of a friend of a friend and kept it beside her bed. She found out where he lived and learned his telephone number. She rang it several times, but always hung up as soon as anyone answered. She tried to dream about him at night, without success. At lunch, she repeatedly looked in his direction to see if he was looking at her. He never was. To this day, it is unlikely that Brian Overthrow ever realized how infatuated Fiz Plant was for those two tormented weeks.

It came to a climax one day after school. He was standing by the main door, leaning against the wall, waiting for his mates. Fiz came through the door and, as soon as she saw him, very nearly ran back inside. But she didn't do that. Mustering all her courage, she walked right past him, staring intently at the ground.

Then, at the top of the steps, she stopped. It was agony! It had gone on long enough. Something had to be done. She turned and walked straight up to him. For a moment she just stood there without speaking. She sort of smiled. Brian Overthrow smiled too, without knowing why. Hastily she rehearsed the speech she had prepared. She would tell him openly and honestly exactly how she felt. Either he would be able to accept it or not. She looked into his eyes. Brian Overthrow, naturally, did not have a clue what was going on and by this time was no longer smiling.

So she kicked him in the leg.

She turned and walked away not knowing quite why she had done it, but feeling that it was somehow appropriate. She got over him very quickly. It was to be her only dip into love's troubled waters for quite some time.

Fiz looked away shyly and Gran smiled.

"'Love is a many-splendoured thing'," she commented wisely. "So is ice cream: enjoy it while it lasts, but don't expect too much. And don't go waiting around for it to magically transform everything either. The important thing is to have a life, not to have a man. As for all that 'better or worse, richer or poorer, sickness and health' stuff, that's a myth if you ask me. You might as well look for fairies at the bottom of the garden."

Fiz knitted her eyebrows together and studied her broken fingernail. She nibbled at it and examined it again, dissatisfied. Gran finished putting her kit back together and walked around behind it.

"But you know, Fizzy, hardly any advice is ever worth taking. You have to find out for yourself.

Find your own way. Maybe you'll settle down with some nice boy and live happily ever after. Who knows?"

"Ha! *As if!* How can you even use the words 'nice' and 'boy' in the same sentence!"

Gran shrugged and smiled to herself. She sat down and thumped her kick drum. She looked around the room.

"We'll have to get someone in to sort out those windows. But they can wait till Cornelius gets back. Let's take it from the top, shall we?"

Fiz picked up her guitar, still lost in thought.

One floor below, Jack was sifting through his used laundry trying to locate a particularly favourite T-shirt when the walls began to vibrate. After a throbbing intro, he heard his sister wailing:

> *I don't wanna eat your watercress*
> *And I don't wanna wear that stupid dress*
> *I don't wanna be a girl called Tess*
> *I just wanna be depressed*
> *I wanna be, MIS-ER-A-BLE!*
> *I wanna be, MIS-ER-A-BLE!*

Drums pounded, cymbals crashed and wildly distorted guitar chords fuzzed like an infernal bit of factory machinery gone wrong. The tune was quite catchy, in that it consisted of just one note – that made it easy to remember.

Jack sat amid a pile of clothes, flinging socks and shorts to either side. Surrounding him on the walls were pictures of girls and sports cars and posters of Wright, Adams, Bergkamp and the rest of the Arsenal line-up that won the Double in '98.

At last he found what he was looking for and passed it under his nose. Having survived the sniff-test, he changed, looked in the mirror and pushed his sandy hair around a bit. With a little trial and error, he managed to set his baseball cap at precisely the correct angle. He grabbed a pair of sunglasses and rode the lift down to the kitchen to meet Duncan.

Scribbling a brief note for his sister and Gran, he said, "C'mon. Let's go before they notice. I hope there's something other than celery to eat."

They went out across the garden and disappeared into the bush as Fiz launched into her second verse:

I don't wanna go to Trinidad
And I don't wanna snog your cousin Brad
I don't wanna wear a shirt that's plaid
I just wanna feel real bad
I wanna be, MIS-ER-A-BLE!

CHAPTER ten

As Fiz's raucous tones assaulted the unsuspecting air above the KlΞrM5 rainforest, Cynthia Howells in Reading stopped filing her rose-blush fingernails and stared with renewed alarm at her computer screen. What had moments ago shown as a temporary power surge was now lurching back to life as a prolonged drain of incalculable proportions. Particularly worrying was that, although all of London was in the dark, something in Neasden was sucking power out of the system as far away as Birmingham. Within seconds her telephone started ringing, confirming her worst fears. She did her best to reassure callers:

"Yes, Lord Chalfont, we are aware of the problem . . . *sorry*? What? Your electronic loo-paper dispenser? *Really*? And no manual override . . . I

see. So you can't, er, you're not able to . . . I see.
Yes . . . yes, that is dreadful, Lord Chalfont, but
you'll be pleased to know that entirely one half of
our staff is presently engaged in rectifying the situation. I assure you he is doing all he can."

Cynthia put down the phone and decided not to
answer it any more. It was too distressing. Instead
she gave them a looped tape of Celine Dion with
the repeating message:

*"Your call is important to us. You are being held in a
queue and will be answered sometime this month."*

Then suddenly the graph on the screen went bal-
listic, warning buzzers sounded and red lights
started flashing all over the console. Quickly, she
rang Herb on his mobile.

"Herb? Oh, Herb, I'm so glad I caught you. It's
started up again – the surge I mean. All generators
are at full capacity, but it's not enough! Alarms
are going off everywhere and now we've lost
Wolverhampton! My mother lives just near there in
Lower Codswallop, you know, and I'm just so worried about her and Fluffy. Fluffy's her pet carp. He's
so cute, Herb, he's half white and half orange and
he does loads of tricks, you know, like he blows
me kisses and when I wave to him he waves his
little side fins at me and once he jumped right out
of the tank and spent the night on the carpet! *Haha*,
that's funny, isn't it? A pet carp on the carpet! Do

you get it? *Heehee*. He was doing an impression of Dad. Dad used to pass out like that all the time. But he didn't die cause he's so clever. Fluffy, I mean, not my dad. My dad died. But he's always had a light above his tank, you see. Fluffy, I mean, not my dad. And now there'll be no light and no pump and no little bubbles in the corner and he'll get so distressed – I just know he will! And then Mum will be upset and, Herb? Fluffy is all she's got! If anything were to happen to him . . . I just don't know. Oh, Herb, I'm so frightened!"

A fit of sobbing choked the line. Herb paused until it subsided.

"Listen, kid, pull yourself together," he said firmly. "We're professionals. Don't ever forget that. I don't want you losing your pretty little head, now."

Cynthia sniffled.

"I know I'm being silly. The slightest things upset me so. Just hearing your voice makes me feel better. I'll try to be brave. It's just that the whole country is blacking out! Tell me what I should do!"

"There is something you can do, kid. Something important. I've got the problem narrowed down to this one street. I've made enquiries at every house, door by door, all except one. It looks empty, but the neighbour says she saw people going in and out this afternoon. It's a long shot,

Cynthia, but I've got to check it out. The country depends on it. I want you to get on to the police. I need an entry warrant for that house and I need it pronto. Tell them it's a national emergency. Will you do that?"

"Oh yes, I'll do anything you say!"

"Good. Now listen: the address is 37 Albemarle Gardens. I'll be waiting next door at number 35. You got that?"

"Oh, yes, I've got it, Herb. I'll tell them. But. . ."

There was a silence on the line . . . a terrible silence that Cynthia Howells felt herself falling towards. She badly wanted to say something meaningful and dramatic; something that would truly express everything she felt. . .

"Herb? I – I. . ."

"What is it, kid?"

"Be careful, won't you."

"Yeah. Don't worry. I will. Catch you later."

Chuckling to himself, Herb slipped his mobile into his jacket pocket.

Silly thing . . . crying over her mum's goldfish. Just a kid, really . . . pretty though. Nice legs too.

He leaned back on the sofa and toured the room with his eyes: the romantic glow of the coal fire, the candles flickering softly on the mantel, the soothing music emanating from a battery-operated cassette player. A beautiful woman with long dark hair appeared in the doorway, carrying two mugs on a tray.

"I hope I've made it strong enough," she said apologetically.

They had only just met. A small round man had appeared on her doorstep enquiring about the blackout, and the next moment she found herself inviting him in for coffee. She couldn't possibly have said why. He wasn't her type at all. She set the cups on the coffee table and sat down next to him.

"It smells divine, Sylvia," he smarmed. "And so do you."

Sylvia slipped off her shoes and tossed her hair from side to side, tucking her feet up underneath her. She turned and snuggled up to the stranger on her sofa, giggling coquettishly. She loosened his tie and ran her fingers through his comb-over.

"Now . . . where were we?" she purred seductively.

CHAPTER eleven

"Are you sure you know where this place is?" Jack asked, beating his way through a dense wall of leaves.

Duncan sniffed the air.

"No prrr-oblem. Rrr-oyals have a very particular smell. It's the in-breeding that does it. Shallow end of the gene pool, if you know what I mean. I had a date with a corgi once. Nice girrrl, too, but stupid. And short."

"Short? Hey, I hate to break it to you, but you are not exactly tall."

Duncan shrugged.

"I don't care. I've just always had this thing about legs. Know what I mean? *Long hairy legs.* Now, take Julia . . . Julia is absolutely my type."

"Julia is an Irish wolfhound. You'd need a stepladder just to sniff her bottom."

"*Oh, yes please* . . . gimme one of them leggy Irish bitches every time!"

"You are a complete animal, you know that?"

"That's the nicest thing you've ever said to me." Duncan shook his head with disdain. "You think it's an insult, but humans are not half as clever as they think they are."

"Well, there's nothing looks more stupid than you humping someone's leg. Funny how you don't see many rocket scientists doing that."

"Yeah, yeah . . . just let me rrr-emind you that there were astrodogs before there were astronauts. First Earthling in space was a Rrr-ussian bitch called Laika: Sputnik 2, 1957. It took another four years for a human to figure out how to drrr-ive the thing! But that's not the point; it's not that humans are *actually stupid*, it's what they do with their intel-ligence – *that* is what's stupid."

Jack grunted, unimpressed. "Just look at this for a sec, willya. The map says we should——"

"Stuff your map, Jackie. Trrr-ust me. The nose knows. This-a-way!"

They pushed on through virgin forest. There were no trails to speak of and, for Jack in particu-lar, the going was very slow. The ground was damp and spongy. The air was hot and muggy. Bright clusters of berries dangled from vines and fabulous purple bell-shaped flowers turned to watch as they passed by, sticking out their honeyed tongues. Riotously coloured parrots streaked from branch to branch.

Gradually the forest thinned out and the undergrowth was less obstructive. They came to a rocky clearing where hundreds of head-high stumps were crested with ferny crowns. The sense of openness was a great relief after the closeness of the jungle. Jack paused and took a deep breath.

"So which way, brains?"

Duncan waved his nose about and announced, "This way. About another mile." He lifted his leg against a stump and added, "And don't forget to mark your territory. I haven't seen you do it even once! How you ever gonna get any rrr-espect?"

The walking was much quicker now. The ground was dry and Jack stepped easily from rock to rock in between the stumpy ferns. Out of the shade of the jungle canopy, the sun was warm and he removed his hat to ventilate his head. He put it back on and adjusted his sunglasses. When he looked up again, Duncan was standing very still, tilting his head from one side to the other.

Jack stopped too. He listened but he couldn't hear a thing.

"What's up?" he asked.

"Rrr-rr!"

Silently, Jack moved nearer to where Duncan was.

"Stop making that rrr-acket!" the dog growled. "I think someone's coming. They smell sort of blue."

"They smell blue. Good. Very good. I don't suppose you could smell something useful, like their credit card number?"

"Shut up. I think they must be Technical Staff. Too big to be anything else."

The two of them moved forward more slowly. Duncan rustled ahead, barely visible in the knee-high grass.

A moment later, Jack stepped around a massive chunk of limestone that thrust out of the ground on his left and came face to face with a long and legless blue floating blob coming the other way. It was carrying numerous giant panes of glass on its head. Jack stopped. He tried to smile and took a cautious step backwards. Duncan jumped vertically out of the grass to get a better view, then cowered back, growling.

The blob set the panes of glass down very carefully against the rock. Its skittle-shaped body was a bit smaller than Jack's torso. The face looked almost human, but for the lack of eyebrows or eyelashes or hair of any sort. The nose was small, but its eyes were large and round and they blinked very slowly. Where the head narrowed into a neck, two thin arms protruded. They both waved rather jerkily. The lower part of its body stopped some distance from the ground, like a helium balloon with no string. Its deep-blue lips stretched into a broad smile.

"*Bweeb!*" it said.

Jack's father had come across a pair of Bweebs on his very first visit to KlΞrM5. Of course, he hadn't realized then that they were Campus Technicians, responsible for all the housing, travel and general maintenance requirements of the visiting lecturers. Native residents of KlΞrM5, there are only about three thousand of them on the whole planet. Along with humans, Bweebs are among the very few beings in the universe who are *not* telepathic. Their spoken language, however, is considered impossible to learn, consisting as it does of a single word with over a hundred thousand distinct intonations, many of them inaudible even to Duncan.

On their first meeting with Professor Plant, the highly intelligent Bweebs responded as they had been taught to respond when encountering a rogue *Homo sapiens,* i.e. they fled as one might from a rabid, drug-addled werewolf. Having subsequently been assured that the Plant family ate only celery and were truly innocuous, Jack was honoured with the traditional Bweeb greeting. Rushing forward, it threw its arms around his neck and kissed him a few hundred times all over the facc.

The boy was so startled that he tripped over

backwards and landed in the grass with the blue blob on top of him, still snogging furiously. Duncan did not immediately grasp what was going on, and he started barking and darting in towards the two on the ground and then retreating again.

Releasing Jack, the Bweeb said, "Bweeb b-weeb bweeb bweeb b-wee-eeb," and, grabbing Duncan, proceeded to smother him in kisses as well.

"Enough! I can shake a paw, you know," Duncan protested, all four legs paddling in mid-air.

Jack got up and wiped his face on his sleeve. The Bweeb put Duncan down and retrieved its sheets of glass. Balancing them on its head, it did some more vigorous waving with both arms.

"Bweee-eeeb!" it sang – then zoomed off so fast that it was well out of sight by the time Jack could pick up his cap.

CHAPTER twelve

With a spectacular flourish, Fiz finished the twen-
tieth and final verse of "*I Wanna be Miserable*" which,
with all the repeats and instrumental breaks, had
succeeded in depleting the total power reserves of
all Great Britain. Factories fell silent. Underground
trains rolled to a halt in their tunnels. From
Southampton to Stornaway, not a single sixty-watt
bulb was left burning.

Removing the guitar from her shoulders, careful
not to disturb her hair spikes, Fiz said thoughtfully,
"You know, Gran, I think you're absolutely right.
Romance is a vile myth. Obviously created by
men so women would think there was something
wonderful about washing their socks. You won't
catch me falling for any of that. No way."

CHAPTER thirteen

In the darkness of Central Middlesex Hospital, Agnes Plant jerked herself awake and sat up in bed. She had only dozed for a few minutes, but was nonetheless disorientated by the strangeness of her surroundings. Her brother was slumped in a chair in the corner asleep, but that wasn't much of a clue. She tried to move her left hand and found it heavier than usual. A sharp pain twanged inside the cast and it all came back to her. She was in hospital. She was going to have a baby.

The nurse had given her a sedative and a painkiller an hour previously, but for Agnes it was still mid-afternoon and she didn't want to sleep. She had palmed them both and only sipped the water. Now she took another sip of water with her good hand and slunk quietly out of bed. She stepped past Cornelius. He snorted briefly and shifted in his chair, but didn't wake. Next to Agnes's, a second bed was curtained off where a Bengali woman was recovering from a hip operation. Agnes had spoken with her earlier, but now she could hear snoring from within.

Silently, she put on her shoes. She took her bag and went into the bathroom to redo her make-up. There was hardly any light to see by, but at her age, make-up was something she could do in the dark. She noticed that she was low on blue eye shadow and made a mental note to buy some satsumas. Taking her overcoat from the hook by the door, she slipped it on and stepped into the corridor. . .

CHAPTER fourteen

"What are you talking about? You call that a palace? It doesn't look anything like a palace. Have you ever even seen a palace? Apart from that corgi's doghouse?"

"Rrr. No question about it, Jackie. This is the place. You'll see."

Jack removed his cap, pushed back his hair and replaced it. Peering through the trees, he tried to get a better look at their supposed destination.

"There's no way this can be right. I mean, look at it! It's more like a high-tech greenhouse or something."

"I'm telling you, boyo, there are five hundred rrr-ooms inside. And about thrrr-ee hundred people. Trrr-ust me."

Hesitant and scowling, Jack scuffed the ground

and moved forward again disappointedly. It was not at all what he'd been expecting. Palaces had high white walls with domes and turrets and stone lions flanking grand, marble steps. Palaces were built in spacious grounds, with breathtaking vistas and elegantly landscaped gardens. The thing they were approaching could not by any stretch of the imagination be described as palatial.

Huddled in a valley between three huge trees and glimpsed through the underbrush, it looked like a giant, mirrored hatbox: round with a flat roof, no more than two metres high and about four across. Boy and dog crashed down the ravine towards it through a thicket of strangling figs.

At the bottom was a grove of vast fruit trees that loomed high above their heads. The misty air seemed to absorb all sound and Jack silently circled the strange building. It wasn't made of mirror. It was made of . . . *what*? A sort of wobbly, iridescent glass? Or water even, somehow held in shimmering vertical sheets? They couldn't see through it and the silvery blue-purple surface gave off no reflection. They walked all the way around looking for some kind of door, but the wall was utterly seamless.

Duncan went a little nearer and sniffed.

"It's made of light," he whispered. "Light locked in an intensified prrr-essure field. You just walk thrrr-ough it."

Saying this, he stepped up to the edge and pushed his nose forward. His entire head disappeared, swallowed up by the wall of light . . . then abruptly, he jumped back and turned to Jack.

"*Rrr!* This is the place all right," he said with a laugh. "Ye of little faith: *prrr-epare thyself!*"

Jack looked down at Duncan. He was suddenly less than sure if he wanted to go to this party after all. Three hundred people in a hatbox four metres across? How would that work? He bit his lower lip and scratched his head under his hat.

As if reading his mind, Duncan tried to reassure him. "Don't worry, it's a lot bigger on the inside. You're going to like it. I think. Something to tell your grandpuppies."

With that, the dog trotted up to the wall and carried on straight through, vanishing into the weird, watery cylinder. Jack took a deep breath and dropped his shoulders. He took a long look around him. He gazed up at the soaring trees, wreathed in low-lying mist. He looked back at the rippling light-wall, alive with colour like petrol on water.

"OK. Here we go," he muttered and, closing his eyes, walked straight ahead.

At the fourth step, a jangly rush of energy jolted through him, as if his body were being shot full of cold, electrified air. He took one more step and the sensation passed. Immediately he became aware of music and voices; a chaotic jumble of sounds and words, shouting, shrieking laughter, shattering glass. . .

He opened his eyes. He blinked and wetted his lips. Breathing through his dumbstruck mouth, his eyes swelled wide to take it all in.

He found himself on a gallery that ran all the way around the edge of a warehouse-sized room that wasn't round at all, but rectangular. The walls were blue-black with odd bursts of coloured light blooming florally in unlikely places. The gallery had no railing and Jack and Duncan stepped cautiously up to the edge to survey the scene spread out below them.

Given enough time to think about it, Jack might have been equally struck by its familiarity, as by its strangeness. A great variety of beings were down on the main floor, laughing and talking. Some seemed to be dancing. Food and drink were laid out and music was blaring — especially familiar music. In these respects, the scene was much like any party he had ever been to. This should have been reassuring. But the familiarities were somehow not what immediately sprang to mind.

The image that ambushed his unsuspecting eyeballs, more or less all at once, was that of numerous oversized pumpkin-like things hanging near the ceiling and, below that, a three-headed wolf in a sequinned dress, leaping and pirouetting on her hind legs. . . The pumpkins kept changing colour and shape and drifting apart before quickly returning, like synchronized swimmers, until one of them went off with a green and gold air-snake, both crooning along to Frank Sinatra who was bellowing in the background. In the centre of the room, a half-dozen large-headed beings with glowing oval eyes and skinny, streamlined bodies were nodding vigorously and making elaborate hand gestures. One by one they rose gracefully and went up through the roof, passing on the way a spangly cloudburst of Living Light which consisted of innumerable two-dimensional squares, dazzlingly bright, weaving and dancing, merging and dividing and spelling out words in the air. . .

Huge, translucent cylinders of milky liquid beamed down like spectral pillars with pink, baby-like bodies writhing inside them. Here and there, pairs of large, hairy, ochre-coloured bricks hopped up and bumped each other purposefully in mid-air, then landed, turned ninety degrees and hopped up again to bump on a different side. One of them appeared to be conversing with the Living Light when a blaze of orange slashed through the air and a flock of butterflies on wings of pure flame flashed across the room settling on various shoulders, including those of a badger with a head like a turnip and all six legs in a single row — which suddenly broke in half to form two three-legged beasts and went around one of the liquid pillars in both directions before rejoining and jumping up on to a sort of sofa between a pair of gnarly, disembodied brains who were, presumably, deep in thought.

The sofas were made of the same pulsing, fluorescent light-stuff as the walls, as was a sort of long table near the far wall where a creature with numerous arms and a head that was part iguana and part elephant had its trunk in the punch-bowl, howling with delight at some witty remark uttered by a pair of jeans with octopus tentacles erupting from the waistband who had only to point at bits of food for them to leap off the table into what Jack presumed was its mouth. And then the green and gold air-snake was snogging a red and silver one, their bodies entwining like braided rope, flicking and tickling each other's tongues, and the wolf-thing was holding three different conversations at once, while periodically a wispy, wraith-like plume of smoke with haunted eyes puffed up in one place, vanished, then puffed up somewhere else . . . over there, talking to a legless, faceless mountain of buzzing flies with a dozen wiry little arms that was rumbling towards the drinks, while, above it all, Frank Sinatra did it *His Way* and, there, upside down in a corner, smugly incomprehensible, hung the ultimate, cake-taking, weirdest of the weird: a poster of Garfield wearing an apron.

"Er, Dunc. . ." Jack murmured, trying to assimilate the riotous carnival that was spread out before him, "I don't think we're in Kansas any more."

"Stuff Kansas — this is life!" Duncan exclaimed enthusiastically. "Ever had a thrrree-headed girlfriend before? Check those legs! Let's go."

"Er, yeah, sure. So how do we get down?"

Jack looked from side to side, but as soon as he spoke, a square of blue-black floor lit up pale green all around them and began to sink away from the rest of the gallery. In three effortless seconds, they were transported down to the main level.

Immediately everything seemed much louder as music and voices boomed at them from all directions. People nodded and even smiled, if they happened to have a mouth. Everyone seemed to know each other, perhaps from other intergalactic raves the princess had thrown. Jack felt like a bit of a Martian, which was really odd because being an Earthling was strange enough. The two of them shuffled through the crowd towards the food. Then gradually, about halfway across the room, they started to pick up snatches of conversation:

". . .oh, getting T-shirts to fit drives me *nuts,* but having seven arms does have advantages you know. I can't imagine how you get by with only three."

". . .no, no, you hang a right at the Tarantula Nebula, carry on till Aldebaran and pick up the A303, that way you completely miss the asteroid belt."

Quite apart from the bizarre things he was hearing, what struck Jack immediately was that he could understand them at all.

Why should they be speaking English of all things?

He was about to ask Duncan this when he realized he was already on his own. Craning his neck to see, he spotted his dog doing a bit of preliminary bottom-sniffing with the Wolf-thing, before launching into a lot of yapping and growling with one of its heads, which seemed to understand Duncan's Canine dialect perfectly well.

Jack arrived at the food and drinks table and examined the selection. There wasn't one. Row upon row of light-plates all offered the same little cubes of what looked like cake. Or possibly plaster. His stomach was rumbling.

Suddenly a voice beside him was saying, "Have you tried those? They're good."

One of the squares leaped off the plate. Following its trajectory, Jack turned to see the piece of *whatever-it-was* disappearing into a hole in a face so obscured by warts he could barely make out its other features. With some effort, he managed to identify something resembling a nose, a mouth and several eyes, all irregularly placed and buried among the fungal crop of fleshy outgrowths. Jack grimaced and fought back the temptation to scream or throw up.

"*Eurrh. . .*" he said before he could stop himself, hoping this might be mistaken for a nice, friendly greeting in some other language.

Mastering his reserves of self-control, he smiled weakly. He would have preferred to believe that this person was wearing a latex Halloween mask. The skin was grey and slightly shiny, almost metallic. The little globules of flesh piled on to it ranged from pink to black. A little taller than Jack, his new friend was very squat in shape with powerful legs. Twin dorsal fins ran the length of its spine. He could have swept the Oscars for a film called *Revenge of the Wobbling Wart-thing from Swamp-Planet Zorg.*

"Go on," said Wobbling Wart-thing. The music was very loud and he had to shout to be heard. "Try one. Think of your favourite food and that's what you'll get."

Jack looked back at the squares on the plate. He wasn't sure what to do. After months of eating celery, thinking about what he wanted was easy. But how was he supposed to make it jump? He pointed as he'd seen others doing, but nothing happened. He tried with the other hand. Still nothing. He could sense his face getting red. Quickly looking around, he casually reached out, grabbed one and stuffed it in his mouth.

"Hey, you actually use your arms for picking stuff up? How quaint. What's your name, anyway?"

With his mouth full of the most incredible cheese and pepperoni pizza, he mumbled, "*Jarnk.*"

"Good to know you, Jarnk. I'm qLî~3o."

qLî~3o held out his hand.

Still chewing, Jack looked down at the hand. The sad remnants of fingers had fused together from lack of use. A swollen, squashy mass of wobbling flesh was clubbed on to the end of a stick-like arm. Some of the warts were distended and dangling with quivery little bobbles on the end. Jack had never seen anything so gross in his life. It was like leprosy with a mind of its own. No, it was worse than that. He tried to offer his own hand, but it wouldn't obey. Being friendly was one thing, but he'd have rather groped for pearls in a bucket of cold vomit than grasp the barnacled blob of flesh that was held out to him.

There was a long, uncomfortable moment, then qLî~3o suddenly smiled and nodded.

"Hey, Jarnk, no worries. I understand," he said.

The proffered hand was withdrawn with a casual wave.

"I know how you feel. I get this reaction all the time. You don't want to shake hands cause you're embarrassed about your smooth skin. I mean, that's it, isn't it. Jarnk, listen, it's nothing to be ashamed of. I used to have terrible skin problems. What you need is some wart cream, that's all. You could have skin like this in less than a month – easy."

Jack fixed a grin across his face and sighed to himself, *Just what I always wanted!*

"Er, do you really think so?" he replied, hoping the subject would die a quick and painless death.

"No problem."

qLî~3o smiled patronizingly and was about to develop the subject when he suddenly became distracted.

"Hey, take a look at this," he cried, pointing. "See that girl? The one with the massive pair of fins? Nice, huh? She's the one that does all those dead-sexy WonderWart adverts. You know the ones I mean?"

Jack peered in the direction of qLî~3o's arm to see a creature best described as *Bride of Wobbling Wart-thing from Swamp-Planet Zorg.*

"Er, not really," he answered. "They don't sell a lot of WonderWart where I come from."

"No kidding."

qLî~3o shook his head in disbelief while tracking swamp-girl through the crowd. The music was now so loud it was almost impossible to have a conversation. Jack noticed the Wolf-thing gyrating about with Duncan on her shoulders. Octopus-trousers was juggling three Hairy Bricks, all shrieking with delight. The Floating Pumpkins had bobbed down a little lower and the oval-eyed aliens were heading them back and forth, while dazzling chunks of Living Light wove in between, flashing out the lyrics to "*I Will Survive*".

qLî~3o gaped his lumpy, lipless cake-hole for another food cube to jump into and lost himself briefly to an erotic daydream involving Miss WonderWart. He surfaced and turned back to Jack.

"So . . . what planet are you from, then?" he asked in a totally blasé tone of voice.

The music pounded in the background and Jack took another piece of pizza (with extra cheese). One of the fire-winged butterflies flew so near to his cheek he could feel its warmth. The smoky, wraith-like face manifested on the other side of the table and hoovered up a few litres of fruit punch. Jack began to relax at last; this was going to be a very good party. The universe was such a cool place.

He swallowed and cheerily replied, "*Earth*."

Instantly the music died as if someone had shot

Gloria Gaynor with a silver bullet. A cacophonous chorus of squeals and shrieks erupted on all sides, muffled only by the sound of terrified aliens clambering over each other to get away. Anyone near enough to the outer wall dived straight through and vanished. Those stranded on the dance floor swept back like the tide going out in fast-motion. qLî~3o edged away from his new-found enemy. The panic subsided and everyone stared, petrified, at the dreaded Earthling. One baffled teenage boy stood alone, looking from face to face.

OK . . . why is everyone staring at me? Was it something I said? What did I say?

He fidgeted and tried to smile.

Somewhere immeasurably far away, a Russian icebreaker crashed and heaved through dense pack ice in the bleak Arctic wastes. In the remotest corner of the vast room, a pin dropped. Its distinctive clatter clanged in Jack's ears as he stood, waiting. . .

CHAPTER fifteen

Slouching at the dining table, Fiz chewed her thumbnail and looked out over the garden. The house was empty. Gran had gone jogging and wouldn't be back for hours. The initial excitement of her new guitar had worn off all too quickly and now she felt depressed again. It was that song. Something about it always got her down. She glanced at the note her brother had left. Maybe she should have gone to the party after all. She wanted something to happen. But not a party. She always felt like a freak at parties.

She got up and wandered towards the kitchen, then stopped and went over to the armchair in the other corner. There was nothing to do. Nothing worth living for. She began to think that even school might be better than this. That's when she realized just how depressed she was. She could go and talk to Henry, but that was always a very unsettling experience. She wondered how long her father and Auntie Agnes would be. She dragged herself over to the lifts and started up to her room. She could always redo her hair colour. Or hang herself. As if it mattered.

The ropes creaked and in the depths of the shaft, wheels whirred and cogs clunked. She passed the bathroom and her father's room and then her brother's. At the fourth floor, the ropes stopped. She disembarked, took one step and froze.

Her room was just as she had left it: Gran's drums were set up on the far side and her new guitar lay on the bed. The amp was on standby, its red eye glowing, the speaker conspicuously silent like a sleeping banshee. The walls of the room on all sides were papered with posters of her favourite bands: *Sepulchre City, Pink Electric Love-Babes, Suburban Baby-Eaters. . .*

It was the blue thing over by the window that concerned her. She hadn't a clue what it was. It definitely seemed to be alive, moving on its own . . . a blue floating blob with no legs. Why was it in her room?

It hadn't yet seen her and her first reaction was to go straight back down to the kitchen. But that would mean calling down to Henry and the thing would hear her. Without breathing, she continued to watch it. It picked up a huge pane of glass and started fitting it into her empty window frame. Finally she twigged that this must be one of the famous University Technical Staff. She'd heard about them before, but had somehow imagined them differently. It finished what it was doing and turned around at last. A big blue smile broke over its face.

"Bweeb!" it squeaked, waving both arms enthusiastically.

Fiz made a feeble little wave in return and tried to smile.

An anchorless, air-cooled, blue-rubber love-sponge, Bweeb rushed over, threw his arms about her neck and covered her face with dozens of wet, blue kisses. After three minutes or so, he paused in this affectionate onslaught to stroke her hair and her cheeks. Lovingly, he gazed into her eyes with unmistakable adoration.

Holding her face against his, he sighed, "Bwee-eeb b-weeb bweeb."

Fiz was stunned. At first she felt physically assaulted, but in the wake of that came a powerful, palpable love-wave that, however confusing, was hard to resist. Taking her by the hand, Bweeb led her over to the window, pointing proudly to the newly installed glass.

"Bwe-eb," he said, pointing to himself.

Fiz swallowed, cleared her throat and straightened her top, trying to recover and unruffle herself. She took a deep breath.

"Er, yes," she stammered. "New glass. Very nice. Thank you."

Smile and nod. Smile and nod.

At the sound of her voice, Bweeb swooned and kissed her several hundred more times. He stroked her face, oozing an expression of such heartfelt warmth and devotion that a stone in a frozen river could not have failed to be moved. He held her hand in his, marvelling at the whiteness of her skin, stroking it, turning it over, kissing both sides, touching each of her fingers in turn, clearly amazed that such a wonderful thing could exist. He regarded her with adoring, puppy-dog eyes.

"Bweeb bweeb b-weeb bweeb," he whispered.

His voice was like music, each tone of the word rising or falling in an endless melody. His eyes held hers and his gaze was steady and utterly sincere. He didn't flinch or waver. His hand was small, but warm, and when he kissed Fiz's hand one last time, he pressed his lips intently against her palm, as if truly giving something of himself.

Fiz was mesmerized. She had never felt anything remotely like what she felt at that moment — except perhaps that time she stepped off a fairground centrifuge and found her stomach in her throat. But this was a nice feeling; a dreamy, floaty feeling, like standing in a deep, warm sea with a giant, feet-sweeping swell breaking over her. Suddenly she felt valued and adored and emotionally inside-out.

Trying to imitate his intonation, she nodded and replied, "Bweeb."

Instantly he let go of her hand and leaped backwards. He seemed surprised and hurt. Then without warning, he exploded into peals of bell-ringing laughter, rolling about on the floor holding his sides. Fiz flapped in consternation.

"Now what? What is so funny?" she demanded.

Between gasps of giddy laughter, he repeated the word exactly as Fiz had pronounced it. She began to feel irritated. Why should he laugh at her like that? How rude and horrible! How dare this ridiculous alien who couldn't even speak English laugh at *her*?! The wonderful, warm, wavy-floaty feeling faded and in seconds she discovered that in fact she hated him intensely and wanted him to disappear that instant.

"Yeah, well, I'm sure that's just hilarious," she said sarcastically, flashing her most lethal *drop-dead-now* sort of look. "So glad you're amused."

She walked over to the window and stood with her back to him.

Bweeb bounced up and bobbed into the middle

of the room. His eyes widened. His mouth turned down and a terrible sadness descended upon him like a dark cloud. His eyes welled up and flowed over. His colour sank to a deep purple and he stared at Fiz's back with his heart about to stop beating. His laughter had hurt her. How could he have been so thoughtless? He wanted to die. He would kill himself that instant. Drifting over to her side, he touched her lightly on the shoulder.

Fiz, who had neither seen nor heard him coming, screamed and nearly jumped out of her skin. Quickly he encircled her in his arms and, laying his head on her shoulder, looked up at her as if he were about to melt. Another palpable wave of pure emotion swept over her and she couldn't help but smile, in spite of herself. She had to admit that being cuddled by a legless blue alien was a lot nicer than she might have imagined. Softly, she stroked his stick-like arm.

Then suddenly Bweeb withdrew and held up one finger purposefully, as if remembering something vital. He zoomed across the room and disappeared down the lift shaft. A moment later, she could hear him babbling to Henry, followed by an echoey reply.

So Henry can understand this guy, she realized. The ropes creaked into life. Fiz stared at them, momentarily stranded by indecision. She checked her hair in the mirror. *Hmm. I guess it can't hurt just to talk to him. . . .*

She grabbed a rope and descended all the way to the basement.

Henry was the name Professor Plant had given to the vast contraption of gears, spindles, levers, pendulums, pinions, pulleys, cogs, cables, counter-weights and flywheels (all interconnected in the most arcane and unlikely fashion), which contrived to control the rope lifts. He had been conceived and installed by one of the other technicians who had once seen a Heath Robinson cartoon and assumed that this was typical of the Earth's prevailing tech-nology. What made Henry unique, however, was that he was made entirely from *Sentient Merkur,* an extremely rare form of solid mercury, intrinsically endowed with perception, understanding and, some say, incomparable intelligence, although this has been hotly disputed.

Fiz disembarked on to a broad platform and then went down three steps to where Henry lived. Bweeb was there already, nodding and bobbing and wearing a huge blue grin.

"Good afternoon, Ms Fiz," Henry said politely.

Henry did not have a mouth or ears as such, but spoke and heard directly by emitting and receiving subtle vibrations through the various bars and tubes of his framework.

"Our friend wishes to inform you that his grandmother does not wear underpants and so, cannot change them."

Fiz looked at Bweeb, who smiled and waved at her with both hands. She looked back at Henry, nonplussed.

"*Qué?*"

A number of cogs clicked and clunked, releasing a lever that caused a metronome to tick five times.

"I am given to understand," Henry explained, "that in your attempt to speak the native tongue, you expressed three basic ideas: mother-of-your-mother; personal-underclothes; needing-renewal. This is what our friend found so amusing."

"But that's ridiculous! All I said was *bweeb,* for heaven's sake."

"Ah, but I don't think that *is* quite what you said. You see, the precise tone you have just now used refers to a particular itch one feels on the left elbow when brushing against the leaves of the Bardu tree in late afternoon."

"No way! Really? You mean you can say all that with just the tone of your voice? So what if I say '*bwee-eeeb*', like that?"

There followed a deathly silence. Bweeb himself turned pale and looked away. One of Henry's flywheels went into a whirr and a shiny cable slithered through a series of pulleys, raising a large counter-balance a few centimetres. After a long, uncomfortable moment, he emitted a low hum (as he sometimes did when nervous).

"With respect, Ms Fiz, you may have gathered that the language here is an extremely subtle and delicate thing. What you just said is utterly untranslatable and unrepeatable. You must never say it again. Merely to think it would make me rust all over. And I assure you, *Sentient Merkur* does not rust easily. Have you considered that our friend might learn English instead? It is a sadly basic language, but better for you both, I think. In the meantime, I should be only too happy to translate for you."

Fiz shrugged and Henry repeated his offer to Bweeb who responded enthusiastically with a long, poetic melody. A number of Henry's gears and wheels started spinning, thus swinging a large pendulum, which in turn pulled on a string that rang a small bell in his top left corner.

When the bell stopped ringing, Henry said, "The Blobby One wishes to convey the following: '*Lush-greenness-of-your-hair; verdant-mountain-jungle-of-Baramas; sweet-voice-of-your-mouth; singing-melody-of-spring-river; smouldering-eyes-that-shine-by-night; strange-jewels-of-Karak-Cavern; mysterious-hardware-in-your-tongue; elegance-of-your-earlobes; weak-making-swoon-of-eternal-devotion.*' Or words to that effect."

Fiz clapped her hands to the sides of her head and demanded, "Earlobes? What about my earlobes?"

"Begging your pardon, Ms Fiz, I am given to understand that the shape of the earlobe is considered highly erotic. As *Sentient Merkur* has neither ears nor desire of any kind, it is very hard for me to imagine. But it is most certainly a compliment."

Fiz felt strangely immune to compliments. Perhaps because she hadn't heard very many. She almost turned around to see if there were anyone else present who Bweeb might have been referring to.

Then he said something else that Henry also translated: "You are invited to meet his family. They live on the other side of the forest."

Fiz raised her eyebrows, overtaken by a runaway panic. Bweeb nodded vigorously. Now what was she going to do? If he had had legs, she might have kicked him. But that wouldn't work this time. She took a defensive step backwards, suddenly distracted by the compelling need to wash her hair. She hadn't washed it for at least twenty-four hours. Going anywhere was out of the question.

She starched a smile across her face to mask her distress. Why the hesitation? Anyone else and she'd have known what to do without even blinking; *Just say no! Run a mile!* She felt herself floundering amid a welter of irrational fears: afraid of her feelings, afraid of his feelings, afraid of getting involved, afraid of getting hurt, afraid of everything changing, afraid of everything staying the same, afraid of going, afraid of being left behind. . .

This is totally mad. Why should I feel like this? I've only just met him, for heaven's sake! I mean — apart from being blue and hairless with no legs, floating in the air, coming from another planet and actually being capable of expressing a genuine emotion — apart from all that, he's just like any other boy I've ever met. Why should I feel like this?

Ironically, perhaps it was Bweeb's strangeness that made him seem less threatening. His being so strange made Fiz feel less strange — or at least, it made her strangeness seem OK. *Normal* people could be such hard work, so much pretence. Bweeb nodded again, open and encouraging . . . she summoned all her resources and reassured herself that it would all end quickly in disaster and regret.

She shrugged and mumbled, "OK."

Bweeb sighed and swept over to her, drawn by some irresistible magnetic force. He lavished her with yet more kisses and caresses while Henry nonchalantly pretended to rewind his mainspring.

Then he pointed to his shoulders with great deliberation and it took Fiz a moment or two to figure out what he was on about. Finally she got the message and wrapped her arms around his neck.

Together they floated up through the lift shaft, across the kitchen and out through the big double doors into the garden.

Rising up above the trees, they zoomed away to the south. His skin was smooth and rubbery and not easy to hold on to, but she locked her hands together and managed to feel quite safe in spite of the height. The view was breathtaking; an ocean of green, unsullied by any brutish skyline, unviolated by roads or rails or telephone lines. She could see Gran jogging across a clearing on her way back to the house. Fiz called out to her, but she was much too high to be heard. A long way up ahead, the mountains of Baramas loomed on the horizon.

Squinting her eyes and stretching her imagination to the limit, she thought, *If that's what my hair looks like I'm shaving my head tomorrow.*

Glancing back over her shoulder, the great white tower had already vanished.

CHAPTER sixteen

"PC Rather," the uniformed man at the door announced.

"Ah, Constable. I've been expecting you. I'm Dribbling, Central Electric."

The two men shook hands vigorously.

"You've got the warrant?"

"I have indeed . . . right here."

PC Rather handed Herb the document. Sylvia held her candle a little higher while Herb glanced, grimaced, grunted and nodded.

"Excellent. Perfect. You've done me proud, Constable. You can always count on a British bobby to come through in a crisis. Envy of the world, they are. I'll see there's something in this for you, my man."

Herb winked and handed back the warrant. Then he turned to Sylvia.

"Fetch my coat, will you darlin'?"

A moment later, Sylvia returned and asked in a low voice, "When will I see you again?"

"Hard to say, baby. I got other things on my mind just now, understand?"

Herb put on his coat and straightened the collar. When he looked back, he saw that her eyes were filling.

"Yes, I understand," she said, looking down. "I won't try to stop you . . . but I'll wait. I'll wait for you because, because you're—"

She broke off, suddenly lost for words. Herb looked away. Outside a light rain was falling and the London sky was blacker than he could ever remember seeing. Blue streaks from the squad-car lights chased each other across the fronts of the houses opposite. How many times had he played this scene? More than he could count. Why was it that every woman in London was coated in Velcro from head to foot? PC Rather rocked on his heels just out of earshot, water dripping off his helmet. Herb edged towards the door, but Sylvia touched his arm.

"Herb? You'll call me, won't you? I know we've only just met and everything, but I really want to see you again. I will see you, won't I? Please say something. . . Say that, *just maybe,* we could – ?"

Herb turned to face her.

"Listen, kid, 'maybe' is the longest word in the world. But if you want me to, I'll say it. What we had was beautiful. Maybe we'll meet again. Who knows? There's a whole world out there just waiting to come between us. You know what I'm saying? So don't wait for me. Life's too short. I gotta go. Ready, Constable?"

"When you are, sir."

Herb took Sylvia by the shoulders and pulled her towards him, as close as his belly would allow. Raising himself on his toes, he kissed her violently.

"So long, baby," he whispered, and he strode out into the cold, unforgiving night.

Sylvia sniffled and closed the door. In a heartbeat she was left holding a candle and a few precious memories. The October rain fell relentlessly and all of London held its breath, waiting for a hero.

Women — they're all the same! You look at 'em twice and they think it's a marriage proposal. Always trying to trap some poor sod. Just look at Anthea . . . stupid cow. Went and got herself knocked up, didn't she. Thought she could catch me like that. In her dreams! Didn't see me for dust.

At the age of thirty-six, Herbert Dribbling could not remember a time when he had had a full head of hair, or was able to see his toes, let alone bend over and touch them. But neither could he remember ever being anything other than one

117

hundred per cent babe-magnet. He didn't understand it in the least. But ever since that school trip
to France when he was ambushed in the corridor
and dragged into the girls' dormitory, only to
escape hours later with his pants in his hand and
love-hearts lipsticked all over his chest, he had been
forced to accept it as his cross to bear.

The two men walked out through the gate of
number thirty-five and up to the door of number
thirty-seven.

"Foul night, eh, Rather?"

"Rather."

"Wouldn't send a dog out in this weather. Still,
somebody's gotta do it, eh? How do we get into this
place?"

In the shelter of the porch, PC Rather produced
a pocket torch and studied the front door.

"It's double locked, but that shouldn't be a problem. We'll need the Big Key though."

Returning to the squad car, he came back a
moment later with a twelve pound sledgehammer.

"Best you stand back, sir," he cautioned. "It could
be messy."

Checking his stance and his swing, PC Rather
drew back the hammer. One well-aimed smash
should suffice. Again he checked his swing –

– just as a shrill woman's voice rang out through
the rain:

"OI, YOU! *YES, YOU!* STOP RIGHT WHERE YOU ARE! What do you think you're doing, you *hooligan!*"

Herb Dribbling and PC Rather turned to look as an elderly woman in a bulky overcoat came up the path.

"That's my Corny's house, I'll have you know! He just painted that door last summer. Clear off the both of you before I call the police!"

"Begging your pardon, ma'am, I am the police."

Agnes stepped a little nearer to the one with the sledgehammer and looked him up and down. It was very dark, but he did seem to be wearing some sort of uniform with a silly hat.

"Well, what's got into you then?" she exclaimed. "Don't they pay you enough that you've got to go breaking into people's houses as well? You ought to be ashamed of yourself! Go on, sling your hook."

Agnes elbowed him aside and stepped up to the door. She was soaked through and her hair hung in bedraggled strands as she rummaged for her keys. Her plastered arm hung in a sling inside her coat. The two men exchanged a weary glance. Herb stepped up behind her.

"Listen, love," he started, but Agnes wheeled around unexpectedly and belted him with her handbag before he could get any further.

"Don't you '*love*' me, you hooligan. You don't

love me at all. We haven't even met. I cannot abide young men getting familiar. You're not a policeman, I can see that straight off."

"Er, no. Right."

Herb rubbed his ear. He tried again more cautiously.

"Look, Mrs —?"

"Miss, if you please. Miss Agnes Plant. And who are you when you're at home — *which you're obviously not.*"

With great deliberation, Herb produced his ID.

"Herb Dribbling. Central Electric. Power Investigator. You may have noticed we have a little blackout. I'm trying to get it sorted. We think the cause of it may be in this street. We need to check your house. That's all."

"Blackout? You should be down at the hospital! That's where the blackout is, I'll tell you that for nothing. I've just come from there. In a right state, they are. This house is blacked out because I'm not home yet. That should be obvious, unless you're thick as well as rude."

Herb sighed and looked down. The fingers of his right hand passed tenderly across his forehead. Rain drizzled on his bald spot. He held his coat closed at the top to stop the water from trickling down the back of his neck. He could feel the night stretching out tediously in front of him.

PC Rather cleared his throat and raised his voice, "Excuse me, sir, but it doesn't seem you'll be needing the Big Key after all. Nor the entry warrant neither."

"What? Oh. Yes, quite right. You can go now, Constable. Much obliged."

"Yes, you run along," Agnes added. "Go do something useful. Catch some terrorists. Bashing people's doors down . . . the very idea!"

PC Rather turned and walked back to his squad car, greatly relieved.

Suddenly remembering she was in a hurry, Agnes unlocked and went inside. She was about to close the door when the electrical hooligan made as if to follow her.

"Just where do you think you're going?" she barked.

"I'd like to read the meter. If you don't mind."

"*At this time of night?* Come back tomorrow! There'll be no one here then."

She tried again to close the door, but Herb got his foot in the way.

"How I wish I could. But this is urgent. Very, very urgent. There's a blackout, remember?"

Agnes scowled. She could not possibly see how reading her meter was going to help the blackout at the hospital. She was cold and wet and her arm was sore. She badly needed to get back to her own planet. In fact, she had every reason to close the door in his face. But she hesitated, regarding the drowned rat on her doorstep with a mixture of pity and disgust. Pity prevailed by a hair.

"Oh, come in then, if you're quick about it. But I won't have you getting familiar, do you hear?"

The electrical hooligan stepped inside.

"The meter's just there, under the stairs," Agnes directed. "Wait while I turn the light on."

Agnes flicked the switch but nothing happened.

"Hmf," she muttered. "The bulb's blown. I must tell Corny."

"Never mind," the hooligan replied wearily. "I've got a torch."

Agnes disappeared upstairs to collect some clothes and things left behind at the time of the move, cursing every time she flicked a switch and discovered another blown bulb.

Under the stairs, a round pool of light crossed the wall to where the meter should have been. It was only barely recognizable. All the plastic parts had melted away and dripped into a puddle on the floor. The dials were still spinning like little propellers. Herb let out a low whistle under his breath. He flicked off the power supply and on the other side of the universe a tiny red standby lamp dimmed and went out.

From his pocket, he produced a hand-held

computer. He switched it on and tapped in the account number. He entered the new meter reading and pressed "print". A tongue of white paper emerged. He studied it by torchlight.

"Thirty-one million, four hundred and forty thousand, nine hundred and ninety-eight pounds . . . and fourteen pence?!" he blurted out loud.

This was inconceivable. He read it over and over. He double-checked all the figures. He cleared the entry altogether, retapped the numbers and reprinted it. Same result.

"Well, this is going to make somebody's day. Isn't it just."

He began checking the house for faults, starting in the two front rooms. There was nothing that looked suspicious. The place seemed deserted. It was hard to imagine anyone actually living there, let alone using thirty-one million poundsworth of power. Further down the hall was a loo, and then a small kitchen, but none of the power points had anything connected. In the back was the dining room. It was empty as well, and the yellow torch-beam swept all around the skirting boards. Everything seemed to be in order. . .

Herb was just about to go and check the upstairs when he spotted it.

There, in the corner nearest the back door, a blackened cable hung from a single socket. The plastic plug was long gone. With a screwdriver, he tried to prise the pins out of the wall, but the contacts had melted together. He tried to pick up the flex but it burned his fingers. Following it with his torch, he traced its path out through the back door, across a small patio and up two steps to a raised garden. Steam rose up from where it lay in the rain. Herb tracked it across the lawn, following the distinctive smell of burnt grass, singed in a dead straight line and pointing to the rhododendron in the corner. He put away his torch and picked up the cable, slightly cooled by the rain. Hand over hand, step by step, he followed where it led. There was an unmistakable tug on the line that reminded him of deep-sea fishing in Florida.

To the right of the rhododendron lay an old mattress, soaking wet and starting to smell. Herb stepped past it. He reached the corner of the garden and the trail went dead. There was nothing to be seen. When he let the cable drop, all the slack was taken up immediately. Immobile, he stood in the rain, hands in pockets, staring at the low bush. Water trickled down his face and he blew the droplets off his moustache. He looked at the mattress. He looked back at the bush. Nothing made sense. The cable vanished into a hole in the ground. But why? What could it possibly be servicing?

Underground heaters to keep the plants warm? Some kind of electronic pest control? A secret bomb shelter?

It didn't add up. None of it did. Herb got down on his hands and knees and peered under the bush. He tugged at the cable. The cable tugged back. He crawled a little nearer and took his torch out again. He pushed aside the lower branches and flicked it on. No matter where he shone the light, the beam bent towards the hole and vanished – as did all the rain that fell around the bush. He'd never seen anything like it. An unholy howl emanated from the ground. Warily, Herb Dribbling reached towards the hole. . .

A minute later, Agnes Plant came downstairs with a well-stuffed carrier bag.

"Oi! Are you finished then?" she called out.

There was no reply. Assuming that the electrical hooligan had done what he came to do and left again, she shrugged and double-locked the front door. Then she hurried into the garden and over to the rhododendron.

"Now, who's left that cable there?" she grumbled. "A body could trip over that. I must tell Corny. Never got my satsumas, either. Got something else, though . . . won't Mum be surprised!"

CHAPTER seventeen

. . .for the icebreaker to arrive. When finally it came, it was courtesy of Duncan. Quickly assessing the situation, he jumped down from the Wolf-girl's shoulders and ran over to Jack.

Addressing the room in general, he barked loudly, "It's OK! It's OK! He's with me. I prrr-omise he won't bite anyone or pee in the corner or anything like that. I've got him trrr-ained. Watch!"

The tide came back in a little as the braver of those present angled for a better look.

The dog turned to the boy and ordered, "SIT!"

Jack looked down at Duncan, speechless. His lip curled in an expression of disgusted amazement that said, quite unequivocally, *Are you out of your doggy little mind?*

"Rrrrr. *Sit, you fool!*" Duncan repeated. "JUST DO IT! *Rrr-rarf rarf!*"

Jack looked out around the sea of faces and non-faces and all the shapes and sizes of wild and weird beings in the room. It was somehow apparent that they wholly expected him to obey his dog. Some edged in a little nearer.

Duncan growled and whispered, "Don't embarrass me in frrr-ont of my new girlfriend. Just do as I say and it'll all go fine."

Boy gazed blankly at dog.

Me embarrass you? I am supposed to take orders from my dog in a room full of strangers and you *are worried about being embarrassed?*

Nervously, Jack took off his cap. Everyone gasped and leaped back again – perhaps fearing a live grenade concealed beneath it. He waved the empty hat reassuringly. It was obvious that they considered him to be truly dangerous. If he started arguing with Duncan, or refused to obey, it would only confirm their suspicions. There could be a stampede. People could get trampled fleeing the terrible Neasdenite. He decided to sit down.

A great sigh of relief whispered through the room.

"Good boy!" Duncan cried enthusiastically. "Now, rrr-oll over!"

From his position on the floor, Jack and his dog

127

were almost eye to eye. The dog was clearly basking in his moment of glory and Jack swore to himself, *I'll get you for this, you pompous flea-bag. You just wait.* But for the time being there was no point in resisting. He rolled over. He closed his eyes, held his arms and legs in the air and played dead. There was muted applause and expressions all around of how well Duncan had done to tame such a ferocious beast.

"I can tie him up outside if you want," he offered generously, "but rrr-eally, he won't be a prrr-oblem. C'mon boy, up you get!"

Jack got to his feet and put his cap back on.

One of the oval-eyed aliens then stepped up and asked, "So, are you a Toyota or a BMW?"

Jack blinked at him, trying to see into his glowing eyes.

"Am I a *what*?"

The alien looked from side to side, suddenly unsure of himself. One of his friends stepped forward to help him out.

"Earthlings always print their names on the backs of their shells. You know, Toyota, Volkswagen, GLXi 2.0 16V . . . so what are you?"

"Oh, he's a Ford Escort, this one," Duncan piped up. "Common as muck."

"His name is Jarnk," qLî~3o informed them, suddenly all too proud of having been the first to befriend the dangerous stranger. "I thought he was an Arcturan."

"So did I!" the air-snake added. "I'd never have come if I'd thought there were going to be real Earthlings."

"Hmm. Never heard of a Jarnk before. Do you have fuel injection, central locking, twin air bags? Rear head restraints? Are you advertised on television?"

"Are you an *astronaut*?"

This question was followed by gales of laughter and Jack quickly got the idea that the Russian and American Space Programmes were taken about as seriously as a kangaroo on a trampoline.

The air-snake did a perfect Neil Armstrong, complete with the crackly radio static: "*This is one small step for man. . .*"

"Understatement of the century. Couldn't even get out of his own solar system!"

"*Whitney Houston, we have a problem.*"

There was another roar of laughter, and one of the wolf's heads snorted, "As if *he* could do anything about it!"

From then on, the bombardment of questions was relentless. Open-mouthed, Jack turned helplessly from one face to the next.

"Why did you invade Kuwait? Why did you bomb Serbia and Afghanistan?"

"What is it you really like about car parks?"

"Why do men have nipples?"

"Are you a Capitalist Pig, or a Commie Bastard?"

"Hey, if you get olive oil from squeezing olives, does that mean baby oil comes from – ?"

"How many people have you killed?"

"Why do Kamikaze pilots wear helmets?

"Is Elvis *really* dead?"

"Why do you keep chickens cooped up in concentration camps? Are they dangerous?"

"You should never have made that film, *Mars Attacks!* Martians are such nice people. And *Independence Day* – that was scandalous! Hey, do you think I'll ever get to be on *X-Files*?"

"Why are you poisoning your planet?"

"Why do you spend so much time kicking those black and white balls around?"

"What is a 'God'?"

"What is a 'condom'?"

"What is a 'Double-Whopper-with-Cheese'?"

Jack felt utterly exasperated and increasingly claustrophobic. Voices were closing him in, shouting questions from all sides. It was impossible to hear himself think.

"*SHUT UP!*" he shouted.

Instantly the crowd fell back and the voices shrank to a frightened murmur. Duncan growled a warning to keep his human in its place.

"Look, I'm not a car, I'm not an astronaut and my name's not Jarnk, it's Jack. Jack Plant. I'm not a film-maker, I've never been to Kuwait or Serbia and I've never killed anybody – although I do know of a particular dog that may not live very long. Elvis is dead unless someone here kidnapped him. A condom is a wellie for your willy, if you can figure that out. Now, what *I* want to know is, *how come everyone in the universe speaks English?!*"

After a moment's silence, one of the Hairy Bricks hopped forward and squeaked like an un-oiled wheel, "Because of Earth television, of course. We watch it all the time."

"You get English television way out here?"

"And French and Chinese and Brazilian and all the rest. But more English and American than anything else. It's everywhere, night and day. The first Batman episodes are reaching the furthest stars by now."

"Yeah, but that doesn't mean you have to watch them. Don't you ever switch it off?"

"Can't. That's the problem. When you're telepathic, you receive television signals directly into your brain. You can't ever switch them off. I'm picking up three or four hundred different channels right now: CNN, MTV, Hockey Night in Canada, Man U at Stamford Bridge (2-nil at half-time), a documentary about chilli peppers, some Egyptian quiz show, Delia Smith on treacle tarts, *Buffy the Vampire Slayer* in Polish, Dutch pornography, *Songs of Praise*, repeats of *Dallas* and *Sesame Street*, three different James Bond films (one dubbed in Swahili) . . . loads of other stuff. It just goes on and on and on, all at once. More new stations come in every day."

"Hundreds of programmes all at once – inside your head?" Jack exclaimed. "That would bend my brain!"

"Tell me about it."

"Yeah, sure," Jack sympathized. He thought for a moment, then added, "But, hang on . . . if you're all so telepathic, how come you talk to each other?"

The iguana with the elephant's nose spoke up: "Because otherwise, everyone would think it was just another television signal and ignore it. Apart from really backward places like the Earth, spoken languages died out thousands of years ago. They're so inefficient. But when the tele-invasion came, we all had to start speaking again. English was something everyone could understand. So that's what we use."

Jack nodded, trying to take it all in.

"What are you doing here anyway?" the Living Light spelled out in dazzlingly bright letters. "You are a long way from home."

"Oh, I live here. My dad's with the university. He's a philosopher."

There was another explosion of laughter. Obviously the idea of an Earth "philosopher" was even more ridiculous than an Earth "astronaut".

"So what's he working on? A justification for the wholesale slaughter of all known forms of life?"

"Universal dominance by televisual hyper-stimulation?"

Jack bravely tried to face down these slanderous accusations.

"There are other things to do on Earth than just watch television and kill people, you know." This did not sound entirely convincing.

"Yeah, some of them are doing really important things," qLî~3o chipped in sarcastically. "Like kicking footballs around."

"Or gaping at pictures of naked women. I could never understand that. You seen one, you seen 'em all."

"So what is your father researching, then?" Octopus Trousers asked. Speaking to him/her/it was quite unsettling because the trousers were cut away at the front and the face was where the groin should be.

Jack was very reticent to discuss his father's work. For one, he didn't really understand it and secondly, he sometimes had the sneaking suspicion that his mother had been right about the little rubber washer thingies.

"Oh, it's something to do with——"

Just then, his attention was diverted so completely that he could no longer commit a single brain cell to the subject of his father's research. His voice trailed away and he raised his eyes above the assembled heads.

A red dress was descending from the gallery with something distinctly female in it. Amid the zoo of foreign bodies, it was startling to see such a standard configuration of arms and legs. Jack couldn't take his eyes off her. Everyone turned to see what he was looking at.

"Is that the princess?" he asked worshipfully.

"The *who*? Oh, no no no," one of the skinny aliens replied, slightly horrified. "She's an *Arcturan*. Infinitely more advanced than Earthlings, of course, but physically similar. Reminds me a bit of that bulbous one in Baywatch — those same unfortunate growths on her chest. At least you don't have that tragic deformity to worry about."

Jack continued to follow her with his eyes. *I think this girl has some very nice deformities. Really.*

"So?" Octopus Trousers persisted. "What is he working on?"

"Eh? What? Who is?"

With superhuman effort, Jack wrenched his focus away from the truly, divinely, wonderfully deformed Arcturan.

"Oh," he sighed. "Grommets. He's working on grommets."

Octopus Trousers twitched his tentacles. Two of them arched forward, pointing rather menacingly.

"*What* is a grommet?" he demanded.

It was a fascinating question; arguably the most fascinating and important question anyone had yet asked. But the conversation was doomed. Every synapse in Jack's cerebellum was firing in one direction only. The room collapsed into an irrelevant blur with one sublime figure held in sharp focus. He floated in timeless suspension as aeons rumbled by . . . calendar pages scattered in the wind, empires rose, flourished and crumbled; supernovas exploded gloriously and died away, unnoticed . . . the great tide of time swelled and thundered by, unremembered.

Without tearing his eyes away, he moved his mouth and replied, "*Why* is a grommet. Not what, *why*."

Those around him glanced from one to another, momentarily dumbfounded. Some of the more far-sighted thinkers nodded pensively, clearly impressed, but Jack did not notice. He was present in body only. This was of no real account because his novelty had begun to wear off. The crowd gradually returned to whatever they were doing before all the commotion. Conversations rekindled. The music came back on and suddenly there was more dancing and singing and shouting. Those who had fled in the initial panic reappeared one by one. Duncan barked at his human to be a good boy and ran back to Wolf-girl. qLî~3o wandered off in pursuit of Miss WonderWart.

Utterly oblivious to anything else, Jack swam into the eyes of the most enchantingly beautiful girl he had ever seen or dreamed or imagined as she came gracefully through the crowd, smiling and laughing and nodding to various friends.

Her ivory hair was cropped short and flat across the top. Her wide-set eyes were large and violet in colour – as captivating as the sea but brighter, as if lit from within. Her lips were a natural blood red and her skin was like milky coffee. She was slim and shapely, statuesque in a scarlet, spray-on dress; no vpl. It was hard to say how old she was . . . perhaps a little older than Jack, but with a wide, girlish smile. She proceeded directly towards him.

If someone had told the boy that his mouth was hanging open and his expression conveyed a combination of terror and slavering imbecility, he would probably have done something about it. Unfortunately, no one did.

The girl walked straight up to him and in a deep, confident voice announced, "Hi. I'm Zaÿfa."

Jack smiled. That was very important. Thinking about it afterwards, he was very pleased that he had remembered to smile. True, it was a no-brain, village-idiot sort of grin, but a smile nonetheless. The faculty for making recognizable sounds in any formally joined-up fashion completely deserted him. He might have done better if she had said, "*Quick — what's the second law of thermodynamics?*" He could have looked it up in a book! A right answer existed! But, what was the right answer to, "*Hi. I'm Zajfa*"?

By the time he figured it out, he found himself staring at a luminous tattoo on her back, nestling cosily between her elegant shoulder blades as (having got a drink and something to eat), she receded into the crowd again.

"Hi. I'm Jack," he called out.

It was a good answer. An excellent answer. Perhaps the best possible answer. But she didn't hear it. She was already dancing with somebody else.

CHAPTER eighteen

"Life's road may be treacherous; its travellers deceitful. But The Way of the Grommet is broad like the sky and knows not these perils. Seek the Grommet of Inner Peace and your trials will be as dew on the morning grass." The Way of the Grommet, page 192

Herbert Dribbling winged into the dining room and out through the double doors, colliding bodily with Jack's gran who was just coming up the stairs after her run. The two of them tumbled into the grass and had some difficulty disentangling themselves.

Gran was first to her feet and, planting one foot firmly on the intruder's throat, informed him, "One move and I'll break your neck. Who are you and what do you want?"

Herb's face turned a curious shade of puce.

"Gllbrrlgrkl . . . glrk —"

Delia lessened her pressure just a touch.

The man gasped, "Dribbling. Hhherb Dribbling . . . Central . . . Elecch—"

His hand moved towards his pocket and Gran

threatened to squeeze cider from his Adam's apple. The hand stopped. Without removing her foot, she bent down, reached into his coat pocket and came out with a plastic card wallet. She flipped it open and checked his ID. She took her foot off his neck, leaving the sole-pattern from her trainer imprinted on his skin. She stepped back.

"So what do you want? We don't have electricity here."

Casually, she tossed the card wallet at him. It landed on his chest. Herb sat up, holding his throat. His eyes were bugging out of his head. He got up and put his ID away, grateful that he could still breathe. That was a good thing. The less-good-thing was that he had no idea where he was.

A minute ago, it had been a wet October night in NW10. Suddenly it was sunny, spring daylight in the middle of a jungle. What had been a perfectly ordinary, Victorian terraced house was now a massive tower-like affair made of opalescent slabs. He began to suspect that Sylvia might have put something more than milk and sugar in his coffee.

He tried to pull himself together; he was a professional, after all. He'd seen a lot of strange things in his life and he was trained to ignore everything that did not concern him. Producing a comb from his inside jacket pocket, he carefully dragged his stringer into place. Personal appearance is very important when dealing with the public.

"Er, do you know anything about a house in Neasden . . . 37 Albemarle Gardens?" he asked, almost casually.

Gran narrowed her eyes, trying to work out where this enquiry might be leading.

"Yes," she said slowly. "I used to live there. The electric supply is still in my name I believe."

Herb produced a piece of paper from his pocket and studied it for a moment.

"Ms Delia Plant?"

"*Yes. . .?*"

Herb sniffed, rubbing his throat. He handed her the slip of paper.

"This is your electricity bill. It seems, er, unusually high. I wonder if you could tell me something about that."

Delia squinted at the paper. She scowled and held it a little further away.

Pointing at one of the long rows of figures, she demanded, "This bit here, is that the account number?"

"No, that is the amount owing: £31,440,998 . . . and fourteen pence."

Silently, Delia studied the paper in great detail: the date, the account number, the name and address, the previous meter reading, the current reading, the units of electricity consumed, the rate per unit, the amount owing. She turned it over and looked at the back. It was blank. She looked at the front again, which still said the same thing. A hollow feeling developed in her gut. Her natural inclination would have been to protest that there had obviously been some mistake . . . but she had the disabling intuition that it might actually be correct. She handed the paper back to him hoping to make it go away.

"That's yours," he said. "That's your copy."

A breeze stirred the grass around them. She heard his voice as if from a long way off: "*That's . . . your . . . copy. . .*" She did not especially want a copy of a bill for thirty-one million pounds. She began to feel slightly dizzy.

"Perhaps we ought to go inside and talk about this," she suggested.

But, just as they turned towards the house, the white door gushed open and out flew Agnes – one empty sleeve flapping in the wind, her good arm holding tight to her handbag. There seemed to be an exceptionally large bulge under her coat. Herb leaped out of the way as she came hurtling down the steps, but Gran managed to wrestle her to a stop before she fell. A moment later, a stuffed carrier bag flew out and smacked Herb on the side of the head. The white door slid closed.

"Agnes! What are you — ?" Gran started to say.

But before she got any further, the bulge under her daughter's coat suddenly slipped. Delia watched as the bulge dropped a little further . . . then further still.

There was a soft *ffflump* as it fell to the ground. Everyone looked down.

Below Agnes's overcoat, the edge of a pale blue hospital gown showed. Below that, her legs were bare. On her feet was a pair of soggy slippers. Between her feet was tall, green grass. And in the grass — robustly pink, completely naked and still wet-behind-the-ears — was a newborn baby girl. Luckily, she had landed on her bottom and the grass cushioned her fall. She gave a bit of a start, arching her back and throwing out her arms reflexively. With a wrinkly wince, her rosy, gummy mouth twitched open, ready to wail if necessary . . . but then it closed again. She wasn't hurt. Without a sound, she went straight back to sleep.

Feigning enormous surprise, Agnes raised her hand to her mouth and exclaimed, "Goodness gracious — I've had a baby! Who'd have thought it?"

A stunned silence issued from two half-opened mouths. Herb sighed and passed his hand over his forehead. Half covering his face, he continued to eyeball the baby, just to make sure he wasn't hallucinating.

142

"Agnes Plant, what is going on?!" Delia demanded. "Where did you get this baby?"

Her daughter recoiled and put on an intensely puzzled expression.

"What do you mean, *where did I get it?* I've been to the hospital and now I've had my baby. Just like everybody else. You needn't make such a fuss. Didn't even hurt — not like they say it does. *Oi!* What are *you* doing here? And stop gaping at my baby, you pervert! You'd turn your back if you were any kind of gentleman — *which you're not.*"

Respectfully, Herb turned his back. He took the opportunity to remove his overcoat and he folded it over one arm. He still hadn't a clue where he was, but he was trying his best not to think about it. Raising his eyes to the purplish sky, he whispered a plea for strength under his breath. Delia quickly stooped to pick up the sleeping baby.

"He's a right hooligan, that one," Agnes explained to her mother. "I caught him breaking into the house. You ought to thank me for that. About to smash the door in, he was."

"Yes, yes, but Agnes — *the baby!* I mean, whose is it really?"

Agnes returned a stony look.

"I told you that already," she insisted. "She's mine. She's mine and nobody else's. I'm her mother and I'm calling her Mary."

Still facing the other way, Herb began to whistle softly to himself, swaying back and forth on his heels. Delia glanced at him briefly and then turned back to her daughter.

"Really? Is that so? Who's the father then?" she demanded.

Agnes took the baby, cradling it in her one good arm.

"*Father?* What's she want a father for? I never had one. Isn't she cute, though? And so quiet. That sedative worked a treat. Must get me some more of those."

"AGNES! You do not give *sedatives* to newborn babies!"

"Oh, keep your hair on. I'm not stupid. It was only half a one. 'Cause she's so little. I kept the other half for later."

Agnes picked up her carrier bag and started towards the house. Herb turned around, cleared his throat and straightened his tie.

"Excuse me, Ms Plant, but about this bill. . ."

Delia looked at him and then back at her daughter who was on her way up the steps. One of these disasters would have to wait. She turned back to the electricity man.

"The bill, yes, the bill. Thirty-one million, you say."

"And four hundred and forty thousand—"

"Yes yes yes, and the rest, I know. It is a bit high, isn't it? Will you have a cup of tea?"

"Just had coffee, thanks."

They started towards the house. Some men might have been gobsmacked by the sight of a massive, seven-storey tower rising majestically out of the jungle, the predominant whiteness of its walls throwing off glinty flashes of gold and pinky-blue. It was impressive, to be sure, and like nothing else Herb Dribbling had ever seen . . . but not the sort of thing that held his attention for very long. Another man might have been astounded by the unsullied beauty, the rampant fecundity of the surrounding rainforest — the weird flowers, the exotic fruits and berries, the soaring trees strung with vines . . . but no, that did not float his boat either.

No, on the short walk to the house, Herb found himself giving Delia Plant the once over instead; up and down, back to front. She was wearing a pair of grey tracksuit bottoms over a simple lime-green swimsuit. Her arms were tanned and, after her run, she exuded a raw sense of health and fitness. With the practised scrutiny of a used car dealer, he assessed her appeal:

Not bad at all for her age . . . early forties, I'd say. Good figure — nothing too saggy. Can't see the legs. Nice eyes. Good cheekbones. A bit flat-chested. Could do with a face-lift. But all in all, not too bad — for her age. Must have been something special when she was young.

But Delia Plant was not young and so scored a mere 4.5 on Herb's demanding yardstick. This was insufficient to trigger any major charm offensive, so he got straight down to business.

"Forgive me for asking," he started, "but where are we exactly? I mean, I get the feeling this is not quite Neasden any more, is it."

Delia gnawed at her lower lip. Her hugely capable brain was doing several gymnastic routines at once, working out the best way forward. Her immediate plan was to play very dumb, at least for the time being. This would hopefully buy enough time to decide what to actually do.

"Oh, well, it is . . . in a way. It's sort of, *Outer* Neasden, you might say."

She went through a mental inventory of her financial assets: a studio in Munich owed her seven-thousand pounds for session work; her second novel was selling well but the advance had already been spent; in New York there was talk of a retrospective of her paintings which should raise a few bob; there were the royalties she received from having invented a particularly successful aluminium smelting process and, in Hollywood, she'd been promised a much bigger role in the sequel to her last film. She definitely had money coming in. But all put together, it was nowhere near thirty-one million. Clearly, *paying the bill* was not an option.

"Outer Neasden?" Herb repeated sceptically.

He nodded and glanced over his shoulder at the surrounding forest.

"Like, how far out?"

He could not believe he was having this conversation. He tried to remind himself that only minutes before he had been groping about under a rhododendron in the rain. They reached the top of the steps. Inside, on the wall opposite, he noted two large doors, black and white. Off to the right, the crazy woman with the baby was shouting into a hole in the floor:

"Henry, this is my new baby, Mary. Say hello nicely, Baby Mary."

She had removed her overcoat and managed to loop the baby into the sling that supported her bad arm. Pulling one of the ropes towards her with her good hand, she clutched it between her knees with a well-practised iron grip. The rope lurched upwards. Mother and baby disappeared.

"Do be careful, won't you, Agnes," Delia called casually.

She turned back to the rotund meter-reader, *bringer-of-bad-news-who-ought-to-be-shot*. "Have a seat," she ordered.

Delia indicated a dining table on the left. Herb sat while she got herself a glass of water, further stalling for time. The inside of the tower was made of the same stuff as the outside and the walls danced with a subtle swirl of colour. Herb's eye travelled once around the room before coming to rest uneasily on a familiar-looking cable emerging from under the white door. It trailed across the floor, then jerked up and out of sight, parallel to the rope lifts. He stood abruptly, like a mentally retarded hunting dog finally picking up the scent.

"What is that cable for?" he called out aggressively.

"Cable? What cable?"

"You said you didn't have electricity here."

"We don't. Well, not really."

Herb flared his nostrils and snorted, "Either you do or you don't."

"Oh, I always liked multiple choice. Let me think . . . no, we don't."

"So what's that cable for?"

"What cable?"

Herb looked away and muttered something inaudible. He took a deep breath and exhaled loudly. Marching across the room, he picked up the extension lead between his thumb and forefinger.

"*This*. This cable right here. This *electrical* cable.

This electrical cable which looks remarkably similar to the one trailing out the back of your house in Albemarle Gardens, across the grass and under that bush in the corner. The very cable that drained off thirty-one million quid's worth of juice in the space of half an hour, blacking out the entire country. Now listen, sister, I have had a very long day and my patience is running thin. I want some answers and I want 'em fast. What precisely is on the other end of this?"

Delia raised both eyebrows. Nothing impressed her less than a short, balding male in a cheap suit throwing his overweight around, even if she did happen to owe him an obscene amount of money. Paradoxically, the more aggressive he became the more calm and unconcerned she felt.

"Ooh, I'm not sure," she cooed. "A double socket, I should think. Or is it a single?"

She raised the glass to her lips. The image of a cartoon bull pawing the earth came to her mind briefly as Herb started huffing and puffing through his nose. The front string of his comb-over flopped down between his eyes. His professional detachment was ebbing away, replaced by an all-consuming, apoplectic rage. He was not at all accustomed to women giving him the wind-up — especially some old bird who was not even worth flirting with. Standing on his throat was bad enough, but this was going too far. He stepped up dangerously close to her.

"And *what,* is plugged *into* that socket?" He very nearly spat the words in her face.

Delia shrugged.

"A guitar amplifier, if you must know. Hardly the sort of thing to pose a problem for a big strong power company like yours. You can take a look if you like."

She waved one hand towards the ropes. Herbert Dribbling started in that direction and stopped immediately. Something was not right. His professional instinct told him so. What about the rain and the rhododendron and the terraced house in Neasden? The woman wasn't being straight. She wasn't giving him the whole story.

He wagged an accusing finger at her and said, "You're not being straight. You're not giving me the whole story, are you?"

Delia sipped her water.

"Of course not," she said. She paused and set down the glass. "But I will if you want."

Stepping right up to him, she walked him steadily backwards as she spoke: "You fell through a black hole and now you're on another planet on the other side of the universe. Does that make you feel better? Well, you're a way out of your area, aren't you. So, as they say in America, you can take your electric bill and cram it sideways. Do what you like. Call the police. Tell them an old woman who lives in a hole under a bush won't pay up. See how far you get. Right now, I'm ready for my shower. Goodbye."

Delia manoeuvred him as far as the black door. Reaching over his shoulder, she wrenched it open with one hand and, shielding herself behind it, smiled cheerily and waved. Herb was stretched out till he was considerably wider than he was tall, then vanished trailing a blood-curdling scream. His raincoat was sucked off the back of the chair and the water glass went with him as well. The door slid closed again.

Delia sighed and ruffled her hair with both hands. She had to laugh, just thinking of the pompous, puffed-up look on his face.

Men! They're so pathetic!

She crossed the room and closed the garden doors to keep out the draught. . .

CHAPTER nineteen

"Pleased to meet you, I'm ᘯώᶘ. Everyone says I look like Margaret Thatcher. Do you think I look like Margaret Thatcher? She is thought to be very beautiful, is she not?"

Jarred from his reverie, Jack tore his bereaved eyes away from Zaÿfa's receding tattoo and turned to see two bone-coloured triangular shapes, each the size of a half-deflated football. They were joined horizontally by a fleshy and pulsing transverse muscle. The two sides had one eye each, and in between hung a hinged mouth that looked like an optional, bolt-on accessory. From under each half, a long, stick-like leg, no thicker than coat-hanger wire, extended to the floor. The legs were jointed at the knee, but had no foot as such.

With great deliberation, Jack studied 𝒮ώ𝜁 from various angles. He nodded slowly.

"You know, there *is* a certain resemblance . . . in the eyes, I think. Definitely. And the mouth. You're virtually a dead-ringer. Where are you from?"

"Oh, a little place near Alpha Centauri, not at all far from Earth, actually. What is it — four, maybe four and a half light-years? It's amazing we haven't met before."

"Amazing."

"Of course, everyone on 𝜌✳◄ — that's my planet — is dreading the day that you Earthlings get the hang of Deep Space Travel. Every time you have one of those silly shuttle launches, property prices plummet."

Bending one wire leg up towards her face, 𝒮ώ𝜁 jabbed herself in the eye with the sharp end. She flicked her ankle and the eyeball emerged with a dull *pop*. Raising it high above her head, she rotated it from side to side, presumably to get a better view of the room, all the while standing on her other impossibly thin leg.

"Er, that's . . . quite a good trick," Jack observed, trying to keep his reactions in check and his mind in one piece. He hoped that if he could just keep the conversation going, he wouldn't have to stop and think about what he had just seen.

"So, do you live here or have you just come for the party?" he asked.

"I live here. I'm a student. Like everybody else."

"A student? Oh, like, at the university, you mean. So you're reading philosophy."

Ⴢώζ replaced her eyeball.

"Of course. Say, what do you think of this Pleiades Theorem postulating the meaning of life as the square root of $\Psi_b \odot^{3/8}$?"

Jack thought for a moment then said the first thing that came into his head: "Nah, the meaning of life is more like Arsenal 3, Tottenham nil."

Ⴢώζ suddenly twisted her head to one side and said, "Will you excuse me? I have to go empty my brain."

Jack nodded and waved.

As he turned around, qLî~3o reappeared, nudging him on the arm and saying, "Hey Jarnk, you chatting up Ⴢώζ? Amazing legs, eh? Looks a bit like that queen of yours – what was his name again?"

"Margaret Thatcher."

"That's the one. What a sexy guy."

qLî~3o shuffled back into the crowd and was soon dancing a sort of tango with a giant glass trout. Jack stood on his toes, trying to spot Zaÿfa, but he couldn't see her anywhere. He wandered about, craning his neck over the mass of bodies.

Twice he glimpsed a shock of ivory hair, only to lose it again.

He began to lose his bearings as well. From the gallery, the room had appeared to be one huge, open warehouse, but as he walked about it became more labyrinthine, with partitions and corridors, nooks and alcoves he hadn't noticed before. He could have sworn the spaces were changing size and shape as he walked. He hadn't gone more than five metres, but when he looked around a wall had grown up behind him, cutting him off from the main room.

He stopped in his tracks, studying the walls. They were definitely alive . . . moving, growing and dissolving of their own accord. He stood still as a different room brought itself to him; the floor flowed past on either side, with walls looming forward as others receded. Different people, different music and a different atmosphere came with it. He walked on, cautiously.

He'd totally lost track of Duncan, but that didn't bother him too much. Duncan could take care of himself. In fact, he had the uncomfortable feeling that his dog might be having a better time than he was. Everywhere he turned there were people of every conceivable description, doing all the usual party things: laughing, drinking, snogging, bouncing off the ceiling – plus other activities of a more intimate nature. Sirians danced with Casseopians. One of the Pumpkin-things was cuddled up in a corner with a Hairy-Brick. Neither of them had arms, so it was hard to tell what was going on. Something quite cosy, by the look of it.

Jack began to feel a bit strange. This was strange in itself because everyone was at least as strange as he was. No one was normal. There were no more than three or four beings of any one species, so what could "normal" possibly have been?

But in spite of this, and perhaps without being aware of it, he somehow harboured the assumption that, while everyone else was an *alien*, he, Jack Plant, was a *human*. "Human" was the right and true and good thing to be. How could they fail to realize this? He found it very hard to accept that, far from being the crown of creation, he was counted among the most feared, despised and ridiculed creatures in the cosmos. On top of that, he felt a complete pillock for having blanked out so badly with Zaÿfa. He'd clearly blown his main chance and now he couldn't see her anywhere.

The only normal-looking person in the place and I reacted as if she were the weirdest! Why did I do that? Why didn't I say. . .? Oh, what's the point — she wouldn't be interested in me anyway. Probably has some body-built barbarian boyfriend with a magic sword called Tharg. At least I smiled. I think I smiled. But I could have asked her where she was from. I already knew where she was from. She didn't know that I knew where she was from. But that's so boring! It just sounds like some tedious line of chat. Yeah, so what else? "Hail Zaÿfa-of-Arcturus! I am Jack-of-Earth! Behold my magic sword whose name is Shirley!" Too idiotic. "Hey baby, I didn't know angels could fly this low. . ." Pure Gorgonzola! Why didn't I just say "Hi, I'm Jack"? That's only as boring as what she said.

He wandered aimlessly. Stepping through a short corridor, he entered what seemed to be a separate space where a pair of lime green Orionese stood on the left hand wall at 90°. This was some curious thing and he stepped up for a closer look. But as he approached the wall, his gravitational alignment seemed to shift and he stepped off the floor on to the wall with them. Then the wall felt as if it were the floor. The Orionese didn't have arms or hands but they waved their eye-stalks at him. Jack waved back. He felt as if his stomach were stuck between his lungs.

"Hey," he called. "What happened? Did the room just turn on its side or what?"

They looked at each other ponderously. They looked at Jack.

"No," one of them said. "Your consciousness did. Gravity is a state of mind. Didn't you know that?"

Jack smiled weakly and nodded as if it were the most obvious thing in the world. Of course he knew that. Everyone knew that.

"Oh. Yeah. Right."

He waved and laughed and the Orionese scuttled away on their very short legs. Turning around again, he noticed a door straight ahead of him. Above it was a flight of light-stairs — glowing rectangular planks supported by nothing at all that created a series of steps spanning wall to ceiling. The door opened and Zaÿfa appeared upside down, standing on the top edge of the doorframe. Jack called out to her as she "descended" the underside of the stairs, hanging straight down by the soles of her feet. She gave him a funny, upside-down smile, waved in what seemed like slow motion and then disappeared through another doorway that opened into the ceiling.

Totally confused and disorientated, he ran towards the door she had just come through but, just as he reached it, it slid shut. He whirled around as the stairs above him faded away to nothing. The room was completely sealed off. Never having been in a closed room with no doors or windows, he felt close to panic. A moment later, a new portal materialized in the wall in front of him and instinctively he dashed towards it. It slid open, emitting a flood of pale yellow light. Jack fled straight through it —

— and immediately found himself tumbling, not down, but forward in a face-first free-fall from the ceiling of a round, bright space. Light poured in all around him . . . a wavy, watery surface rushed up to meet him . . . his arms flailed, trying to right himself in mid-air. He felt a wet slap against his face . . . he heard a splash . . . and after that, all sensory impressions altered radically.

There was the sound of water splashing and swishing around the edge of the room. Deeper, within the water, there was the *shush* of shifting currents, gently folding into each other. But he couldn't so much hear that as feel it. He had the dazzling sensation of light flooding in on all sides, above and below, but he couldn't have said whether his eyes were open or closed. He felt neither hot nor cold.

In fact, he lost track of his body altogether. He could feel himself moving — a slithery, slippery, swelling sensation — and yet, waves seemed to pass right through him. There was no clear distinction between Jack Plant and the surrounding liquid. He had become the water of the pool.

Jack had heard of people with bodies losing their minds, but never a mind losing its body. Curiously, the first thing that bothered him about this was that his dad would be cross if he lost his new trainers. Then the broader implications took hold and in a desperate, scatterbrained panic, he erupted all over the surface trying in vain to break out, to throw himself back into the air, back into human form. . .

But his thrashing was futile. There was nothing to be done. Very slowly, the horror subsided and he became deeply depressed. He would have to be siphoned off and carried home in a bucket. He'd spend the rest of his life sloshing around in the bathtub . . . until he evaporated.

How could he possibly explain?

"Dad, I'm really sorry, but I seem to have lost the body you gave me . . . and, er, the trainers as well."

It just sounded careless in the extreme. A bus fare, an umbrella, a sock, yes – but not your entire body. He didn't even have a mouth to say it with.

Jack's disembodied consciousness floated for what seemed an eternity. All sense of time was suspended . . . until at some point, he became aware of a certain rotation to the water. It was barely perceptible at first as there was so little to judge it by. But he could definitely feel himself revolving.

As the spin accelerated, he also realized that the level in the pool was dropping. The water was draining out through the bottom. Being liquefied was bad enough, but going down the plughole was decidedly worse. Struggling against the draw of the whirlpool, he splashed and thrashed and forced himself out to the edge where the pull was weakest. The whole room was now whirling around a plunging vortex in the centre. A great slurping *suck* gurgled and echoed around the walls, vibrating through the liquid remains of Jack Plant. The water level dropped steadily till there was only a few centimetres left.

Then, just as he felt himself draining dizzily towards certain oblivion, he felt a reassuring bodily sensation. His cheek bumped and juddered against the slick, wet floor of the pool. His legs came back: his knees, his shins, his feet . . . *his shoes!* Suddenly he was all there again and he skidded to a halt, face down with the chrome-rimmed sinkhole just one centimetre away from his left eyeball.

He rolled on to his back, lying slightly downhill. He took a deep breath and exhaled. *What was that about?!* As an experience, it was something he could well have done without and his sense of relief was euphoric — like thinking yourself dead and then discovering you were still alive! He found himself remembering the word *"reconstituted"* that he had seen on orange juice cartons. For a long moment, he lay panting and gazing up at the luminous vault above him. There was no hint of the door he had fallen through. The walls and ceiling were like frosted glass, brilliantly lit from the other side. He felt achy all over and he stretched his arms and rotated his shoulders. Very slowly, he sat up.

Two things he noticed almost simultaneously: he wasn't wet. He was absolutely dry. Even his clothes were dry.

But . . . they weren't his clothes.

Jack jumped up and looked down at his feet . . . not a Nike tick in sight. He seemed to be wearing a dusty pair of well-worn cowboy boots, complete with spurs. His astounded eyes travelled up his body: a stiff pair of jeans were tucked into the boots . . . gun-belt and holster, low-slung around his waist . . . red checkered shirt . . . suede waistcoat. Knotted around his neck was a blue and white polka-dot bandanna. On his head, a ten-gallon hat. Jack fingered this fancy-dress kit with repugnant disbelief. Lifting one heel, he reached down and flicked the silver spur.

Too naff for words. . .

He had never really been into cowboys. They were just not his sort of thing. But at least he was in one piece; that was the main thing. Being a cowboy was better than being a pail of water. But this party was getting weird beyond compare. Time to find Duncan and go home. He took one step in no direction at all, then jerked around in total alarm. He nearly tripped over his boots. That's when he noticed the third thing.

It wasn't his body either; he was over two metres tall, broad-shouldered and barrel-chested.

This realization defied all bounds of horrification and instantly he changed his mind; it would have been better to stay a pail of water. Having no body was better than being in the wrong body! He'd been reincarnated before he'd even died. He'd only barely had a go at being Jack Plant from north-west London — now he'd have to start all over being somebody else!

And yet, in spite of this unspeakable, unthinkable outrage, he could not seem to respond in any adequate way. He wanted to scream. He wanted to pull his hair out, tear his skin off . . . he wanted to rip open that massive chest, jump free and throw himself through the wall — *now! Immediately!* He wanted to wrestle himself to the ground and beat himself up. . .

But he couldn't do any of that. He wasn't in control; the hulking brainless brute had a mind of its own! He saw and heard his toe casually tapping. He watched as the fingers of his left hand started to click on the offbeat. Raising his head, he found he had a rich baritone voice — only slightly nasal — so he sang a little song made famous by the immortal Gene Autry:

"*I got spurs that jingle-jangle-jingle,*
as I go riding merrily along. . ."

The melody resonated around the room. Jack sang verse after verse of a song he had never heard before, a song that would haunt him for the rest of his days. Imprisoned in a musical cowboy, he tapped the toe of his dusty right boot, jangling the aforementioned spur. He clicked the fingers of his manly left hand. He wanted to pull his ears off. He wanted to weep or scream, or both. But his mouth would not obey. It just went on singing.

Eventually the cowboy ran out of verses. He chuckled to himself and, for no apparent reason, whipped his pearl-handled pistol from its holster and twirled it on his finger before replacing it again, all in one smooth, well-practised action. He sucked his teeth and hitched his trousers.

"Why, shucks," he drawled, "wonder where I left my durned horse. Better mosey about and have myself a gander."

Swaggering up to the glowing wall on bowed legs, he pushed his way through and was gone, taking the hapless Jack with him.

CHAPTER twenty

Herb Dribbling hurtled through the air and squelched on to a soggy mattress that had been left in the garden for that very purpose. He sat up, gasping for air, as his coat flew up behind him, wrapping itself around his neck. A second later, a heavy-bottomed water glass cracked him on the back of the head. He groaned and rubbed his bonce, plastering his hair into place. It was drizzling again. He stood up and slipped the raincoat on.

He was back where he'd been a half-hour previous. That was some relief, but it was also profoundly disturbing. Because he had definitely been somewhere else . . . somewhere that wasn't London . . . somewhere warm and sunny. There was a tower in a jungle. And that crazy woman with the baby. But then — she'd been here as well! She was the one who'd let him in in the first place. What about the other one then? The one who stood on his throat . . . the one that owed the thirty-one million quid? He'd just been speaking to her! They'd been virtually nose to nose! But, *where exactly?*

Herb turned a slow, full circle on the grass. Sealed by the black door at the other end, the white hole he had just been flung from was completely invisible. There was nothing untoward to be seen. It was as if the night sky had just hawked and spat him out. He felt deeply troubled. This was something he hated to admit, even to himself. He was simple and practical by nature, not easily ambushed by the bizarre and irrational. He cherished his certainties: he was a man and all men were warriors. A woman was a warrior's reward. A house was a house. A bush was a bush. These things he knew and understood. They constituted the bedrock of truth from which the modest edifice of his life rose with confidence.

But, *a hole in the ground?* What was that? Suddenly, he wasn't at all sure. For the first time in his life, he felt he might be losing his grip.

Tell them an old woman who lives in a hole under a bush won't pay her bill. That's what she said. But . . . but. . .?

He looked at the bush and he looked all around

the garden. Rain pattered on the roses and the honeysuckle. It splashed into shallow puddles on the sodden mattress. Since cutting the supply to 37 Albemarle Gardens, power had slowly returned to London and between the houses in the next road he glimpsed a row of sodium streetlights, haloed by the slanting rain. In the house next door, Sylvia's bedroom window gave off a warm, enticing glow.

Herb raised his head, letting the water stream over his face and drip from his chin. Heroically, he raised both arms. Pointing to all the little yellow lights, he cried out to the impassive sky: "I did that! Every one of them, turned on by *me*! Where there was fear and darkness, I brought hope and light. I gave the people back their pride, their dignity. I gave them back their electric toothbrushes and their Sony PlayStations. *I gave them something to live for!* And what thanks do I get? I get stepped on by some old wrinkly who owes thirty-one million quid!"

This was not acceptable. He would get to the bottom of it if it were the last thing he did. He blew the rain from his moustache. He mopped his brow with a soggy sleeve. Looking down, he nudged the mysterious extension lead with the toe of his shoe. This was where it had all started.

Crawling on his hands and knees, Herb followed

the lead once more across the lawn to the rhododendron. There was just enough light from Sylvia's
window for him not to need his torch. The material surrounding the hole looked the same as the
stuff the tower had been made of. But that tower
could not possibly be under the ground. It was too
big. Too sunny. Too jungly. He picked up a pebble
and dropped it into the hole. There was no sound
of it hitting the bottom. He tried another. Still
nothing. Picking up a third, he chucked it through
the opening then quickly put his ear up to the hole
to listen.

Invisible forceps reached up and seized him by
the lugs, stretching him out like a ribbon and
whipping him off his feet. A bit of old chewing
gum on the sole of one shoe was the last thing to be
seen as Herb was dragged screaming into the bot-
tomless blackness. . .

For seven seconds, someone played Greensleeves
badly.

Then the big white door zipped open and he was
propelled across the living room, only to *whump*
bodily against the closed garden door. As he
collided, his belly and his face flattened and spread
sideways, but the glass proved uncommonly strong.
He bounced, staggered, danced three steps in
reverse, tripped and crashed to the floor, flat out on
his back.

In the bathroom, one flight up, Gran was under the shower and didn't hear a thing. At the top of the tower, Agnes was singing and cooing to Baby Mary when she thought she heard a *thump* followed by a *thud*. Briefly she stopped and cocked her head towards the lift shaft. She wondered if her mother had fallen in the bath.

But surely she'd call me if it were serious, Agnes told herself. *I mean, if she'd knocked herself out or something like that. . .*

As no other sound came, she carried on playing with baby.

Herb tried to sit up and immediately fell back. He lay contemplating the ceiling for a little longer, then tried again more successfully. He could see a smudgy imprint from where he'd bounced off the glass. The knees of his trousers were soaked and grass-stained. He tried to massage his nose back into place but it was too sore. Very carefully, he got to his feet.

He studied the room with great intent. He went to the dining table and glanced at the note that Jack had left. He looked out over the garden. Bathed in sunshine. You couldn't even call it a garden. It was wild. A jungle. This was no "Outer Neasden". It wasn't even England. It was more like Australia. *Maybe I fell right through?* Herb dismissed this thought as far too idiotic. He glanced back at the pair of doors in the back wall, noting the guilty extension lead still snaking out from under the white one.

That's the door I came in by. . .

He went slowly over to the flex, leaving a trail of muddy footprints. He picked it up. He looked over to the lift shaft where it trailed away upstairs. The sound of running water tumbled in the distance and, more faintly, there was the sound of a woman singing and laughing. He looked back at the cable and dropped it. He settled his raincoat on his shoulders. He straightened his nose. Stepping up to the black door, he examined it very closely.

This is the door I went out by. . .

He stared at the latch, fingering it as if it were a priceless antique. He paused to stroke his moustache. With an irretrievable *click,* he lifted the latch. He edged the heavy door open just a couple of centimetres. An unearthly moan howled from the black crack and the room darkened visibly. He put his eye up to the opening, just for a peep at what might be – *zooop!*

Seven seconds later, he was back on the soggy, squelching mattress in Neasden feeling as if he'd been sucked through a letterslot.

Bounding to his feet, he turned and started kicking and cursing the mattress at the top of his lungs. He kicked it all around the lawn. At one point he began to walk away, then immediately returned to give it another good thrashing.

Hearing the racket, Sylvia got out of bed, twitched her curtain and peered down into her neighbour's garden. A short, round man was abusing a mattress. She had often wondered what that mattress was for. Hooking her hair behind one ear, she angled for a better view. It looked a bit like Herb, but it was very dark and anyway, it was impossible. He'd only gone in to check the meter and that was ages ago. Why would he be out in the rain, maltreating a mattress? She shrugged and went back to bed.

Having vented his impotent rage, Herb stood with hands on hips glaring viciously at the naked rhododendron. He huffed and puffed until his heartbeat settled, then he went and kicked the bush as well for good measure. Thrusting his hands into his coat pockets, he chanced one last look underneath it from a safe distance. He shook his head and swore. He hadn't the foggiest clue what was going on, but whatever it was, he had had enough. It was all too weird and implausible.

Defeated, he strode up to the house and jerked open the back door. Luckily, due to the cable lying over the threshold, Agnes hadn't been able to close

171

it properly. At least he hadn't been locked out. He marched purposefully up the hall to the front door, only to discover he'd been locked in.

Gritting his teeth, he bit down hard on a cry of utter frustration. He wanted to pummel the door into matchsticks, except he took a very dim view of property crime. He groaned and leaned back against the wall, breathing slowly and deeply: in, out, in, out . . . he looked at his watch. 1:30 am. He sighed and went into the front room to check the windows, but they were locked as well. If the key was anywhere around, it was very well hidden. The room contained one old wicker chair and Herb sank heavily on to it, deaf to its objections. His clothes were wet and his hair was dripping. His shoes had leaked. Cold and miserable, he sat staring at the back of the fireplace, dreaming of a roaring blaze.

Hmf. Probably wouldn't draw even if there was anything to burn. Obviously hasn't been cleaned in years . . . just about as black as you could get. The only thing blacker than that would be. . .

His mind drifted. He thought of Cynthia. More specifically, he thought of Cynthia's legs and her shapely pink jumper. How was he going to seduce her without getting all tangled up? He hated that. Women were so clingy. He'd have to get her transferred to Huddersfield. But not just yet. No point in getting ahead of himself. He thought about her father passed out on the floor.

So her old man was a drinker then . . . blacked out on the carpet . . . black black blackety-black . . . blackjack, blackmail, blackbird, black coffee, black market, black pudding . . . blackblackblackblackblack, very, very, incredibly, awfully black.

Why did this word have such a special resonance? He couldn't imagine why. He was overtired. His mind was playing tricks on him. Why should he get all exercised about the word *black*? The only mention of anything black was when what's-her-name said something about a bla —

His mind wandered again. He glanced out of the window where the sky was stained a dirty grey from light pollution thrown up by the city. Earlier that evening was the first time he had ever seen a truly black sky over London. The effect had been quite eerie. Made the whole city seem dead. That was obviously why the word had stuck in his head. Because of the power cut. The blackout. . .

But, no, there seemed to be something else. . .

Sylvia had lovely black hair . . . natural or from a bottle? Bottle. English girls never have hair that colour. That one in Bradford — what was her name? — Mangit. She had truly black hair. But she was from Calcutta. Hmf . . . the Black Hole of Calcutta. That's what what's-her-name said. She said, "You fell through a —"

In a flash that had taken a very long time coming, Herbert Dribbling sat bolt upright in his chair and spoke aloud: "You fell through a black hole and now you're on the other side of the universe. That's what she said. That's what she —"

Something inside his head made a little *click* and, jumping to his feet, he bounded for the door, stopped, turned around and immediately sat down again. He glared at an empty mayonnaise jar on the mantel. He bit his upper lip. With callipers of thumb and forefinger, he stroked his cheeks, listening to the rasp of his own stubble. Summoning all his resources, he urged his weary brain to leap the terrible hurdle that had been placed before it.

A black hole . . . in Neasden?

It was absurd. It was totally and utterly un-believable. But it did make sense of what had happened. And for a man like Herb, an absurd explanation was far preferable to no explanation at all. Taking out a giant, mental wrecking bar, he began to prise open a space in his cranium where this new concept could be entertained.

Just imagine . . . what if there actually were a black hole? he asked himself. *And nobody else knew about it . . . just me and a couple of losers on the other end?*

He got up again and paced slowly back and

forth. What would a black hole be good for? It must be good for something. A theme park, for example . . . conveniently located, just minutes from the tube: *The Neasden Black Hole Experience!* He could buy up all the surrounding land, bulldoze the houses and charge a hundred pounds for admission. People would queue as far as Bulgaria just to throw money at him! He'd be as rich as Croesus! Mega-babes from all corners of the world would beat a path to his gold-plated front door!

But that would take a huge amount of capital to get going. There must be something else . . . something simpler, more immediate.

There was also the trifling problem that the property containing the black hole did not actually belong to him – *but who did it belong to*? Surely a thing like that belonged to science! It belonged to the whole world and the whole world should benefit from it! Not just a couple of new-age flakos living in the jungle and trying to keep it to themselves. That was criminal in itself! Robbing science of this extraordinary advance!

This line of rhetoric had considerable appeal; it sounded noble and heroic. Herb Dribbling would return nature's heritage to the people, for the benefit of all! Naturally, as the great liberator, he would benefit more than most. That was only right and proper. No one would begrudge him that.

Without him, the thing would still be languishing under a bush!

As luck would have it, Herb knew of a particular branch of science that could properly appreciate such a discovery. He grabbed his mobile and jabbed one of the speed-dial numbers.

After eight or ten rings, a sleepy voice grunted, "*Ermf?*"

"Walter? Dribbling here. Listen up. I'm on to something big and I think you should be interested."

"Who? What did you. . .? *Herb?* It's two in the morning. What do you want? Do you want to speak to your sister?"

"No, it's you that I want. I want to solve a little problem of yours and make us both a fortune in the process. Are you awake yet?"

"No, I'm not. Can't it wait?"

"No. It can't wait. It's that big. Very, very big. You're going to thank me."

There was a long silence on the line, punctuated by the reluctant sound of a man sitting up in bed. The man was K. Walter Finch, Herb's brother-in-law, who also happened to be the director of the UK's largest atomic power station and nuclear reprocessing facility.

"OK, let's have it. This had better be good."

Herb paused for dramatic effect . . . then, speaking slowly and enunciating his words with great care, he asked, "What would it be worth to you, to get rid of your *entire stockpile* of nuclear waste — *cleanly and efficiently* — with no conceivable comeback from those meddlesome, tree-hugging *troublemakers* at Greenpeace? *Hmm?*"

CHAPTER twenty-one

"The Grommet of Life is an empty cup. Its fullness lies not in that which exists, but in that which has the potential to become..." The Way of the Grommet, page 51

Jack-the-cowboy stepped through the light-wall and found himself, not back in the main room where the party was, but in a spacious, low-lit bedroom. It was decorated throughout in 1960s kitsch with a white shag-pile carpet. Against the far wall was a mini-bar laden with bottles and glasses; to the left, a zebra-skin sofa. A ceiling fan lazily churned the air. A psychedelic bedspread was thrown over a vast brass bed. On either side of the bed were a pair of orange lava lamps, looking like they might be some highly intelligent life form . . . or just a couple of bedside lamps. On the bed reclined Marilyn Monroe: living, breathing, pouting – resplendent in a diaphanous baby-doll nightie trimmed with pink fur. Desperately embarrassed and feeling like an actor walking on stage in the wrong play, the cowboy immediately turned to leave.

"Hey there, big-boy," Marilyn sang. "Not going so soon, are you?"

Running one hand upwards along her leg, she stretched and writhed cat-like. Curling up on her side, she hugged her pillow, peering over the top of it through straggles of hair that tumbled over her face. The cowboy stopped and turned, gaping speechless.

"What's the matter, honey? Cat got your tongue?"

Quickly he remembered to take off his hat in a lady's presence and stood with it in both hands, fiddling with the rim.

"Howdy, ma'am. Hope I'm not intrudin' none. This sure is a swell place you got, Miss – ?"

"Call me Princess. That's what everyone calls me. I've been waiting for you. You've just won first prize."

From inside his slow-witted carcass, Jack felt like he was peeping through a keyhole. The view was memorable, if slightly unbelievable. *Marilyn Monroe?* He knew her from pictures he'd seen: those eyes, that hair, that body . . . definitely that body. But why? What was she doing here? Was this where dead movie stars went to? Surely not.

"First prize at what, Miss Princess?" the cowboy asked.

"Why, the John Wayne Memorial Door Prize, silly. I must confess, it *was* rigged. You were the only contender. I've always had this *thing* about Earthlings, you see. Nobody else likes them, but I do. I used to pick one up now and then on holiday in Bermuda. You could say I'm a bit of a fan. I just *adore* all those old films, don't you? Newman, Brando, Redford. . . So naturally when I heard that some real humans had appeared on the event horizon, I just had to get my hands on one."

Her guest obviously looked gobsmacked and Marilyn flopped one hand casually in the direction of the bar.

"You look like you need a drink. Help yourself."

"Oh, why thank you, ma'am. I sure have got a mighty thirst." The cowboy hunkered over to the bar, calling over his shoulder, "You wouldn't have a nice cold glass of milk, would you?"

The princess rolled her eyes. "In the fridge, if you must."

The cowboy rummaged behind the bar. He poured out a pint and downed half of it in one gulp. He wiped his mouth on the back of his sleeve. Marilyn propped herself up against the headboard and smiled, patting the bed.

"Come on over here so we can get friendly. . ."

The cowboy took his glass and sauntered over.

His legs were so bowed that a child on a tricycle could easily have ridden through them without touching the sides. He sat down beside her, grinning around the room, trying not to meet her eye.

"That's quite some pistol you got there, loverboy," she sighed, gently fingering his holster. "Hope it didn't get wet during your little swim. Do you think it'll still shoot OK?"

The cowboy wrinkled his brow. "Swim, ma'am? I don't rightly recall any—"

"No, of course you don't. You don't remember a thing, do you? It's one of the beauties of morphing fluid."

Morphing fluid, Jack repeated to himself. He remembered it all too well.

The cowboy sat nursing his puzzlement, trying to concentrate. He was clearly out of his depth, which may have only consisted of a few millimetres.

"You see," the princess went on, "whatever goes into it, comes out more or less as what I'm thinking about at the time. So I just lay back dreaming of Big JW, as I do from time to time, then lo and behold –"

Marilyn's eyes went vacant for a moment and then became troubled. She examined her guest. He certainly looked like John Wayne, but something wasn't quite right. Surely The Duke never drank milk. She frowned, then dismissed the thought with a toss of her blonde curls.

"The main drawback is that it can't cross species," she continued, "which is why I had to have some kind of human to start with. I mean, it's not that you weren't kinda cute the way you were, but I am in need of *a real man,* honey. I've heard so much about them and they are so hard to come by . . . a man who knows how to handle *a real woman.*"

Arching her back, she sighed and rolled her shoulders, pushing out her chest.

"'Cause I can be quite a handful, if you get my meaning. I had to beef you up a touch, for your own protection. You don't mind do you?"

Do I mind? DO I MIND?! Are you talking to me? On a scale of one to ten, I mind five million! And I want my trainers back!

"Why, shucks, ma'am, I is happy to be of service," the cowboy replied. "Would you like t'hear me sing? I can yodel too. Back home they call me *The Texas Warbler.* But golly, if you're lookin' for a real hunk of a man, you come to the right place! My daddy always said I was strong as a ox and almost as smart. He was jokin' of course. I'm not really *that* strong. But I bet I could lift this entire bed clean over my head. You wanna see me lift the bed? I can do it, you know."

He started to get up, but she touched his arm.

"I was kinda hoping you might help me to hold it down."

The cowboy looked at her blankly. He wasn't at all sure what the subject was, so he decided to change it.

"My-oh-my, you sure are purty, Miss Princess. You look jus' like that movie star — I forgit her name. I ain't never set eyes on no princess before."

"Well, I'm not really a princess. It's just a nickname. On account of my fondness for tragic blondes: Grace Kelly, Lady Di . . . but I can be darker if you'd prefer."

In an instant, everything about the princess changed and she took on a sultry Spanish look . . . hair and eyebrows went from blonde to jet black, eyes from blue to dusky hazel, skin from cream to olive. . .

The inhabitants of Tau Ceti are famous for being adepts of polymorphism. It was their natural evolutionary response to the limitations of a fixed body; in particular, the body's inconsiderate habit of dying. By mutating into a form of pure consciousness that could take on any form desired, they thereby attained a kind of immortality, as well as a certain omnipotence.

The cowboy gaped and gulped. He shook his head and started to panic.

"Er, no — no, ma'am — you were just fine the way you were. Honest. I, oh . . . that's better."

The princess changed effortlessly back into blonde bombshell mode. "I can be anything you want," she whispered, blowing him a kiss.

Try four legs and a tail, Jack muttered to himself. *Try a banjo-playing donkey. That might turn him on.*

"Marilyn has always been my favourite though," she went on. "So dreadfully misunderstood. . ."

The princess let out a long sigh. The fingers of her right hand traced a perilous path along the cowboy's leg. He held his breath and looked down. A little storm erupted in his glass as his hand began to quake. The other kept a white-knuckled grip on the rim of his hat. The princess ran the tip of her tongue around the inside of her parted lips. Tex watched, mesmerized, horrified. Reviewing his situation, Jack clung to his sanity and tried to stay calm — not that he could do anything, even if he panicked:

I am sitting on a bed with Marilyn Monroe. She is blowing me kisses and stroking my leg — but it's not my leg, for I am imprisoned in the body of a straw-brained yokel who would rather be singing to his horse! Get me out of here! Duncan? HELP!

"How about it then, cowboy?" the princess purred. "Wanna have six?"

Her guest's head jerked away involuntarily. He held up his glass.

"Why shucks, I ain't finished my first one yet!"

Climbing to her knees behind him, she started kissing his neck and devouring his earlobes.

"No, not *six*," she whispered. "That's the wrong word . . . I mean, *sacks* . . . don'tcha wanna? Huh?"

Tex was stymied. His face went blank and he stared into the middle distance, ignoring the hands that were unbuttoning his shirt.

"Sacks? *Sacks-o'phones?*"

"Tex, honey, don't be a tease . . . I never said my English was perfect. But you *know* the word I'm looking for, don'tcha, honey . . . you know what I want . . . just watch my lips."

The princess kissed and bit his neck playfully and a little light went on in the cowboy's head. He was a little slow getting there, but there are some things any man can understand, even when the words are all wrong. He disentangled himself and got to his feet. He turned to face her, wagging a knowing finger.

"I know the word you're after, Miss Princess. Don't you think I don't. But you oughta be more careful with yer vowels. A girl could get herself into a whole heap o' trouble! I know esackly what you want – and I'm gonna give it to you!"

185

He hung his hat on the bedpost. He set his glass on the bedside table. Bending down, he removed one boot and then the other. Standing straight, Tex smiled and pointed down.

"Now *this* is what every woman needs —"

The princess looked down.

"— a darned good pair of socks."

Jack cringed and wanted to leave the room. The embarrassment was painful. What had he ever done to deserve this? The princess glowered. Her nostrils flared with each breath. The cowboy jabbered on regardless.

"Bought these in Dodge City last June and I wash 'em once a month whether they need it or not. They're yours if you want 'em. Darn, I shoulda offered earlier! First thing I clocked when I come in was you weren't wearin' no socks."

Teetering on one leg, Tex bent to pull off his sock while the princess fumed.

"Six . . . sacks . . . socks," she muttered, her anger growing in a steady crescendo. "*This sucks! I'll show you what a real woman is made of!*"

The cowboy looked up and dropped his jaw. Rising before him, hideous of face, murderous of eye, loomed a midnight-skinned, bloody-tongued incarnation of Kali, four-armed goddess of destruction. In one hand she brandished a gleaming sword, in another an astonished giant's pop-eyed head, dripping red from the neck. Her throat was garlanded with rats' skulls, her waist girdled with severed hands. An obscene, protruding tongue lolled from her mouth. She growled and swayed ominously.

Tex gulped and whimpered, "Oh, *Christian Aid!*"

Hopping backwards on one leg, still trying to get his sock off, he fell back on to the zebra-skin sofa. Swinging her sword in front and behind, Kali danced towards him, demonic eyes set to incinerate any small, flying insect that might cross her line of vision. Smoke squirted from her ears and the reek of sulphur crushed the air. Whipping out his pistol, the cowboy clapped one hand over his eyes and was about to fire blind when he heard a tiny voice say:

"*Ba-a-aa-a.*"

He peered out between his fingers. Kali was gone and a newborn lamb bleated up at him helplessly. The lamb hopped into his lap. Tex smiled dumbly and stroked its head. He truly loved animals. The lamb peed on his leg. He struggled to get up, but suddenly the lamb vanished and the sofa around him came alive: warm and fleshy and all-embracing. A big motherly face beamed down at him beatifically. Encircled by great matronly arms, the little cowboy perched in her lap sinking slowly into her cleavage. Then, just before he was entirely engulfed, he clunked abruptly to the floor and found himself looking up at Marilyn Monroe again, this time power-dressed in a pinstriped suit.

"I also have a doctorate in every subject you can think of and an IQ that's higher than you can count. Get the picture? I told you I was a bit of a handful. A full-bodied, red-blooded, multi-faceted handful. I'm all those things and a dozen others as well. I never stay the same and I don't necessarily make sense. I need a man who can keep up. Understand? No, of course you don't. But that is what it would mean to be '*a real man*'."

She went to fix herself a Martini.

Jack felt shell-shocked. If he had had a head, it would have been spinning. He could feel the cowboy quaking with fear. He looked as if he were about to wet himself if the lamb hadn't already done so. Tex got up shakily, not taking his eyes off Marilyn's back for a second. He holstered his pistol and quickly pulled on his boots.

"Um, er, Miss Princess?" he squeaked, retrieving his hat. "It sure has been a pleasure meetin' you and all, but I need to get along home now. I got my choir practice tonight and—"

The princess silenced him with a flash of her eyes.

"You are not going anywhere except back in the soup, honey-pie. I'll make a man out of you if it's the last thing I do! I might try Schwarzenegger this time . . . or Stallone. He seems a big tough guy. Let's see what he's really made of."

She strode forward. Locked away in the cowboy's cranium, Jack was quietly freaking out. He could see his entire life becoming a package tour of other people's bodies. . .

Marilyn took a sip of her Martini, then chucked the rest of it in Tex's face. Within seconds, the effect of the morphing fluid was neutralized and a pale, naked fifteen-year-old stood before her, more than a little nonplussed. It took Jack a moment or two to realize he was back in the corporeal world . . . and another few after that to twig that he had no clothes on. At least he remembered his lines:

"Hi! I'm Jack," he said and, with a perfunctory wave, he turned and fled straight through the light-wall —

— which proved to be uncommonly solid. With both hands occupied in protecting his modesty, front and back, there was nothing to break the impact. His recently regained body thudded dully. His forehead cracked. Staggering backwards, he crashed into unconsciousness on the soft, white, shag-pile carpet. . .

CHAPTER twenty-two

"The Grommet of Heaven will perish, and the Grommet of Earth will pass away, but The Way of The Grommet is eternal and everlasting."
The Way of the Grommet, page 211

Waking up groggily in Central Middlesex Hospital, Cornelius Plant was still blinking at his sister's empty bed when he heard voices coming from the corridor.

". . .just last night, during the blackout! Apparently the mother was putting it up for adoption in any case, but even so! Janet, the charge nurse in maternity, she's in pieces. She's still being questioned by the police."

"But that's just awful! How did it happen?"

Two nurses paused just outside the open door. Cornelius strained to hear the rest of their conversation:

"Apparently a dozen '*Call*' buzzers went off one after the other. There was only her and Christine on duty, so she left the nursery unattended for, like, *three minutes* – just to go check on the patients. But all the ones that had buzzed were fast asleep. And when she got back, the baby was gone!"

"How terrible! Who do they think did it?"

"No idea. There's going to be an inquiry. . ."

The two carried on down the corridor and Cornelius grabbed his face with both hands. He had a depressingly good idea who did it. Silently he got up and checked behind the door. His sister's coat was gone, along with her shoes and her hand-bag.

Agnes Agnes Agnes! How could you do this! Didn't she say something about wanting a baby? It must have been her! This is a total disaster!

But what if they suspected *him*? An accomplice! An accessory to the crime! He wasn't a registered patient. He shouldn't even be there. *They'll think we planned it all together.*

Cornelius began to feel very edgy. He was still trying to decide what to do when the Bengali woman in the next bed called out, "Doctor is coming?" and he nearly jumped out of the window.

"*What?* Where!? What doctor? No, he's not!"

He tried to pull himself together. He needed to focus his energies and concentrate. What do you do when your sister steals a baby? What was the correct and honourable course of action? *To inform on her?* Even if it meant the police dragging her off to gaol? Even if it meant their discovering the black hole, his family being thrust into the merciless glare of publicity and all hell generally breaking loose? *Even if it meant him losing his professorship?*

Cornelius gave all these issues their due consideration. He was no stranger to life's many intractable dilemmas; he had a lifetime's study of ethics behind him! He thought long and hard for over thirty seconds, applying the full rigour of his philosophical training. And when he arrived at his conclusion, he found that it was not such a difficult decision after all. He knew in his heart of hearts that, regardless of the consequences, he had only one credible option:

Stuff ethics and run while he had the chance.

Grabbing his bag, he made his way through the hospital unchallenged. Stepping through the main exit, his eyeballs were assaulted by a blast of brilliant sunlight. There was a cold wind as well and he buttoned his coat quickly as he walked. He turned left into Acton Lane, then carried straight on to the bus stop where he waited nervously for the 260. . .

In Albemarle Gardens, Herbert Dribbling slept fitfully on the floor of a damp, unheated, upstairs room. He had been lucky enough to find a moth-eaten blanket that had kept him from freezing, but only just. He was having a frustrating dream about trying to get into a pub whose doors were all locked. It was obviously open for business because he could see people talking and drinking inside. He rattled the front door furiously, then he heard a side door open and he ran over to it. But when he got there, it banged shut in his face and wouldn't open again.

He sat up abruptly. His mouth was dry and the side he'd been lying on was completely numb. He felt clammy all over from sleeping in his clothes. He took in his surroundings and felt even worse. He'd been dreaming about a . . . but then he heard a. . .

He threw off the blanket and propped himself up against the wall, listening hard and trying to wake up. He could have sworn he'd heard a door bang shut. Yes, he must have done . . . someone was moving about downstairs. He rubbed some life into his face and raked his hair into place. Appearance is very important when dealing with the public, especially when you wake up in their house uninvited. He got up and opened the door to the room.

Cornelius clomped down the hall and dumped his sister's bag by the entrance to the kitchen. He chucked his keys into a wooden bowl, as had been his habit of many years. He went into the loo and locked the door just as Herb started quietly down the carpeted stairs.

When he reached the downstairs hall, he immediately noticed Agnes's bag, which hadn't been there the night before. He walked towards it. There was a muted groaning coming from the loo. Herb was still three-quarters asleep. He'd virtually forgotten why he was there and he wasn't at all sure of what to do. One thing was certain, he couldn't just wait for whoever-it-was to emerge. They'd probably have a heart attack. He stepped into the kitchen so as at least to be out of the way.

What *was* he doing there? He needed someone to let him out . . . but, but . . . *oh yes!* It all came back to him: the thirty-one million . . . the black hole . . . the fortune he was going to make in the Discount Nuclear Waste Disposal business! How could he possibly have forgotten that?

The kitchen looked even more barren in the light of day. There was no sign of life; no mugs lying about, no kettle, no toaster . . . grey Formica cupboards, an ancient cooker, a fridge with a lone fridge magnet in the shape of a fridge. The only thing of interest was a round wooden bowl on the counter. In the bowl was a plastic Darth Vader . . . and a bunch of keys.

Hmm, Herb wondered. *Keys. . .*

From inside the loo came the sort of shuffling that invariably preceded the flushing of the toilet, which invariably preceded the opening of the door, which invariably preceded the emergence of a person, which would inevitably lead to an encounter that Herb could well do without. He stopped wondering. He grabbed the keys and darted on tiptoe down the hall to the front door. Quickly and blindly, he grabbed a long brass Chubb and fitted it into the mortise lock. Miraculously, it turned. Releasing the latch as well, he pulled the front door open, just as the door of the loo opened. Herb stepped noiselessly across the threshold of the house and Cornelius stepped obliviously into the hall. In one synchronized manoeuvre, they closed their doors behind them.

Cornelius picked up his bag, walked through the back room and out into the garden.

What's that cable doing there? he asked himself. *I must tell Mother. Someone could trip over that.*

The grass was still wet from the evening's rain and by the time he reached the rhododendron, the tops of his shoes were beaded with water drops. He got down on his hands and knees and crept towards the hole. He had always hated this bit. It struck him as ridiculous and undignified, like pretending to be a brain-damaged rabbit or something. He held his breath and let himself fall face-first towards the tiny hole. . .

A few moments later, he catapulted across a big round living room a hundred and ninety thousand light-years away, sailed out through the double glass doors with his legs struggling to keep up, down the steps and across the garden at record-breaking speed. As he sprinted past the garden table, he happened to notice his daughter sitting there. She seemed to be snogging a legless, blue alien. Cornelius skidded to a halt, precariously, but without falling. He turned, gripping the handle of his bag with both hands.

Fiz jumped to her feet, straightened her top and tried to find the right expression of detached defiance with which to face her father.

Bweeb, on the other hand, bounced up like a balloon, smiled, waved both arms, sang, *"Bwee-eeb!"* and rushed over to smother the professor in sloppy wet kisses.

The two collapsed into the grass. A minute later, when Bweeb finally let go, Cornelius's glasses were on his forehead and his normally bleached face was the colour of his tongue. He staggered up, urgently straightening his glasses with both hands. He pushed back his hair, shifted his coat on his shoulders and brushed away the bits of grass. Retrieving his sister's bag, he turned a blank, unblinking gaze on his daughter.

"Dad, I'd like you to meet Bweeb," Fiz announced with artificial confidence. "Bweeb, this is my father."

Sweeping aside all formalities, Bweeb rushed back in to deliver another twenty or thirty kisses, but without knocking the professor over this time. With both arms around his neck, he gave him a big cheek to cheek hug and sighed, "*B-w-e-e-e-e-b.*"

Without speaking, Cornelius succeeded in fending him off solely with his elbows, so as not to have to touch the blobby blue body with his hands. Bweeb bobbed back over to Fiz's side.

"He doesn't speak English yet, but he understands a little," she explained. "And he's learning really fast."

Bweeb thought she was referring to her father. He smiled and nodded sympathetically, although it did seem odd. The professor did not respond. He kept looking from daughter to blob, uncomprehendingly.

"I've spent the day with his family. He has ninety brothers and sisters and they live in a tree."

As these words echoed in her head, Fiz's confidence faltered a little. It didn't sound right at all. She sensed it was going badly but she didn't know quite what to do about it. She started speaking faster and faster.

"Er, you'll really like them though. I told them all about your work and everything and I'm not sure, you know, if he understands what a grommet actually is, but I sort of drew a picture and he seemed genuinely interested. Maybe you could—"

"Fenella," her father interrupted, "could you come inside for a moment please."

He walked across the grass and up the steps without even looking back at the blue blob holding his daughter's hand. Bweeb smiled and waved vigorously at the professor's receding back. Fiz turned to him sadly.

"I have to go," she said.

The immediacy of his feelings was overwhelming. He turned a deep purple colour and his heart broke into a thousand pieces. Enormous tears rolled down his cheeks and when he threw his arms around her neck, he made both their faces wet. How could she leave him? Why did she have to go? How could he bear to be without her? Fiz pulled away and stood gazing into his eyes. He sniffled and gently fingered her eyebrow stud.

She held his hand and sobbed, "I'll see you very, very soon. . . I hope. Think of me."

She retreated a little, allowing Bweeb's hand to

slip slowly through hers. As their fingertips lost contact, he let out the most mournful sigh, as if all life were ebbing out of him.

"*bweeb,*" he squeaked in a very small voice.

His hand hung in the air where she had left it. He didn't move. Fiz walked backwards through the grass and then turned to climb the steps to the tower. At the top, she looked over her shoulder. He still hadn't moved. She waved. He waved back. Reluctantly, he turned and bobbed away into the forest.

Fiz went in through the double doors. Her father was sitting at the table like an Egyptian statue with an Umbro bag across its knees. She sat down opposite him, trying to compose herself. She would be straightforward and mature. Above all, she would stay calm. She would show him that she had thought things through properly and she wasn't going to do anything rash or childish.

There was a prolonged and stony silence. Finally her father cleared his throat and said, "Fenella, I don't think you should be seeing this, er, this—"

Fiz leaped up as if a gun had gone off. Her chair clattered over backwards behind her.

"I KNEW IT!" she shrieked. "*I knew it, I knew it, I knew it!* I *knew* you were going to say that! *AND*

WHY NOT?! Why shouldn't I? You can't make me! You can't tell me what to do! I'M SIXTEEN AND A HALF. I know what I'm doing. I've thought this through properly, you know. *Bweeb and I are in love!* I feel perfectly calm and mature about it. We're going to get married and you can't stop us!"

"But, Fenella—"

"*AND DON'T EVER CALL ME FENELLA!* It sounds like a fabric conditioner. But *what?*"

"I just think that perhaps you should . . . would you mind sitting down, please?"

Fiz erected her chair and perched on it, scowling. Her father passed a trembling hand over his forehead. He hated arguing with his daughter. She could be so ruthless. Learned it all from her mother, of course.

"I mean, I'm sure he's very nice and they are meant to be highly intelligent and everything . . . but he is, you know. . ."

"Why don't you just come out and say it? He's *blue*. Is that your problem? That he's blue?"

"Well, in a way, yes. Of course, there's nothing wrong with being blue *per se*, it's just that—"

Fiz launched to her feet again.

"RACIST!" she screamed, pointing.

"Fenella, please don't say that."

"Yes, you are. You're a *RACIST*! You think you're so liberal and so politically correct and all that, but

200

when I so much as bring home a blue boyfriend, you loose your rag!"

She folded her arms and posed defiantly in her orange platform trainers. Her anger was glowing through her blanched face-mask.

"It's not that. It's not a question of race. He's just – he's just different from us. I mean, have you noticed, for example, that he doesn't have any legs?"

"HA! *So that's it!* It's the legs. That's just about the most *offensive* thing I've ever heard! You think people without legs don't need love like anybody else? *Huh?* People without legs aren't human, I suppose. Is that it?"

The professor stared at the table. Very quietly, he replied, "Well, in this case, no. He *isn't* human. He's an alien."

"WHAT DO YOU MEAN, HE ISN'T – ?"

Fiz broke off in mid-screech. Her father seemed to have made a point. But, that was impossible. Turning on her heel, she marched towards the kitchen, then spun round abruptly, pointing a long black-painted fingernail: "Being human isn't the only thing there is, you know. What's so great about being human? *Huh?* Did I ever ask to be a human? *No!* I don't even *like* being human, if you must know. I'd rather be a shrub!"

With that, she proceeded straight to the lift shaft.

"Henry?" she ordered. "Take me up to my room!"

CHAPTER twenty-three

Herb Dribbling stepped into the sunlight of Albemarle Gardens, wide-awake at last. He slipped the house keys into his coat pocket, smiled to himself and tapped them twice just to hear them jingle. He unlocked his car and got in. He took his mobile phone from his inside jacket pocket. The first call he made was to the Electricity Board's lawyers:

"Drench? Dribbling here. We've got a little problem that's going to need some legal work. The problem's name is Delia Plant, 37 Albemarle Gardens. Owes us thirty-one million plus change and doesn't want to pay. That's right, thirty-one million pounds. I know. I know. Well, that's definitely the amount. No, of course she hasn't got it, what do you think? There is the house though, a five-bed terrace in Neasden — could be worth, what? Quarter of a million? No, it's not very much, but it is something. I'll need a possession order. What do you mean, that's not strictly legal? *Make it legal!* At least, make it *look* legal, that's what you're paid for. No, I'll come by this afternoon. Good man. Thanks, Drench."

Herb's second call was to his own lawyer:

"Clinch? Herb Dribbling here. Good. Very well thank you. No . . . no, I didn't watch Jimmy Tarbuck last night. Really. What? That's nice. Listen, Clinch, I need you to — what? The Nolan Sisters? No, I don't think so. I'm not a fan. Now listen, Clinch, I . . . oh, that's nice . . . yes . . . but really, I — *CLINCH, WILL YOU PLEASE SHUT UP?* Thank you. That's better. It's OK, it's OK — just listen: I need you to register a company for me in the name of — *are you listening?* — Dribbling Atomic Research Foundation; sole proprietor, Dr H. Dribbling. Yes, of course I'm a doctor. Well, there are a lot of things you don't know about me. I'll need a bank account as well in the same name. Can you do that? Good man . . . no, I need it done yesterday.

"Now, I *also* want you to draw up the necessary papers — *are you listening?* — for that company to purchase a house from the Central Electricity Board. The house is at 37 Albemarle Gardens, NW10. The purchase price is £100,000. Have you got that? The house is to be the registered office of DARF Ltd. No, Clinch — *Dribbling Atomic Research Foun* — that's it. Very good. Yes . . . *yes, of course it's legal.* Yes, I know . . . yes . . . yes . . . I know. Look, just do it, will you? For God's sake, Clinch, which part of '*JUST DO IT*' don't you understand? Fine. Goodbye. Thank you. Goodbye."

Herb rang off, shaking his head, and immediately made a third call:

"Walter? Dribbling here. Have you thought about my little proposal? Yes, I thought you might, *haha.* No, it's my own organization that's handling it: the Dribbling Atomic Research Foundation. Katie didn't tell you? Well, no, she wouldn't, would she — all hush-hush up till now. It's a sort of charitable academic research society, you know, working for a better world and all that, *haha.* The process? Oh, it's a major scientific breakthrough . . . a radical new way of dealing with nuclear waste. *And, it's one hundred per cent safe!* Not as if we're going to go pumping it into a hole in the ground, eh? *Haha!* No, public safety is paramount. *Paramount!* I know . . . I know . . . it's terrible. Those idiots at Greenpeace are to blame. Putting silly ideas into people's heads. As if all we cared about was profit! But this has been *extensively tested* by leading experts . . . well, myself mostly.

"But let's just take a look at your present procedure: to reprocess the spent fuel rods, you have to cool them first, *correct?* Which produces a lot of contaminated water. So, you evaporate the water, turn the residue into glass, seal the glass in steel and concrete and store it for thousands of years. *Correct?* And how much does all that cost, on an annual basis? *Over a hundred million* . . . that is an awful lot of money sealed up in concrete, Walter.

"Now, let's say you produce a hundred thousand litres of high-level liquid waste per week. If you were to supply the transport, the manpower and the pumping equipment, the Dribbling Atomic Research Foundation could dispose of it for just £999,999.99. Annually, that comes to less than half what you're spending now. *You save fifty million quid each year!* Well, I told you it was a revolutionary process. It's out of this world, *haha!* Oh, I couldn't agree more: we would be making the world a *much better place*!

"*Of course* it meets all government safety regulations . . . *of course* it's good for business . . . *of course* it will mean cheaper electricity for consumers . . . *of course* it will mean a massive executive bonus for yourself . . . *massive,* Walter, *massive!* There are fifty million good reasons for you to sign up for this, and every one of them's got the queen's face on it, *haha!* But think about it: a new Roller, public school for the kids, that house in Tuscany you've always wanted. . .

"Just don't think for too long, OK? I'm letting you in at ground level cause you're family, know what I mean? Why don't I draw up a draft contract for you to look at? What's that? *A copy of the safety report?* What would you want that for? I mean, of course I'll send you one . . . er . . . I think they're reprinting just now. But I'll get one out to you as soon as poss!"

Herb rang off and put his mobile away, muttering to himself, *"Copy of the safety report . . . what a wimp!"*

CHAPTER twenty-four

"Rarf! Rarf!"

Jack's head lolled from side to side. Somewhere on the outer fringes of consciousness, he could hear a dog barking.

"Wakey-wakey, Jackie-boy!"

No . . . a dog talking . . . that would make more sense.

He opened his eyes. He was lying on a psychedelic bedspread. Duncan was sitting up beside him.

"What happened?" he groaned groggily.

His face ached from where he'd hit the wall and the back of his head throbbed from where he'd hit the ground. At least he was no longer completely naked. He was wearing a nappy. A big fluffy, white cotton nappy, done up with a giant blue safety pin at the front.

"Nice pants, kiddo," Duncan smirked.

Jack stared with stunned amazement at his new attire.

"Where did this come from? Why am I wearing this thing?"

"I was going to ask you that. Something you want to tell me about? A little prrr-oblem in the toilet department?"

"Shut up. I cannot believe this. Where's the princess? Did you see her? How long have I been out? How did you get in here?"

Jack sat up against the headboard, looking around the room. There was no one else present.

"I just walked in. The nose found you. You were missing the best part of the party so I thought I'd better see what was up. Who's this prrr-incess then?"

"She was here earlier . . . looks like Marilyn Monroe, but she keeps changing – changes her body into anything she wants. And me as well . . . dumped me into this morphing stuff and I came out as a singing cowboy. Then she changed me back but wouldn't let me leave. I nearly broke my nose trying to run through that wall. It's a madhouse, Dunc. You would not *believe* what I've been through. I wonder where my clothes are?"

Jack got up and started looking around for his jeans and T-shirt and the dog eyed him with curiosity and concern. He had always considered Jack to be the only sane member of the Plant family. He looked at the nappy with the big blue pin. He shook his head. All humans were mad, every one of them without exception.

"So what's this prrr-incess got planned, that she wouldn't let you leave?" he ventured.

"Oh, nothing much. Wants to turn me into Sylvester Stallone, that's all. Fate worse than death. She's got this thing about 'real men', whatever that's supposed to mean."

"*Turn you into — ? How?*"

Jack related everything about his experience in the morphing fluid and the circular pool.

"Basically, I become whoever she's thinking about while I'm in there. Don't ask me how it works. What's she done with my clothes?"

"They're not in here — I'd smell them if they were. No offence. But, I just came in through the wall . . . so we should be able to get back out."

"What, dressed like this? I'd rather have my fingernails torn out one by one."

"Well, you could always wear —"

Jack followed Duncan's eyes and came to rest on Marilyn's baby-doll nightie with the pink fur trim, hanging on the bedpost.

"Oh, that's so much better! No chance."

"You know, I never could understand this thing humans have about clothes. Especially those idiotic

210

little jackets they buy for their dogs — *sooo embarrr-assing!* I'd never have forgiven you if you'd made me wear one of those. But think about it — hardly anyone out there has clothes on. They're not even going to notice."

"Yeah, apart from. . ."

"Apart from who?"

"Never mind."

Jack sat down again on the edge of the bed and scratched his head. "How did you get on with your three-headed wolf?"

"Who? Oh, *her.* . . She's nice. Legs to die for . . . but you know how it is: you meet, you talk, you dance, you exchange urine odours . . . she's not on heat again for months. I doubt if anything will come of it."

"Hmm, pity. I know what you mean," Jack replied vacantly.

Duncan had a long thoughtful gnaw at his hind leg. He waited a bit, then said, "Listen, I know it's not much of a choice, but you've got to make up your mind: either you play Rrr-ambo or you go home in a nappy. Which is it gonna be?"

Jack picked at the cotton towel around his loins.

"I am house-trained, you know," he grumbled.

He looked at Duncan despondently and sighed.

"All right, let's just do it. Get me out of here as fast as possible!"

He stood up and waddled a few steps. His nappy bunched up between his legs and he adjusted it as best he could. The two of them walked to the edge of the room, then stopped. Jack paused to straighten his hair. As if that mattered. What a party. He groaned and shook his head, took a deep breath and walked slowly forward: one, two, three steps – then clunked his forehead. The partition was as solid as ever. He pushed on it and pounded it with the flat of his hand.

"Oh, this is great! It let you in, but it won't let me out!"

"Let me try."

Duncan jumped up and clawed at it with his front paws. It wouldn't let either of them pass. The dog ran off, frantically sniffing in all the corners and checking the walls on all sides. Jack turned and slouched to the floor, leaning back against the all-too-solid sheet of light.

"Forget it, Dunc, it's no use. We're trapped."

Duncan came back and sat looking up at him, cocking his head from side to side. He licked his lips and had a little scratch. Jack sighed and hung his head, shading his eyes with both hands. A heavy silence hung in the room as the full impact of their predicament settled over them. Cautiously, Duncan cleared his throat.

"You know, *er*, there are prrr-obably worse

things to be than Sylvester Stallone. . ." he offered sympathetically.

"Oh really?" Jack looked up. "Well, right now I can't think of any. I'm going to spend the rest of my life as a sweaty, bull-necked lunkhead with a torn T-shirt and a toothpick hanging out of my mouth. The guy can barely string a sentence together! How would *you* like it? How would you like to suddenly become some brainless Rottweiler?"

"OK, OK . . . I was just trrr-ying to be positive."

The two looked at each other without speaking. Neither of them knew what to say. Jack sniffled and smirked and shook his head. He reached out and stroked Duncan under the chin. Then he scooped him up in his arms, and the dog licked his neck and his cheek.

"What a way to go, eh?" Jack murmured. He tried to sound coolly ironic when in fact he was on the verge of putting his nappy to good use. "Never in a million years could I have imagined. . ."

His voice trailed off. He couldn't bring himself to finish the sentence. Duncan curled up in his lap. The party was over. Everything was over. There was nothing to do but wait. . .

A minute passed, then suddenly the dog raised its head as if remembering something extremely important. It wriggled out of Jack's arms and stood beside him, looking up. A reluctant spark of hope leaped in the boy's heart . . . could it be that Duncan was going to save the day after all?

"There's one thing I need to know," the dog announced flatly. "This is absolutely crr-ucial and we haven't much time!"

Jack stared intently. Was there some obscure detail he had missed? Something he hadn't thought of? Was it possible that Duncan's unerring canine instinct would find a way out of this mess?

The dog began pacing back and forth excitedly, his brain working overtime. Finally he stopped and asked:

"*What is this thing that humans have about thrrr-owing sticks?* What is the point? You go out with a human, they get a stick and they thrrr-ow it. '*Fetch the stick,*' they say. Dog fetches stick. Brrr-ings it to the human. Then what? They throw it away again! And the dog has to go and get it, over and over and over. *What is all this about?* If you want the stick, why don't you keep the stick? And if you *don't* want it, why get *the dog* to fetch it? *AND WHY THE DOG?* Why can't you fetch your own stick! You thrrr-ew the thing! It just bends my brrr-ain. I mean, if this really is the end, you've got to tell me now: *What is the meaning of thrrr-owing sticks?!*"

Jack barely had time to open his mouth, when a flash of red lightning split the room. There was a thunderous *KRAKK!* and a tower of blue smoke billowed and swirled up from the floor. As it cleared, a haggard woman with a broom, a pointy hat and green, warty skin appeared.

Extending a long bony finger, she croaked, "So, my pretty! You've brought your little *dahg* with you, ay?"

The witch threw back her head and let out a cackling peal of hideous laughter. Duncan jumped back into Jack's arms.

There was another puff of smoke and the witch vanished. On the other side of the room, a girl with brown plaits and a blue dress popped up, shouting, "*Run, Toto, run!* Oh, Auntie Em! Auntie Em! There's no place like home!"

Then, with a loud *POP,* Dorothy disappeared as well and Marilyn Monroe was back, now in a white blouse with a pencil-thin leopard-skin skirt and matching pillbox hat.

"Sorry for the melodramatic entry, darlings, but I do *adore* that movie, don't you? I've just never had a real live *dahg* to play it out with before."

Swinging her hips over to the bar, she offered Jack a "Drink? No, of course not. You're much too young. Does that diaper fit, by the way? I mean, that is what baby humans wear, isn't it? Best I could come up with, I'm afraid."

Marilyn fixed herself another Martini. Jack set

Duncan down and got nervously to his feet. The dog started growling.

Marilyn bent from the waist and cooed, "Oh, what a cutesy-wootsy little poochie-coo-coo!"

Duncan snapped at her.

She straightened up and snapped back, "Wrap up, mutt, or I'll skin you for a hand-towel." She turned to Jack. "So. You've had your little afternoon nap? I've been killing time, waiting for you to come around. For some reason, the body swap doesn't work so well if you're not fully conscious when you go in. Ready for your dip?"

"No, I'm not, actually. I'm not ready and I'm not doing it. This is ridiculous. You can't invite someone to a party and then go changing them into someone else!"

"No? Oh. Why not?"

Marilyn teetered on her stilettos over to the bed. She sat down and kicked them off. She sipped her drink.

"*Why not?* Because you just can't, that's why! It's not on. You just don't do it. Recycling people is wrong!"

She set her glass on the bedside table then leaned back on her elbows. She shook her head patronizingly.

"I think you have an attitude problem. After my letting you win the door prize and everything. So ungrateful."

216

"But it doesn't even work! Just look at that cowboy — he was hopeless! You had some fantasy of what he was going to be like, but he turned out to be completely different. People are the way they are. You can't change them, or remake them into what you want. It doesn't work."

"Hmm . . . I did a Humphrey Bogart once who came out all right. Except he snored."

"Well, I don't care. I'm not doing it and you can't make me. I want my clothes and I want to go home. Now, if you please."

"*Auntie Em, Auntie Em!* You forgot your ruby slippers, baby-face."

Marilyn stood up and wriggled forward in her impossibly tight skirt. Jack backed away. Duncan started yapping and growling.

"Oh, do shut up!" she barked back. Then to Jack she added, "Are you sure you don't want to play my little game? I could show you things you'll never learn in school . . . things you'll *never* forget. And you know, a woman *always* gets her way, one way or another."

Jack glanced over his shoulder. He was less than a metre from the wall. He reached out with one hand just to touch it, but as he feared, his hand went right through. On the other side he could hear the sound of the pool filling. He could also hear Duncan going berserk.

When he turned around again, there was a leopard crouching on the floor directly in front of him. Slowly it advanced. It hissed and spat and took a swipe at his bare legs. He jumped back, teetering on the very edge of the room.

Just then, Duncan darted forward and sank his teeth into the cat's tail. The leopard snarled and spun around, but as it did, the dog swung out through the air on the end of her tail. The faster the big cat turned, the faster the dog flew. The two of them made one, two, three rotations, snarling and growling, steadily gaining centrifugal momentum — until on the fourth pass, the terrier slammed into Jack's nappy, knocking him backwards through the wall.

Duncan heard a groan . . . a scream . . . a splash — followed a moment later by the almighty crash of bottles and glasses. As the leopard's tail vaporized, the dog had sailed across the room and collided with the bar. A gin bottle toppled on to his head. He yelped and jumped up on to the sofa out of the way.

The princess was already poised on the bed in the lotus position, now dressed in a simple, white cotton shift. Her eyes were closed and she was clearly sinking into a deep meditation. Duncan scampered over and leaped on to the bed. His only hope was to somehow distract her and derail her thought process. He started with a lot of yapping and barking, which had no effect at all. He ran around in circles. He did a backflip. He rolled over and played dead. He jumped up and licked and slobbered all over her face. Her concentration was total. She didn't even bother to push him away.

Duncan wracked his brain, trying to expand his repertoire of attention-seeking behaviour. He stood on his hind legs and recited Shakespeare:

> *"The quality of mercy is not strrr-ained.*
> *It drrr-opeth as the gentle rain frrr-om heaven*
> *upon the place beneath. . ."*

No result. He tried his Elvis impersonation:

> *"You ain't nothin' but a hound dog,*
> *crrr-yin' all the time —*
> *Ahr-rrooOOooOOooo. . ."*

Not so much as the flicker of an eyelid. He squatted for a scratch, thinking, *This girl is really not easily impressed.*

Grabbing the edge of her robe, he growled and tugged and ripped off a great piece of it. He grabbed it again and tugged some more. Still clutching it between his teeth, he jumped off the side of the bed hoping he could topple her over.

The princess remained immobile as a marble Buddha, while Duncan dangled and grumbled on the end of the white cloth. Releasing her dress, he leaped back up and nipped her on the forearm – just hard enough to draw blood. Without disturbing any other part of her anatomy, the arm swung out like Tiger Woods teeing-off and – *fffump* – walloped the dog off the bed, sending him tumbling head over heels across the shag-pile carpet.

Down in the morphing pool, the water began its broad rotation as it started to drain away. Jack swirled and plopped and splashed, bodiless and helpless. Never in his life had he wanted so badly just to be himself. What a gift! What perfection! *To be ordinary Jack Plant!* (He would have liked some ordinary clothes to go with it.) The vortex expanded and accelerated, he felt himself being drawn down and around and around in a dizzying whirl. . .

Duncan jumped to his feet and charged back to the bed.

"I'm not afraid of you!" he yelped. "*I am a Jack Rrr-ussell!* Named and bred by the famous Sporting Parson of Devonshire in 1822!"

Flying with legs at full stretch, he landed back in the ring with a ferocious flurry of brown and white fur. This was no time for Mr Nice Guy, this was personal. He went straight for the throat –

– and nearly broke all his teeth. She had turned herself to stone.

The whirlpool was at full spin and the water level was dropping steadily. It slurped and gurgled vulgarly in its relentless swirl down the drain. What was left of Jack's consciousness scattered in a panicky welter of worst-case scenarios. At any moment, he would judder to a halt along the bottom of an empty pool in *somebody else's body,* with somebody else's mind in control. The word *somebody* had never seemed so poignant. There were only a few centimetres of liquid left. . .

Duncan stared perplexed at the statue before him. Draped over it, the long white dress was unchanged, but this was not playing fair. How could he be expected to disturb the ruminations of a stone statue? Behind the expressionless face, he could only presume that the same obsessive thought was held, fixed and immovable. How to move it? How to break through that seemingly impregnable power of concentration, even for a few crucial seconds? There was only one thing left to try . . . his ultimate resource . . . the one thing that was *guaranteed* to get anyone's attention.

Lifting his leg, he peed all over the front of her nice white dress.

Pandemonium ensued.

The statue erupted into life. Arms flew, legs

kicked, the mouth screamed, as stone became flesh once more and struggled to get up. Duncan ran to save his hide from the volcanic onslaught of threats and imprecations. The princess peeled off her soiled shift and flung it after him, shrieking and swearing and cursing. . .

. . .while across the bottom of the pool, the water eddied and trickled into tiny little rivulets, until every last drop ran silently down and away through the inky-black, chrome-rimmed plughole.

CHAPTER twenty-five

"The grommet that can be expressed is not the eternal grommet."
The Way of the Grommet, page 19

Cornelius Plant got up wearily from the dining table and took off his coat. He picked up Agnes's bag, trudged over to the rope lifts and asked Henry to take him up. He passed the bathroom. He passed his own room and tossed his coat on the floor. He carried on up, passing his son's disaster area.

As he passed the fourth floor, he called to the prone figure on the bed, "Where's your brother gone?"

Fiz screamed into her pillow, *"I'M NEVER SPEAKING TO YOU AGAIN AS LONG AS I LIVE!"*

The ropes creaked and complained and continued their ascent. When he reached the top, he stepped off into his sister's room. His mother was there already, sitting on the bed with Agnes beside her. Cornelius's worst fears were instantly confirmed: in the crook of her left arm she held a well-swaddled baby. He plonked her bag on the floor and adjusted his glasses. The two women looked up at him without speaking. Instinctively, Agnes tightened her grip on the bundled baby.

The room was painted ivory with a border of blue and yellow flowers. Just under the border, a fancy bit of lace ribbon swung loopily all around the room. Each loop was pinned up with a pink bow. The overall effect was like a giant, inside-out wedding cake. Between two of the windows were shelves displaying more than four hundred teapots. Other walls were plastered with newspaper clippings and pictures of kittens and puppies and the occasional carburettor. There was a wall chart of the EC Common Agricultural Policy and, above the bed, a framed portrait of the King of Zambia. Don't ask. The bed was piled high with pillows covered in *broderie anglaise*.

Twelve years separated brother and sister, and, when Cornelius was very young, Agnes had, in many ways, been more of a mother to him than Delia had. A strong bond had formed between the two and, as Agnes grew increasingly eccentric, Cornelius had never dismissed her as mad. After all, he was no stranger to eccentricity himself and they shared a deep mutual understanding. Over the years, they had developed a remarkable way of communicating.

"How is your hand, Agnes?" he asked.

"She's my Baby Mary, and I'm keeping her."

"The doctor wanted to see you. He was very upset that you had gone. The nurse was upset too."

"So she should be! Which nurse?"

"The nurse who was upset."

"Pah! Calls herself a nurse! Where did she get her training? Off the back of a cereal box? Leaving my Baby Mary unattended like that!"

Cornelius pushed his glasses up on his nose and said, "Cereal boxes have feelings too, you know."

"I know that."

"Of course you do."

"Do they?"

Cornelius nodded. Agnes looked down at the baby, then back at her brother.

"Agnes, you really must take the baby back," Delia said softly. "You can't keep her. It's not right."

"I certainly can keep her! She's not going back to that hospital where any Tom, Dick or Harry could walk in and steal her, that's for sure! What kind of mother would I be then? I've got responsibilities!"

Cornelius sighed. His mother had never understood that, with Agnes, the direct approach never worked; you had to come at the subject as obliquely as possible.

"We have to put the clock back tonight," he commented casually.

"What, already? It feels like spring!"

"I know. But it's not. It's October. That's why it has to go back. Even if we don't feel like putting it back. Even if we don't *want* to put it back. We have to do it. Don't we, Agnes."

"Er, well, yes . . . the clock . . . if you say so."

Agnes looked down at Baby Mary.

"Because it's time, isn't it. It's October. That means we have to put it back. Even if we don't want to. Would you like me to put it back for you, Agnes?"

Agnes sighed and didn't reply. She held Baby Mary closely and her eyes filled with tears. She'd always longed for a baby of her own . . . to be somebody's mum . . . but now it had to go back. Just like the clock. Corny said so. He must be right; he was a grommet professor.

Cornelius stepped towards her very slowly. Through her tears, Agnes continued to gaze lovingly as he leaned down to take the baby from her. There was a moment when it was not at all sure if she would let go . . . but then she did, reluctantly. It was a touching scene. Delia sniffled and couldn't help but feel sorry for her daughter, in

226

spite of her having done such a dreadful thing. Agnes's lips wobbled and she dabbed her eyes on her sleeve.

Cornelius straightened up. The baby stretched and arched its back. It opened its eyes. Startled by seeing a new face, it opened its mouth as well, as if to cry –

But the baby didn't cry.

"What do you have to do to get a drink in thish place?" it demanded.

Agnes screamed, Cornelius jumped and tossed the baby back to his sister like a sack of flour. Everyone stared in alarm.

"Hey, go easy willya? I only jusht got here!"

Due to a distinct lack of teeth, it spoke with a pronounced lisp:

"Derek Wilkinsh, painter and decorator; besht rugby fullback in all Easht Anglia! Drank fifteen pints and wrapped my GTi around a tree . . . never shoulda had that last one. *Such a shtupid washte!* Such a beautiful car! Sixteen valve, metallic green, alloy wheelsh . . . at leasht no one was hurt – eshept the tree, *ha!* I didn't feel a thing. What the hell, that'sh life, innit! Tell the wife I'm OK, willya? You know, new body and everything. I am sure gonna mish that car though. Total write-off. But hey – *what eshactly?* I sheem to be mishing shomething elshe . . . am I a girlie now, or what?"

Cornelius groped behind him for a chair and sat down rather heavily. He and his mother struck an identical pose with one hand on their respective foreheads. After the real shock of a speaking terrier three months ago, a speaking baby was comparatively ordinary. The bad news was that any practical hope of it going back to the hospital was quickly receding from the agenda. There was no telling what other effects the passage through the black hole might have had. Agnes was clearly delighted.

"Baby Mary!" she exclaimed. "You're awake! And so clever! One day old and talking to beat the band!"

"*Mary?*" Derek Wilkins cried. "You cannot be sherioush! They'll never let me play rugby if I'm a girlie. And I'll have to kish boys. Never! Not in thish life! I'll never forgive you for thish, Mum."

"She called me Mum! You see? Did you hear that? She called me Mum!"

Cornelius and Delia were too stunned to reply.

"Yeah, so who'sh my dad then? That geek with the hair and the glasshes? The one what jus' pitched me acrosh the room?"

"That's Corny. He's my brother. But I'm sure he wouldn't mind. Shall we ask him? Corny, would you like to be Baby Mary's daddy? You'll have to be her uncle as well. She's a painter and decorator and she likes rugby. You like rugby, don't you Corny?"

Cornelius looked up at his sister with a face like an empty page: blank, white, immobile. Delia looked from son to daughter. She suddenly felt unusually old and tired. Life was so long and she'd seen so much . . . maybe too much. The more she saw the less she understood. Perhaps some things were never meant to be understood. It was better that way. She sighed and got up.

It will all work itself out, she told herself. *Things mostly always do. . .*

She walked over to the rope lift.

"I think I'll go and lie down for a while," she said without turning around. "I'll be in my room if anybody needs me."

"I don't want your brother for a dad!" Derek Wilkins wailed. "I want a proper dad. My lasht one was hopelesh. And say, aren't you a bit old to be my mum? You look about ninety. This is not shtarting at all well. I really need a drink. Make it a double."

"Baby Mary!" Agnes scolded. "I'm going to smack your bottom if I hear any more talk like that! Do you want a smack on your bottom? Do you?" She laid the baby on the bed. "Now look what I've got for you — a nice bottle of celery juice!"

Derek Wilkins wailed forlornly. Cornelius stood up. There was nothing more he could do but pray. His sister was going to make a wonderful mother. A wonderful mother.

"Oh, stop your blubbering," she exclaimed from the bed. "You're a grown man, for heaven's sake!"

The baby continued to whimper and Cornelius dragged himself over to the lifts. On the way down, he called out again, "Fenella, where have Jack and Duncan got to?"

"Up on the roof! I'm not talking to you! *AND DON'T EVER CALL ME FENELLA!*"

The rope continued its descent.

What are they doing up on the roof? Nice view, I guess. At least they can't get into much trouble. Jack is so sensible. I never have to worry about him. What a relief.

The professor arrived in the kitchen. He made himself a celery sandwich and carried it to the dining table. What a day it had been: Agnes's broken hand, the stolen baby, Fiz's blue boyfriend . . . where would it all end? Maybe the move had been a mistake after all. Maybe they should all just go back to Neasden. But what about his work? The universe had such high expectations of him. He couldn't just walk away from something like that.

He sat down, pulled a sheaf of papers from a battered folder and started leafing through them. His first big lecture was coming up and he hadn't even begun to prepare for it. It was for level-three students as well, which meant they'd been studying philosophy for two hundred years. It would have to be good. He began to collate his notes, scribbling extra bits in the margins and drawing coloured arrows and lines to connect various related passages. It looked like a sort of psychotic treasure map. Bundling it all together in what seemed to be the right order, he began to read it through.

He got halfway down the first page and groaned. He flipped ahead, scanning one page after another. It was a mess. It lacked cohesion. The argument was muddy and the central idea was unclear. He took a pair of grommets from his pocket, toyed with them for a while, then set them on the table in front of him. What was it about these enigmatic rubber rings that fascinated him so? How was he to unravel their deepest secrets?

Diving back into his papers, he went over it all again, simplifying and clarifying. He scratched out huge sections and drew yet more coloured lines and arrows. These were the moments he truly lived for. He became so absorbed in the vitality of his hypothesis that all other concerns melted away. He gave it his fullest concentration; being the moral and intellectual guardian of the universe was not something he could afford to be cavalier about. Everything depended on his capacity to put across a clear, concise argument in words that anyone could understand. . .

After two hours of revising, he leaned back in his chair and read aloud:

"*The grommet that relinquishes its grommet-nature for the perfection of non-existence, by existing, ultimately negates this negation and becomes that which, as perfect, it cannot be:* itself. *This sacrificing of representational-object meaning is signified by the grommet's reduction to the pure flux of becoming* – not *by its necessary self-obliteration. Thus, the entire objective-representational is evacuated and, insofar as one can say,* 'This is a grommet', *the representational constative is reversed into a performative.*"

Cornelius put the page down. He threw back his head and closed his eyes. It was good and he knew it. It was very good. If his work was going to have any impact on the real lives of real people, then this was the calibre of writing he had to aim for: clear, direct, unambiguous. But it was only a beginning. He could have no rest until he put some flesh on these bare bones. With a broad sweep of his forearm, he cleared aside the acres of notes and bad first drafts. He set a clean sheet on the table in front of him, gave his biro a shake and launched back into the fray.

For another hour he laboured, totally absorbed in his subject. So absorbed in fact, that when the white door zipped open, he only dimly registered a short round man skidding across the room and out

232

into the garden. A large brown envelope fluttered after him. The door closed again. A moment later the man reappeared, now holding the envelope and brushing bits of grass from his coat.

He stood for a long moment waiting to be acknowledged, looking around the room to see if there was anyone else he might speak to. There wasn't. He pulled a sheet of paper from the envelope and did a quick name-check.

"Excuse me," he said, "I hate to barge in like this, but I'm looking for a Mr Cornelius Plant."

Cornelius carried on writing and muttering to himself, his forehead propped heavily on his left hand. His long scraggly hair curtained his face. He couldn't bear to be interrupted, especially at such a critical moment. Without speaking or looking up, he held up one hand to ward off the intruder. The man frowned and stroked his moustache. He narrowed his eyes and tried to read the notes scattered over the table. Incomprehensible garble. He decided that the raised hand must be a confirmation of identity. He cleared his throat to proceed.

"Mr Plant, my name is Dribbling. Herb Dribbling. Central Electric."

He flicked open his plastic card wallet and displayed his ID to the curtained side of the professor's head. He flipped it closed and put it away again.

"It's about your house at 37 Albemarle Gardens? I presume your wife Delia told you about the bill? I spoke to her earlier."

Cornelius mumbled what he had just written:

". . .the grommet as pure flux must be considered an 'event'; the subject qua the void of negativity that mediates the self-relating signifier chain."

This was not quite right and he shook his head, frowning.

"Ah. She didn't. No, she wouldn't, would she. You see, it was a bit high this quarter: a tad over thirty-one million, in fact."

As he said this, Herb leaned a little to one side to get a glimpse of the man's face. Not a flicker. He paused and looked away, quickly scanning the room. He cleared his throat and recited loudly: "The rain in Spain falls mainly on the cucumber."

Still no response.

Must be on drugs, he decided. But there was no one else he could deal with. It had to be the owner of the house. He pressed on.

"*Ahem*. . . Obviously, Mr Eggplant, the Electricity Board is a bit concerned at this level of debt. But following discussions with our legal and finance departments, we have decided that, for the sake of good community relations, we are willing to completely write it off . . . I said, *completely write it off* – hello? – *are you listening?*"

Herb leaned in a little closer and raised his voice. "We are willing to completely write off your wife's debt, Mr Plantpot, *in exchange for the title deed to the property.*"

Again he paused to gauge the man's reaction. There wasn't one. Cornelius carried on writing, regardless.

"I am sure you can appreciate that this offer represents enormous generosity on our part. The house cannot possibly be worth anywhere near the amount owing. You do understand that, don't you?"

Cornelius was impervious, unreachable, sunk in his own deep and vital world, wrestling with ancient demons that had forever plagued the human mind. He reviewed his last paragraph:

"*. . .viewed from within the symbolic order, the over-determined grommet appears as its own irreducible/constitutive performative, a self-referential circularity; the non-symbolizable kernel that disturbs its own over-determined circuit.*"

As he muttered, he held up his pen absently and waved it in a circular motion, to help animate the idea. Herb interpreted this as a gesture of impatience and a willingness to get on with signing the paperwork. Quickly, he opened the brown envelope and produced a ten-page possession order.

"Quite right. I understand how busy you are. I should never have troubled you with the tedious details. Just a formality really. What do you care about silly little houses on far-away planets? Now if you could just sign here please . . . there, at the bottom."

He thrust the papers in front of the mumbling half-wit and suddenly the professor balked. Something had disturbed his universe. What was this before him? These were not his papers. He could see the word, *Signature,* followed by a long dotted line. Where had it come from? At last he looked up. There seemed to be a small round man in the house. Why? What was he doing there? Cornelius gazed at him blankly.

"Ah, awake at last. Central Electricity Board. Just need a wee signature. Right there if you don't mind."

Cornelius blinked for perhaps the first time in his life. In fact, he blinked two or three times.

"Central . . . Elec. . ." he repeated to himself flatly. *. . .that would be the substantive / constitutive / performative electricity board?* He looked back at the paper. *. . .an event in the flux of becoming, in need of a signifier . . . no, a signature.*

He nodded and grunted. He took his pen and made a few trial passes in the air in preparation of signing — just as Henry rumbled and whistled.

Agnes could be heard, distantly, singing to Baby Derek as she clambered on to the ropes. Inwardly Herb groaned at the sound of her voice. She was certain to foul everything up, just when he was making real progress! On the other hand, he did need someone to sign as a witness. And it would have to be someone fairly mad. No one else would do it. Perhaps her arrival wasn't all bad news. He turned back to the professor.

"Mr Plantation, you were just about to sign, I believe," he urged.

"You mean, to signify."

"Yes, that's right. You just signify right here on this funny little line."

"Yes . . . but, what exactly?"

"It's to settle your electricity bill. You needn't worry, just signify it."

The professor blinked again. His hand made a few more preliminary passes above the page, then stopped. He riffled the pile of papers.

"Seems awfully long for an electricity bill. Are you sure it's— ?"

"It's a special quarterly statement, you being a very special customer. It gives you far more information than usual. Just look at all the information you're getting, at no extra cost!"

Cornelius stared at the page. He felt as if he were in a foreign country. His mother had always dealt with the running of the house. But he didn't want to wake her up if it was just a bill. And he certainly didn't want to go wading through ten pages of it. He could lose the thread of his lecture altogether. He put pen to paper – then stopped again.

"But surely – " he started to say, just as the rope lift came to a stop.

"Listen, you used the electricity and now you have to pay. Simple. So just sign it, all right? I. M. Corny Eggplant. Like that. Here. Let me help you."

Taking hold of the professor's hand, Herb quickly moved it to the right place on the page, just as Agnes alighted from the rope lift with the baby slotted through her sling.

She took one step, pointed violently at Herb and spat, "*You again?* I thought I could hear voices down here. Corny, you didn't let that hooligan in did you? And what's that you're signing, you plonker!"

Corny signed.

"I'm just signifying the electric bill," he said. "Nothing you'd understand."

He returned the pen to the electricity man. Agnes scowled. It was true, she understood even less about such things than her brother did, but even still, signifying an electricity bill seemed a bit excessive.

Herb smiled. "Miss Plant, I wonder if you wouldn't mind signing as witness?" He offered her

238

the sheaf of papers, holding up his chewed biro in the other hand as if it were a prize-winning carrot.

"Well you needn't wonder. I do mind. I mind very much. Get out or Derek here will throw you out on your ear!"

Herb's starched smile crumpled slightly.

"Derek? I thought you had a baby girl."

"He *is* my baby girl. And he's the best rugby full-back in all East Anglia. Now sling your hook."

The baby raised its head and squealed. "Take me with you – *pleashe!* You gotta get me outta here!"

All blood drained visibly from Herb's face. He took on a bluish pallor and struggled with a strong impulse to turn and run. He knew he was over-tired and overworked, but this was too much. He couldn't take his eyes off the thing.

"Agnes, please just sign it so the man can go. I have to get back to my work!"

In fact, the professor had already turned back to his own papers and was about to resubmerge himself, like a fish returning to the sea after a worrying spell on dry land. Agnes hesitated momentarily. Why was the electrical hooligan staring at her baby like that? It was probably best to get rid of him quick, the pervert.

"Oh, give it here then and I'll sign it. What do I care."

Agnes grabbed the papers from him, stepped up

to the table and made a quick scribble. She banged the pen on top and stepped back again.

"Now get out," she ordered.

Jarred from his catatonic reverie, Herb couldn't get away fast enough. He stuffed the contract hurriedly into the envelope, stowed his chewed-up biro in his inside pocket and made for the black door. Flicking the latch, he yanked it open, calling back over his shoulder, "I'll see my own way ou*WOOOOUUouut*. . ."

The door slid shut behind him. The only sounds to be heard were the profound and urgent scratchings of the professor's pen. . .

Then a tiny voice peeped, "That'sh my real dad, innit!"

CHAPTER twenty-six

Jack's watery consciousness swirled and gurgled through a long dark pipe. All he was properly aware of was the blind blackness squeezing him in on all sides, like riding a rollercoaster in a body-bag. He felt himself sloshing around a number of sharp bends, to the left, around to the right, levelling out for a bit, then dropping away —

— abruptly.

Suddenly he came spraying out of the end of the tube. He fell briefly through open air in the form of a thousand separate droplets and then splashed into a glacial, underground pool.

The shock of the heart-stopping cold was enough to wake the dead and then kill them again. Particularly startling for Jack was the fact that he felt it at all. To feel the cold, he had to have a warm-blooded body to feel it with. That was a good thing. But in the same instant that he realized he was back in one piece, he became painfully aware of the disadvantages. Surfacing blindly, all the air was punched out of his lungs in one prolonged shriek of frozen agony. Disorientated, he thrashed and gulped, turning this way and that, still seeing nothing. He flailed his arms and pumped his legs just to keep alive, swimming in any direction at all and hoping for a dry shore nearby.

His knee soon found a rock. Wincing, he kicked more carefully and found another one under his hand. He drew up his legs and crawled on all fours, up and out of the life-sapping ice water. He clambered on to a flat outcrop, teeth chattering like a road-breaker.

Quickly he checked his various bits, relieved to find himself occupying his own body. He could tell that much in the dark: his arms, his legs, his hair, his head . . . *his nappy* . . . his icy-wet, dripping nappy.

Jack sighed and tried to stand up, but banged his head on the cavern ceiling. Immediately he sat down again. He couldn't see his hand in front of his face. The cave might have been three metres across or thirty, it was impossible to tell. Somewhere out to his left, was the *plip, plip, plip* of dripping water. The only other sound was his own juddering breath. He rubbed his arms to try to generate some heat, coaxing his blood to keep moving through his veins.

Then, he became aware of another sound.

He stopped breathing and listened. To his left the *plip, plip* was unrelenting, but away to his right he could definitely hear something else . . . an erratic, slapping, scuffling noise. It stopped. He breathed as lightly as possible . . . ice-water trickled from his hair and ran down the back of his neck . . . his heart pounded. There it was again . . . like something inching its way over the rocks with wet, flapping hands . . . flippers maybe . . . some fish-like thing, or – *what?* Something unmistakably alive and coming steadily towards him.

He crept down off his perch and tried to feel his way along the water's edge in the opposite direction. It made no difference at all whether his eyes were open or closed. He groped his way over smooth rocks and jagged rocks, pawing at the air in front of him. His only orientations were the rock wall on his left, the water's edge to his right, a low ceiling above and a mysterious scuffling noise somewhere behind. He stubbed his toes and scraped his knees. Twice the ground ahead of him suddenly gave way and he found himself back in the water with an icy jolt, scrambling to get out.

He stopped again to listen. When Jack stopped,

the thing stopped as well. It seemed distinctly further away. After a long, cold silence he heard a small splash . . . *a pebble, perhaps? Or. . .?* Every sound was amplified by the hard acoustic of the cave walls, and even further by Jack's hyper-alertness. There was another splash a few metres away, then more of the flapping, slapping, dragging sound – louder and very much nearer. Whatever it was, it moved much more quickly through water than on land.

Jack lurched forward and cracked his forehead. Frantically trying to see with his hands, he found only a solid wall in front of him, with no way around it that did not involve swimming. The glacial water was deterrent enough, but the thought of sharing the same inky pool with some slinky, slimy swimming thing, that might come up from behind and through his legs . . . no, thank you. He would do better to deal with it on land, if it came to that.

He turned around with his back to the wall. He was too scared to shiver. He tried not to breathe. A huge hammer was pounding in his chest. In the distance, the tedious *plip, plip* dripped like torture. The other sound was much nearer; a thing dragging itself over the stones with great effort. Whenever it stopped, there was a taut absence of sound . . . a gulp of cold breath rasped like a bellows . . . silence again. In the black intervening space hung the sound-vacuum of two beings listening out for each other. . .

Two stones scraped together and it edged a little closer. Jack pressed himself back and away, a little nearer to the water's edge. In the dark, distance was impossible to judge but it now sounded no more than couple of metres away. How big was it? Like an otter? A seal? No, smaller than that. . . It hauled itself forward and now Jack could hear a faint moaning, almost a whimper. He considered stepping past it and hurrying back the way he had come, but there was no telling what shape the thing was. What if he stepped on it in the dark, in his bare feet? What if it had tentacles, or arms sprawling out, waiting to grab his leg as soon as he moved?

He inched down to the water's edge. Tentatively, he groped into the pool with one foot, but the shore sloped away steeply and he couldn't even find the bottom. The thing was right in front of him. He could sense it without seeing it. Then it flopped forward once more and this time it landed on his foot: cold, slimy, jelly-like. . .

Jack screamed and flicked it off, but as he did, he looked down and saw a translucent orange oval glowing dully on the ground before him. It was no bigger than a loaf of bread – tapered at both ends. As his starved eyes drank up the light, he could make out short, flat fins on either side. As graceless as a beetle on its back, it righted itself and pulled itself forward with its flippers, coming within a centimetre of Jack's big toe. The light it had generated was already beginning to fade to black.

Jack realized he wasn't cornered at all. He could easily step past it and scuttle away to the other end of the cave. It would be a half-hour before the thing could catch up. But . . . why did it glow like that? It hadn't been glowing before. It only lit up after it touched his foot for that split second. It must have converted the scarce warmth of Jack's body into light. What then, if . . . what if he were to pick it up?

He looked down. The creature nosed forward just far enough to touch the boy's toe. Instantly, its head fluoresced the colour of amber. He could make out the remnants of eye sockets, wrinkled and redundant. Inside the head was a central dark mass he presumed was a brain. Threadlike veins trailed away from it throughout its body like a kind of nervous system. Jack began to feel vaguely sorry for it. It seemed quite helpless. It seemed to need him. Or, perhaps it realized that he needed it? If it really could generate light. . .

Carefully, he knelt down and stroked it with one finger. An orange path lit up along its back. He repeated this over and over. He laid his hand on its back. His arm tingled with a mild electricity and the body of the strange creature gave off a much brighter yellow light. He took it by the fins with both hands and picked it up. Instantly it lit up like a lantern, illuminating everything within ten metres. The walls of the cave suddenly came alive with colour: turquoise and emerald gemstones striped with silver and metallic red. Lumps of rock he had tripped over in the dark appeared to be solid gold.

Jack stared, awe-struck, all around him. The cavern was no more than fifteen metres long and about ten across. In the centre, the water was as black as oil with golden ripples circling out from the drips that plipped from the pipe in the ceiling. Holding his living lantern out in front of him, he crouched and started back along the shore the way he had come. Stepping over dazzlingly bright, jewel-encrusted mounds, he made his way back to the flat outcrop where he had originally been sitting and clambered over it. Shadows lurked behind glittering stalactites and across the water, silver and red flecks glinted. His arms jangled electrically and the weird, oval jellyfish was now radiant with brilliant blue-white light.

He reached the far end of the elongated pool and was about to start up the other side, when the lantern-fish suddenly twisted in his hands. It seemed to be pointing towards a section of wall they had just passed. Jack stopped to look. At first, there was nothing to be seen, but as he looked closer, camouflaged amid the riot of coloured stones, he could make out a distinct circle. He stepped nearer to it and the beast began wriggling frantically, trying to twist free. He set it down and it hobbled towards the water, still glowing brightly.

At chest height, the circle was about sixty centimetres in diameter. Behind him, the blind, luminous creature waited at the water's edge, still lighting up that entire section of wall. Jack touched the centre of the circle and instantly it fell back, revealing an open passage just big enough to crawl through. At the same time, he heard a splash behind him and turning, he saw a trail of light streaking away under the surface of the water. Then it dived deep, away out of sight. The cave went black again.

But no longer entirely black. As he peered into the tunnel, a misty light filtered down, promising the possibility of a way up and out. Jack clambered in, head first. He had scarcely crawled more than his own body-length, when he heard the round door swing closed behind him. The only way was up.

Dragging himself on his elbows, he edged up the sloping passage. The earth beneath him was smooth, but above his head roots and twigs hung down, raking his back. In places, it narrowed so much he could barely squeeze through, then it opened up again, growing steadily lighter. It seemed to take for ever to reach the mouth. Blinking like a mole, his head finally emerged from a hole almost completely overgrown with creepers. He pushed them aside and scrambled out of the ground, filthy and relieved. The change of temperature from the arctic cave to the blast of tropical sun was staggering. He brushed himself down as well as he could and looked around for any clue as to where he was.

It only made sense that he had to be quite near the palace, but it was nowhere to be seen. As if anything about it made sense. He stumbled off, following the line of least resistance through the underbrush. It quickly became apparent that he was not well equipped for a jungle expedition. Some specialist high-tech gear could have been really useful; shoes . . . trousers . . . a shirt, maybe. Within a hundred metres, his legs and arms were raw. He had to clamber around enormous flat roots that grew out from colossal gum trees. Millions of vines and lianas tangled down all around him and giant ferns waved their parasols above his head, blotting out the sun.

Finally, he came to a grassy clearing and stopped to survey his surroundings. As Duncan had been leading on the way out, he hadn't paid a great deal of attention to landmarks. He certainly didn't recognize anything now. The palace had to be around somewhere, but it would not have surprised him if it had just evaporated, or turned into an aubergine. He flopped down on a hummock to rest. The wind rustled the tall grass and, overhead, the violet sky was a vault of airbrushed perfection. He plucked a blade of grass and chewed on it distractedly. The air was fresh and the sun warmed his skin. He noticed it edging steadily towards the north-east where it would set. It would be dark within the hour.

Jack got up again and scanned the horizon. To his left, some three metres away, a lone daffodil waved in the breeze. It looked profoundly out of place – so utterly English and well-behaved, stolidly trying to win a toehold on the verge of untamed wilderness. How could it have got there? *Who knows, who cares.* He shrugged and set off, with no great conviction as to which way to go.

He walked right past the daffodil. For some reason, he couldn't take his eyes off it. In fact, after a few paces, he stopped and went back to it. He scratched his head. He scratched his leg. He was overcome by the sudden urge to bend down and smell it. *Why?* Why should he want to smell this extremely unlikely flower?

Perhaps it was nostalgia for the far-away English spring. Perhaps it was the reassurance of such a harmless and ordinary sight after such a weird and trying day. Perhaps it was the colour or the scent or the way it waved and bowed so bravely – an outpost of civilization amid the riot of raw and lawless jungle life.

Well, why shouldn't he smell it? No reason.

He got down on his hands and knees. The scent was especially powerful, stronger than any flower he could remember. He put his nose right up to it . . . closer . . . closer still . . . until his nose was right inside the bell. The fragrance was delightful but intoxicating . . . almost too strong. He pulled away and tried to get up.

He couldn't get up.

He couldn't get his nose out of the flower.

He pulled his head back two or three times, but it wouldn't let go. He grabbed it by the stem with both hands and yanked on it. The stem stretched a little – then sprang back as if made of indestructible rubber. He tried to jerk it out of the ground altogether, but it clung on with roots of steel. Leaning back as far as he could, he pulled against it with his entire body. He shook his head vigorously from side to side. No result.

He repeated all of the above over and over without success, virtually exhausting himself and nearly pulling his nose off in the process. It was hopeless and, at the same time, utterly absurd – to be kneeling in the grass, his nappied bottom in the air and his nose superglued to a daffodil. It was too idiotic for words.

Then it gradually stopped seeming idiotic and started to be genuinely worrying. No one knew where he was. The sun was setting. He literally could not move from the spot. The flower's perfume was so overpowering he was about to pass out.

The pin! he suddenly remembered. *The pin in my nappy. Maybe I can stab it, or scratch through the stem. . .?*

Jack was just about to remove the pin when he heard a voice. What incredible timing! Help was at hand! He was rescued. . .

"Hi, Jack!" the voice called. "So there you are!"

Footsteps rustled in the grass behind him. Turning his head slightly to one side, he glimpsed a pair of slim, coffee-coloured legs. Zaÿfa! The daffodil wrenched his head straight again and nearly broke his nose. He quickly decided not to undo his nappy for the time being.

"I was looking for you at the party, but I couldn't see you anywhere. So I came out for some fresh air — and here you are! What a surprise. I almost didn't recognize you in your, er, in that thing you're wearing. Why is it all brown at the back?"

Jack Plant blushed to thermonuclear level and

prayed for an earthquake. If only the ground would heave and yawn and swallow him up – anything to make this moment not happen. He tried to speak, but the flower's outer petals immediately clapped over his mouth.

"Oh, I guess it's just dirt. I mean, not that it's a problem or anything if you, you know, if you had a *problem* like that. Lots of people have problems. It's nothing to be ashamed of. In fact, it doesn't bother me at all that you have to wear a . . . a . . . actually, it looks wet. Are you wet?"

Zaÿfa sat down in the grass a short distance away. Out of the corner of one eye Jack could see a flash of scarlet, a part of an arm, a hand, but not her face.

"I'm not embarrassing you, am I?" she asked. "You know, I thought you were really sweet when we first met. So shy and quiet. I like boys who are a bit shy at first. I think it's a sign of real sensitivity. Just like the way you're into flowers. I like that. It's so rare to find someone with real sensitivity these days. You know, someone who's observant and perceptive, who can really tune into another person's situation, who would naturally know if they needed help or anything. I think things like that are really important, don't you?"

"*Hrrrmmlebrrl.*"

"I mean, most people are so wrapped up in their

own world, they hardly even notice other people at all. You know, they like the sound of their own voice so much that they bang on and on and on . . . I have no time for people like that. So self-centred. What do you think of this nail varnish? Isn't it a great colour? Gosh, it's hot."

"*Hlllpf! Mmm bng swlld bythz flwr! Hllllpff!*"

"Sorry? Do you speak Dutch, or what? Earthlings have so many languages. I only know English. Shame really. I was hoping we might get to be friends. In spite of your nasty reputation, I've always wanted to meet an Earthling. I mean, physically we're nearly the same and yet we hear such awful things. Surely you don't really dump horrible chemicals in the oceans and slaughter elephants and whales and explode little children with land mines and stuff like that, do you? No one where I come from could just stand by and watch all that destruction and suffering without doing something. It's unthinkable. Arcturans are very compassionate people."

". . .*hlllpf mm . . . hllf . . . cnt gt thz, thng fff mmm nzzzz. . .*" Jack was at the point of blacking out.

"Hmm, I'm sure you're right. Whatever you're mumbling about. You know, I am roasting in this dress. Would you mind if I took it off? We don't bother much with clothes at home. I guess you don't either."

Zaÿfa stood up. Straining his left eyeball to its

maximum rotation, Jack could just see her ankles. A moment later, they disappeared in a pool of crimson as the dress tumbled to the ground. Raising one foot and then the other, she stepped daintily out of it. Jack could barely breathe. The petals closed more tightly over his nose and mouth, the odour asphyxiating.

"Mmm . . . isn't it wonderful to feel the sun on your skin? Don't you just love it? *Jack?* Boy, you really are shy, aren't you. I don't suppose you could make just a little bit of an effort, even in Dutch?"

Jack could feel all life ebbing out of him. Raising one arm, he pawed listlessly at the air in Zaÿfa's direction.

She laughed and said, "That's a bit formal, isn't it?" Bending over, she shook his hand and let it fall in the grass.

"*Mmbrbl!*"

Zaÿfa sighed and gazed out over the clearing. She looked up at the sky, shaking her head. She would never understand boys.

I may as well not even be here. I mean, what do they really want? Either they're doing the mega-octopus-grope or they've got their nose stuck in a flower. They're just incapable of relating. That's all there is to it: Dutch, Arcturan or otherwise . . . totally incapable of relating.

"I think I'll go back to the party now," she said as

she picked up her dress. "By the way, you need to be careful with flowers. I was told that some of them can be dangerous. See you around, I guess."

Zaÿfa sauntered off, trailing her dress in the grass behind her. Blue in the face and cross-eyed, Jack keeled over on to his side. The daffodil began to emit a high-pitched *hummmmmm*. . .

CHAPTER twenty-seven

"Herbie! Where have you been?" Cynthia jumped up and clattered across the computer room on high heels, throwing her arms around Herb's neck. "Naughty boy! I was beginning to think you weren't coming in today!"

Herb prised himself free and continued across the room to his desk.

"I almost didn't. Been busy elsewhere, kid."

Cynthia pouted and posed with her hands on her hips.

"What do you mean, *elsewhere*? Why didn't you ring me?"

Herb stopped shuffling his papers and closed his eyes. He was feeling badly stressed: finding a black hole under a bush, going way out on a limb to put a deal together with Walter and then, worst of all, that scene with the talking baby – that had nearly done his head in. He was in no mood to deal with a possessive drama queen.

"Listen, kid, I've got a lot on my mind just now. I'm setting up my own business on the side, see. Discount nuclear waste disposal. Big gap in the market. I just need to make a few phone calls in peace, OK?"

Immediately, Cynthia ran up and threw her arms around him again.

"Oh, Herbie, that's so exciting! Our own business! It's going to be a huge success, I just know it! We make such a good team!"

Herb ducked out from under the ring of her arms and snapped, "What are you – salted or dry roasted? Where do you get this *our business* from? What makes you think we're a team, for God's sake? BECAUSE WE'RE NOT! Get it through your blow-dried little brain! It's *my* black hole, understand? *I* found it and it's *MINE* – the house, the bush – *EVERYTHING!* Mine. *Comprendez?* You can go back to Lower Codswallop and blow kisses at your mother's carp for all I care."

Cynthia staggered backwards as if she'd been slapped. Her glossy bottom lip began to wobble. Within seconds her face crumpled, the tear-taps turned on and a mournful wail issued from her lipstick. She didn't cover her face, but just stood there like a distraught toddler, arms hanging limply at her sides.

"You're being horrible to me," she whimpered. "You didn't have to *(sniffle)* say that. I was only trying to *(sniffle)* help and then you have to *(sniffle)* spoil everything!"

Herb sighed loudly. *I cannot deal with this. Not today. Not now.* He took her gently by the arm and led her to the door.

"Listen, kid, just get a grip, OK? I've got a lot to do right now. Once I get a few things sorted out, I'll see what I can do, all right?"

The tear-taps turned off.

"Oh, Herbie, do you really mean it?" Cynthia exclaimed, smiling through her smeary mascara. "I'll let you go then, so you can get on with setting up our new company. Are you doing anything tonight? Maybe we could have a drink after work, so we can discuss everything?"

Herb glared and curled his lip, narrowing his beady eyes into an armour-piercing beam. Cynthia turned and left the room.

Oh my God, they're all the same. Cling like bleeding limpets! She'll be talking about babies next. I can hear it coming. Well, let her try. That's one trick that will never work on me. Didn't work for Anthea either. Must be due by now, poor cow — unless she got rid of it. If she hears I've got money she'll be sniffing around for maintenance . . .

I've got to be very careful. Must get these papers in to Clinch. What if Walter doesn't go for it? No, he has to; he's not stupid . . . but it could take weeks to get the contracts drawn up. And he's such a wimp . . . might change his mind if he thinks about it too long.

Herb sat down and grabbed the telephone.

"Walter? Herb. Listen, I just realized I completely forgot to mention our Special Pre-Christmas Introductory Offer: on all new orders we're taking the first tanker *gratis,* free of charge — that way you save a million before you've even signed the contract! What do you say? Once you see how smoothly it all runs, you'll be itching to sign up! But I can only do it because we happen to have a gap in our delivery schedule for midnight tonight. How's that for you? Excellent! Thought you might. Not much a man can't do for a million quid, eh, Walter? *Haha!* You've got the address? Don't worry about a thing, I'll take the delivery in person!"

CHAPTER twenty-eight

The giant KlΞrM5 sun slunk reluctantly below the horizon, bathing the magnificent tower in a rosy pink afterglow. The evening settled comfortably in the dusky air, promising a few hours' respite from the muggy heat of the day.

Professor Cornelius Plant finished reading through the final draft of his first lecture, placed it carefully on the table in front of him and leaned back in his chair. He drew a breath and sighed the self-satisfied sigh of a man who knows he has done a sound day's work.

He got up from the table and walked over to the French doors. Standing there, he watched the gathering grey clouds pile up overhead, as they did at the end of every long day. A warm breeze puffed up ominously and, as the glow in the north-east began to fade, the first heavy raindrops spattered the stone steps. They arrived as the advance guard of an overwhelming liquid onslaught; every few seconds the number of drops doubled, until great lashings of water were hurtling from the leaden sky, pummelling the ground into submission. With an enormous sense of relief after so many hours of intense cerebral activity, Cornelius strolled down the steps and out over the grass. Within seconds, he was soaked to the skin.

On the fourth floor, Fiz was watching the rain from her window. She looked down to see her father dancing on the grass, his saturated shirt clinging to his skin. On the fifth floor, his mother saw him too, as did Agnes from the floor above that. For several minutes they watched him, as you might regard a mad dog from a safe distance. Then, with the same pitying perplexity, the three women of three different generations all walked over to the rope lifts. One by one they arrived in the kitchen. They came and stood side by side in the doorway, their feet getting splashed as they watched their son/brother/father leaping and pirouetting about in the downpour. None of them spoke.

When Cornelius saw them, he stopped dancing. He smiled and waved feebly. His long, lank hair was plastered to his head in clumpy strands. Still smiling dumbly, he walked back to the house, splashing through warm, swampy puddles. As he climbed the stone steps, the women parted to let him pass, eyeing him carefully, still without speaking.

"Cornelius, are you all right?" his mother asked as he dripped over to the dining table.

"Never better," he answered. "Why?"

"No, he's not," Agnes cried. "I saw him here earlier with that electrical hooligan. It's like he was in a trance, he was."

"The electrical *who*? Was he back? What did he want?"

"Nothing. It's nothing. I simply signified the bill. That's all. You were asleep and I didn't want to trouble you." Cornelius sat down with water streaming off him in a growing puddle.

"You did what?"

"He signed some papers," Agnes chirped. "Ten pages! I told him he was a plonker. But he made me sign it as well."

"*Sign what, exactly?*"

"The bill, mother. I settled the electricity bill, that's all. Honestly, I'm forty-eight years old and still you treat me like a child."

Delia passed a nervous hand over her forehead.

"You mean – *the thirty-one. . .?* No, you couldn't have. That's not possible."

"Thirty-one what?" Fiz piped up.

Delia Plant pulled out a chair and sat down without answering. Agnes stared at her brother, who was suddenly looking much less smug. Fiz looked at her gran.

"Would someone please tell me what's going on?" she demanded.

"It was just an electricity bill," her father explained, his voice wavering slightly. "Wasn't it?"

"Cornelius, no one *signs* an electricity bill. And certainly not if it's ten pages long. It must have been something else."

"Well, he *said* it was to settle the bill. That's what he said."

Gran sighed. "Yes. I'm sure he did. Did he happen to mention it was for thirty-one million pounds?"

"*WHAT?*" Fiz screamed.

No one else spoke. The professor's face went blank, then gradually took on a puzzled expression. He became aware that his glasses were wet and, taking them off, he wiped them with the tail of his soaked shirt. He replaced them no drier than they had been. The rain beat in sheets against the windows, each drop the size of a small egg. There was a prolonged silence.

"Hmm . . . that is a bit high, isn't it," Agnes commented, as if they were discussing the price of fish.

Fiz grimaced at Gran.

"Is this about what I think it's about?" she asked.

Gran nodded. Fiz sat down beside her. Agnes

eyed the two of them suspiciously then she sat down as well. The professor made a second attempt to clean his glasses, with no more success.

How could electricity cost so much? he wondered. *How on earth do people get by?*

He scratched his head. Slowly raking his hair with his fingers, he tried to claw a few strands away from his face. It was all too much to cope with — just when he'd produced such a brilliant lecture. The more he rubbed up against the real world, the less it made sense. Take one step outside the sanctuary of immaculate abstract concepts and suddenly you're ambushed by banality. Electricity bills; he had genuinely hoped he would never have to think about such things ever again. He should have let his mother deal with it. Absently, he picked up one of his grommets from the table and toyed with it, steadily retreating into the world of things that really mattered.

"I'm sure it's of no great importance," he said, trying to sound convincing.

"We'll find out soon enough," Gran shrugged.

They all sat and listened to the rain for a moment until Agnes changed the subject: "My Mary Derek's got it in his head that that hooligan is her real dad. She's crawling already, the little tyke. Sleeping now though. Like a baby. And I've tied him up so she can't come to any mischief."

Agnes capped this statement with a concise nod as if it were clearly the best solution to the problem of errant babies. Fiz had been staring at her father, hoping that he might do something, say something, to redeem the situation. She gave up and swung round to face her aunt.

"What are you blathering about? Who's Mary Derek? Why doesn't anybody ever tell me anything?"

Agnes was quite taken aback. "What do you mean, *who is Mary Derek?*" she huffed.

But Fiz knew better than to engage with her aunt and she looked instead to Gran. Gran cleared her throat with some difficulty.

"She's, um . . . she's Agnes's baby," she said cautiously, pausing to let this sink in. "Your new, er, cousin."

Fiz leaned back and crossed her arms. She did a sort of figure eight with her head, side to side. "Oh yeah. And pigs may fly. No seriously, who's Mary Derek? Is it a she or a he?"

Agnes glowered at her niece.

"Just you mind your tongue, young lady! Why shouldn't I have a baby?"

"Cause you're too old and you're barking mad, that's why."

The shock wave of this bald statement bounced around the table like a billiard ball before coming to rest in front of Agnes, whose mouth began to flap.

"Well, I never! Barking mad, am I? You're not half so clever as you think you are, I'll tell you that for nothing! And as Corny's her father, she's not your cousin either. She's your brother. What do you think of that?"

Corny's her father. . .? An uninvited picture began to form in Fiz's head which she found intensely repellent. She didn't know whether to scream or hurl or wind her watch. The one thing she did not want to do was to think about it.

She jumped to her feet shouting, *"WHAT DO YOU MEAN MY FATHER'S HER FATHER?"*

"Oh, for heaven's sake, don't be so literal," Gran ordered. "How could *he* be the father?"

Fiz looked at her gran, slowly catching up with the absurdity of her assumption. "Yeah, OK, so who is? Where did it come from? Surely they didn't let her adopt it?"

"No. She didn't adopt it. She stole it. From the hospital."

"WHAT?"

"I never stole anything! *I rescued her!* There's no telling what sort of lunatic they might have given her to. She'll thank me for that when she's bigger."

"I'm sure it's of no great importance," Cornelius repeated, still stranded in the previous conversation.

"NO GREAT IMPORTANCE?!" Fiz exploded. *"Stealing a baby?* I cannot *believe* what I'm hearing! How can you say that — and then have the nerve to lecture me about Bweeb! THIS FAMILY IS DRIVING ME INSANE! I can't deal with it. I'm leaving! I'm —"

Fiz was on the point of storming out of the room, when her father turned his unblinking eyes upon her and she paused. He looked perplexed, thoughtful, sincere. . . Once more she found herself hoping beyond hope that he might say something intelligent, something meaningful, something that would make it all OK. . .

He raised a grommet to his eye and, peering through it, asked, "Is Jack still up on the roof?"

Fiz's face contorted into a picture of repugnance and incredulity. She snorted and stomped across the room to the lifts.

"HENRY?!" she bellowed. *"GET ME OUT OF HERE!"*

Outside, the KlƎrM5 twilight deepened to its maximum, which would still have allowed the reading of a book out of doors. The sound of the rain reduced from a thunderous tattoo to a gentle patter. A warm breeze blew in the door, smelling clean and fresh. Delia Plant lit a candle on the dining table.

"What makes you think Jack's on the roof?" she

asked. "He and Duncan went to a party. He left a note . . . it's around here somewhere."

A worried expression wandered across the professor's face. A party? Oh yes . . . very distantly, he remembered something about a —

"But I'm sure I said Fenella was to go with him," he pondered aloud. Actually, he was no longer sure of anything.

"I wish I could have gone," Agnes said. "We could do with some life around here. I haven't been to a party since my fortieth. That Colin Jarvis threw up all over the cat, remember? And I head-butted his wife out the front window. Fourteen stitches, she had. Deserved every one of them. Remember, Mum? No, of course you don't. You were in Timbuktu or somewhere."

"Mozambique. Clearing land mines."

"What time did he go?" Cornelius asked.

"Colin Jarvis? Passed out in the cupboard under the stairs. Couldn't wake him up for two days."

"No, I mean Jack."

"Oh, ages ago," Delia said. "I'm sure he'll be back soon."

Cornelius slipped the grommet into his pocket, stood and squelched towards the door. The sky was a turbulent greyish-puce. The garden was flooded to a depth of fifteen centimetres.

"I'm going to look for him," he said decisively.

He made this statement mostly to himself, as if he needed to regularly remind himself what he was doing so he wouldn't forget.

No one replied or paid any notice. It was obvious that he wouldn't have the faintest clue where to look. The sky sprinkled the marshy garden and the water sitting in pools reflected the slow-breaking clouds. Delia toyed with the candle, leaking the melted wax down the side till it congealed in a blob on the table.

"I'm sure he'll turn up as soon as it's light," she said. "I can't see you accomplishing anything out there now."

But her son wasn't listening. By the time she looked up from the candle, he was wading halfway across the garden.

CHAPTER twenty-nine

Skirting Birmingham on the M42, a great lumbering bear of a lorry signalled and changed lanes. On the trailer was a giant, bullet-shaped tanker and on the back of that was a sign that warned: *Hazardous Chemicals.* As understatements go, this was like saying cluster bombs are unsuitable for children under the age of five.

The driver, Gil Tiplady, hunched slightly forward, hairy forearms resting on the steering wheel. He peered out over the night-time motorway landscape before him: red lights in front, a steady stream of white lights across the central divide, parallel rows of broken lines like weird footprints and cats' eyes staring back at him. Beneath the cab, the engine whined as he changed up a gear.

"Don't you just hate haulin' this stuff?" he grumbled. "I feel I'm about to mutate just being anywhere near it."

In the passenger seat, a gaunt man with sour breath and a three-day stubble grunted unintelligibly. He folded his arms, grimaced and pushed himself back in his seat. On his right arm a dagger tattoo was flanked by two brutish cherubs with the words "LOVE" and "HONOUR" criss-crossed on the blade and finger-guard.

"I mean, have you got any idea how toxic this stuff is?" the driver went on. "You got just one drop of it on your skin, you'd probably get every kind of cancer there is. If we was to crash this rig, it'd wipe out the whole of the West Midlands — women, children, sheep — the lot. No one could go near the place for a thousand years. Maybe more. And if they did, their children would be born with six arms or something. Ever think about that? Eh? Do you?"

Gil Tiplady looked at his passenger, awaiting some kind of response. The passenger, who was called Stretch on account of his being so lanky, jounced in his seat to the relentless rhythm of the road. With every movement, his temples were cudgelled by a merciless hangover. He took a deep breath, exhaled and closed his eyes. He rubbed his nose, then refolded his arms.

"Nope," he said.

"'*Nope,*' he says. You don't think about much, do you."

The passenger gave an exaggerated yawn, exposing the gold tooth he was particularly proud of.

"I get paid to deliver stuff. If somebody smarter than me decides it's safe, that's OK by me. I take my pay and I don't ask questions."

"*Don't ask questions?* I'll say you don't. Have you even looked at the delivery address? It's a house in bleedin' north-west London! *London,* we're talkin' about here, not some ditch in the back o' beyond."

The driver flashed his lights to another lorry that was overtaking them. The passenger sucked his teeth, rolled down the window, hawked and spat. He rolled up the window.

"Don't make no difference to me. Weren't my decision. They could say, '*Take this tanker and pump it out in your mother's kitchen sink.*' Still wouldn't make no difference. S'long as I get paid. Just another job, innit."

"'*Just another job,*' he says. Just another job! You're just another moron, you are. I got a hundred thousand litres of nuclear sludge on the back and a total friggin' moron beside me up front!"

The driver shook his head and the two fell silent. Within minutes the passenger was snoring, lulled to sleep by the rocking of the giant lorry.

The flashing green indicator lamp lit up the driver's chin as he negotiated the merging of the M42 and the M40. He checked his mirrors and rejoined the on-streaming traffic. He sighed and scratched the top of his head. His hair was thinning and his mind was humming. Everything about this job was wrong and he knew it; he could feel it in his bones. Endless lanes of highway stretched out before him, hemming him in, drawing him on, as inexorable as fate. A big blue sign read: London 104 miles.

He drove for another hour. The traffic increased steadily as they neared the capital, but they made good time nonetheless. Marching rows of orange overhead lights striped the gleaming silver flask as it slipped through the unsuspecting Home Counties with its deadly cargo. Stretch snored and snorted and clacked his tongue like a dog. Gil scowled and fretted.

Rummaging through a box in the console between the seats, he produced a cassette and pushed Dolly Parton's Greatest Hits into the tape player. He turned up the volume. He had never particularly liked country music, but he needed something to take his mind off what seemed to be a disaster in the making. He also knew that it would annoy his partner, which seemed a good enough reason to do almost anything. Stretch grunted and roused himself.

"Are we there then?" he asked groggily.

"Just passin' Oxford. Another hour to go."

"What'd you wake me up for then? Do we have to have that howling cow in the cab with us? My head's about to split."

"Helps keep me awake. Some of us have to stay awake, you know."

Stretch was suffering badly from having spent the past three days in the pub. The truth was he had spent the past three years in the pub. For most of that time, he drank to avoid his wife. When finally she walked out on him at the weekend, he drank to avoid his empty flat. His left cheek bore a nasty gash, ringed in purple, inflicted in the heat of an altercation regarding the Queen Mother. He belched vindictively and turned the music down.

The driver flashed an angry glance. He turned it up again. Stretch stared at the knob for a moment, then reached out decisively and turned it down.

Gil turned it back up.

"I said, it keeps me awake. Maybe you can do your job in your sleep but I can't. So just leave it, all right?"

Stretch glared hatefully. He quickly scanned the list of things he felt prepared to fight and die for: Aston Villa FC held the number one spot unchallenged and the Queen Mum was well up in the top five. The right *not* to have Dolly Parton assaulting his earlugs came a little further down the list, but it was there nonetheless. With no further hesitation, he yanked the cassette from the stereo and pitched it out of the window.

"*What the — ?!*" Gil Tiplady spluttered as he hit the brakes and careened over to the hard shoulder. The lorry jerked and wheezed to a halt.

He turned to his supposed assistant and demanded, "What'd you do that for, you moron! I just bought that tape. Cost me eleven quid!"

"I hate that stuff. I'm dyin' of hangover and you got some twinky-tanky hillbilly strangling a cat! I don't have to listen to that. You know I hate country music."

Gil swore under his breath and flicked on his emergency flashers. Leaning over the wheel, he indulged a momentary pause while considering his response. He did not rouse easily; he was not a fighter by nature. But, his taste in music had been insulted, his property violated, possibly destroyed. Dolly Parton's unique vocal talents, which he had only just begun to appreciate, had been viciously slandered. He wasn't about to take all that sitting down. Pushing open the door, he jumped down from the cab and strode around the front of the lorry. He jerked open the passenger door and yanked Stretch out of his seat by one arm.

He had to yell above the roar of the cars going by: "GO AND FIND IT!"

"You go find it. 'Snot my friggin' tape. I wouldn't have pitched it if I was plannin' to go find it."

Gil pushed Stretch in the chest.

"You are going to find that tape or you're not getting back in my lorry."

"*OOOOooooOO!* Get you! It's *your lorry* now, is it?"

"That's right. *I* am the driver. That makes it *MY* lorry and you are not putting one foot inside that cab until you find my cassette. I've had just about enough out of you. All the way down from Cumbria, whinging about how your wife never loved you and how she's taken the dog and the soap dish and the magazine rack you never liked and poor you in your poxy empty flat! I'm just amazed she stayed so long. How did anyone marry you in the first place? Can't you see we're doing a serious job here? We got a tank full of atomic waste to deliver and all you can think about is your bamboo magazine rack! I got half a mind to dump you here."

"Yeah, so how you gonna make the delivery then, wisearse? 'Cause *I'M* the pump operator and if you so much as touch any of those controls, the union'll be down on you like a ton o' bricks."

Gil, who was twice the other man's size, pushed him again in the chest with both hands.

"JUST GO GET THAT TAPE!"

Stretch staggered backwards, steadied himself and shouted, pointing, "YOU TOUCH ME ONCE MORE AND YOU'RE GONNA REGRET IT!"

Gil Tiplady was by now very red in the face. He advanced menacingly.

"Are you threatening me, you little runt? I'll break you in half!"

With that he lunged forward, but, in spite of his size, Stretch was easily the more experienced fighter. By simply shifting his centre of gravity, he soon had the larger man on his back.

With its near-side door hanging open, the giant lorry resembled some weird, prehistoric bird with a crippled wing, recovering by the roadside. The amber running lights continued to flash off and on and the London-bound cars streamed past endlessly. Locked in an awkward embrace, Gil and Stretch tumbled over and over, off the hard shoulder on to the grassy verge of the M40. . .

Zipping by in her Ford Fiesta, Muriel Crump, Headmistress of Picklesfield Girls' School, picked them up in her headlights.

"Oh, I say!" she muttered to herself. "Couldn't they at least wait till they got home?"

CHAPTER thirty

In Albemarle Gardens, Herb Dribbling sellotaped a handwritten sign above the doorbell and stood back to examine it:

DRIBBLING ATOMIC RESEARCH
FOUNDATION LTD PLC
Director: Dr H. Dribbling MSc, PhD, QPR

It seemed perhaps too small and he stroked his moustache disapprovingly with thumb and fore-finger.

No, when you've got a brilliant scam going, you don't need to go shouting it about.

He put out some cones in the street to mark a space for the lorry to park, then went back inside. The house reeked of fresh paint. He had spent the evening avoiding Cynthia and doing up the hall a nice sterile white so it would look more like a proper research facility. The floral carpet was all wrong, but there was nothing he could do about that right away. Removing his jacket, he slipped on a long white lab coat that instantly bestowed upon him an irreproachable scientific credibility. He adjusted the row of biros in his chest pocket, picked up the clipboard he had bought from W.H. Smith for £1.99 and went into the kitchen to make himself a cup of coffee. . .

CHAPTER thirty-one

"The finger that points to the moon is not the moon. The grommet that encircles the finger is not the finger. The grommet that shows the way is not The Way." The Way of the Grommet, page 77

Lying in her bedroom, Fiz chewed her broken fingernail and cursed the fact that there were no telephones. She desperately needed to talk to someone. How could she get in touch with Bweeb? It was miles to where he lived and she wouldn't have known how to get there even if she could. She would have to wait for him to come to her. But that might be days, weeks even. Considering the way her father had treated him, he might not come at all. *Unbearable thought.* She rolled on to her back and stared at the ceiling. Her insides were all in knots. Her mind raced, while the rest of her was stuck in neutral. She felt like a wild animal, tied by one leg. She had to break free — to run and run and never stop until she was so far away that her loony family would never find her. Except Gran of course. Gran would get a postcard from Outer Mongolia. She had to go, she had no choice. *But how?* How could she go without him? That had rapidly become an impossibility.

She got up and went to the window. The sky was breaking open and the forest was washed with a milky monochrome light. Leaning her face against the glass, she traced with one finger the path of the water droplets. A single tear rolled down her cheek. Love was so bittersweet; so rapturous and agonizing. How could it have ambushed her like this? And her being so well defended, so determined to keep her heart sealed and unassailable. . .

She went back to the bed and picked up the unplugged guitar. Gently strumming some mournful chords, she played through the new song she had started that afternoon, pausing now and then to scribble in new lyrics. She played it through again. It was something of a stylistic departure:

Bweeb, I know u're blu
but I'm blu 2 ... tho u can't c it
Bweeb, I'm torn apart
u took my ♥ and tried 2 free it
But I'm just waiting 4 u here
+ I'm just trying 2 make it clear
that u're the only l...
I'm just waiting 4 u now

+ I'm just trying to hope somehow
that I'm your only 1...
Bweeb, I know u're blu
well, I'm blu 2
y don't u come?

Fiz put down the guitar and sniffled. She got up and crossed the room to her dressing table. She sat for a moment frowning at the mirror. She passed her hand over her green hair spikes. Taking her hairbrush, with only the slightest hesitation, she knocked them down one by one and brushed her hair flat. She sighed and put down the brush. Dousing a cotton wool pad with make-up remover, she began wiping away the mask she had worn for so long. She frowned again, then got up and went to the rope lifts.

Riding it all the way to the basement, she descended the last few steps and asked Henry, "I don't suppose there's any way I can get a message to Bweeb, is there?"

Bells rang, whistles whooped, flywheels whirred. . .

"Of course there is," Henry replied. "How do you think he knew about the broken windows? I can send him any message you like. . ."

In the kitchen, Agnes and her mother sat across from each other at the table. The candle had guttered long ago. Delia was leaning on her elbows with her head held slightly to one side. Her daughter looked around the room, her mouth twitching and frowning in time to a never-ending internal dialogue.

"Very peaceful at this time, isn't it," Delia commented. "Reminds me of the Congo . . . had that same smell just before dawn. You look so tired, Agnes. How long have you been up?"

"Hmm?" Agnes half-emerged from her reverie. "Two foot three. Mary Derek's a good sleeper though. I knew she would be. I gave her the other half sedative. She's a good boy really. Just a bit confused."

Delia sighed. She had seen so many of her daughter's obsessions come and go: the teapot collection, her plan to buy the Werther's Originals company . . . now, the baby. These passing fancies invariably gave her a new lease of life, but how long would it last?

"You were a good sleeper when you were little," she said.

"Was I?"

"Well, yes, considering we were being bombed or shot at half the time."

At seventeen, Delia Plant had enlisted to fight in the Spanish Civil War. Agnes was born accidentally during a raid to blow up an enemy bridge near Lérida. The new mum, already a lieutenant, successfully completed the mission and scrambled back behind the lines with a squalling baby in her arms.

"So, was my dad Spanish then or what?"

"Hard to say. It could have been Manuel . . . but more likely Hans. Or Jimmy-the-Wheels."

"You didn't half keep busy, I'll say. No wonder your side lost."

"Or Harry. It could well have been Harry Carter. You've got his jaw, his eyes. It was a strange time for everyone. So young and idealistic."

"It was pretty strange for me, I'll tell you that for nothing. Never met my dad, and I hardly saw you neither for twelve years."

"Oh, that's not true! I used to come and see you whenever I was in London."

"Only to bugger off to the other side of the world on the next plane going! Diving expeditions in the Arctic, painting exhibitions in New York, some malaria clinic God knows where. . ."

"Sri Lanka." Delia looked down at the table. "I haven't been much of a mother to you and Cornelius, have I?" she said quietly. "It's not that I didn't want to be there for you, it's just that, well, there were always so many other things I wanted to do as well. . ."

Delia looked up and smiled wistfully, hoping for a little redemption, but Agnes's face gave away nothing. The two had never been particularly close.

Agnes was not someone you could easily get close to. She lived in such a world of her own. But maybe — just maybe — if Delia had tried harder, if she'd been around more . . . would it have made a difference? Could she have saved her? Kept her on the rails, at least? For a long moment, they gazed into each other's eyes.

Agnes broke the spell. "Well, there's nothing to be done about that now, is there. But my Mary Derek is going to have a proper mum and a proper family, that's all I can say. I've waited a very long time to have this baby and I plan to do it right. She'll grow out of all that rugby and beer-drinking nonsense; it's just a phase. He'll be a well-adjusted little girl and have all the normal things like other kids have. She can even be a boy if she wants to!"

Delia sighed again. She found herself wondering about the baby's birth mother. What could have led her to put her child up for adoption? Would Agnes or Cornelius have been better off if she had let them be adopted? Who could tell? Life worked itself out in such mysterious ways. It would all come right in the end.

"I'm sure you'll be a wonderful mother," she said hopefully.

Agnes stared out of the window and furrowed her brow.

"I just hope I tied that rope tight enough. I didn't

want to cut off the circulation in her leg, you know. But you should see how big he is already!"

Up to his ankles in muck, tripped by roots, lashed by vines, deceived by shifting jungle shadows, Cornelius Plant plodded on through the terrible wilderness. He had no idea where he was going, or in what direction. All he knew was that his son needed him and he mustn't fail. He mustn't for a moment consider either of them as being "lost". Such illusions thrive in the chaos of wrong-thinking. He would tune into the subtle and infinite cosmic field where all things were known, all things inter-connected, all outcomes inevitable. . .

I must try to spend more time with Jack. There's so much I could teach him. He has yet to really find his grommet. Shame he never sees his mother. Must try to do something about that too. I had no idea electricity prices were so high. That's inflation for you. What about this boyfriend of Fiz's, though? It can't be good to date outside your species. She's obviously serious about him. And they are meant to be highly intelligent. That was awful what she said about being racist. I've got nothing against aliens – I just don't want my daughter marrying one. Teenagers! How do you get through to them? Teach by example. Show the way. That's all you can do. Thank God it's getting lighter. I think I saw a patch of purple sky up there. . .

Squinting up through the canopy, Cornelius walked straight into a waist-high Karulu root, fell over it face-first and went sprawling into the under-growth. The last thing he heard before raising his face from the mud was his glasses splashing into an inky puddle two metres away. It was fortunate that he was so tuned-in to the subtle and infinite cosmic field where all things were known, because he was virtually blind without them. On hands and knees, he began groping about on the forest floor. Everything around him merged into a foggy, shape-less blur. . .

CHAPTER thirty-two

Herb heard the hiss of air brakes in the street long before he heard the doorbell and he very nearly jumped up and ran outside, but immediately sat down again. Directors of top-level research foundations do not run into the street for every lorry that pulls up. It wouldn't look right. When the bell rang he waited one full minute, then, with great composure, he slipped his clipboard under one arm and went to the door. On the step were two dishevelled men with ruffled hair and bits of grass stuck to their clothing. Both were in their early thirties: one tall, lanky and unshaven; the other stocky and solid.

"Good evening," Herb said. "You are — ?"

"Who, me? I'm Stretch. This pillock is just the driver. Finch sent us. Got a hundred thou' to dump. Where do you want it?"

Herb nodded.

"Hmm, let me see . . . *Finch, Finch, Finch* . . . I'm sure it's here somewhere." He scanned down the clipboard that had only one name written on it.

"Here it is: K. Walter Finch. One hundred thousand litres. Excellent."

He pressed a button on his watch and wrote down the precise time beside the entry.

"I'm Dr Dribbling. Right this way, please."

Herb led the two of them through the house and out into the back garden. They stopped on the grass. Stretch stood picking his teeth while Gil looked all around in the dark, incredulous.

"So where's the site then?" he cried. "This is supposed to be a Nuclear Waste Depot."

Herb smiled smugly.

"Your reaction is not at all uncommon," he explained, "and very flattering to myself, as the designer of this complex. You see, the site is completely concealed *underground*, so as not to disrupt the local skyline. In fact, we managed to build the entire facility without disturbing a single plant in this garden. Hard to believe, isn't it. It's just one of the many ways we're showing our concern for the environment. In fact, our choice of this location is one aspect of our extensive Community and Harmony in Industry Programme. That's CHIP for short. It should really be Community and Industry in Harmony, but that didn't make such a nice acronym. All the local residents are very enthusiastic about CHIP. Especially when they see the wealth it's going to bring, *er*, to the area."

Gil narrowed his eyes suspiciously.

"I want to see it," he said. "I want to see downstairs. Chips or no chips, I can't believe the council would allow it."

"Shut your gob," Stretch barked, slapping him on the shoulder. "You're just the driver. Your job is finished."

Gil shoved him back and Herb smiled.

"Access to the site is for technicians only, I'm afraid."

Stretch scratched his arse and belched.

"Fine by me. So, Doc, where do I put it? Where do I connect my hose?"

"As your colleague sensibly pointed out, due to council regulations, we aren't allowed to have any actual fittings above ground. It was a great technical challenge, but one we rose to enthusiastically. You just fit your nozzle into that hole in the ground – there, tucked away unobtrusively under that bush – and our staff down below will take care of everything else. You may feel a slight tug on the line. That means you're connected."

"Sounds good to me."

Stretch wiped his nose with the back of his hand

and turned to go. Gil bent over to inspect the rho-dodendron.

"This all seems incredibly dodgy," he countered. "What about spillage?"

"I assure you it is the safest process in the world. Er, actually, it's out of this world."

"And the government safety regul— ?"

"Followed to the letter. Absolutely *to the letter*."

Stretch winked at Herb and cocked his head at the driver: "Dolly Parton fan. You know what they're like."

Gil shoved him sideways with one arm, but Stretch pushed his hand away and warned, "Don't start that again, mate."

Reluctantly, Gil turned away.

Behind his back, Herb punched the air and screamed a silent *YES!* before leaving the garden to follow them back up the hall. When they got to the lorry, he informed them that he would have to personally consult his technicians to double-check all the safety procedures.

"It should only take ten minutes or so," he said. "But whatever you do, *under no circumstances* are you to commence pumping until I get back and give the all clear. Understood?"

Stretch grunted. Gil shrugged. Herb scuttled back into the house, leaving the front door wide open. The driver clambered into his cab. His bit was done. Whatever happened, it wouldn't be on his head. He pushed his recently replaced Dolly Parton cassette into the stereo, leaned back and closed his eyes.

The KlΞrM5 sun pushed its way up through the reddish band of mist that blanketed the horizon. The flooded garden had mostly drained and steam was rising from the damp earth. Delia was crouched at one side of the garden. She got to her feet, admiring the bouquet of flowers she had just picked: lilies and orchids and fabulous blue-tongued blooms that were like nothing on Earth. She walked over to the steps to where Agnes was sitting —

— just as a man in a lab coat came flying through the white door, sprinted across the room, hurdled clear over Agnes's head and landed, not badly, in the grass. Seen from the back, sailing over her head out of nowhere, Agnes thought for a moment it was the angel she had long awaited. Then the moustachioed apparition turned around. Delia's hand with the bouquet fell despondently to her side.

"What do you want now?" she demanded. "I was hoping we'd seen the last of you. What were those papers you made my son sign?"

Herb swaggered up to the two women wearing the sort of smirk that Delia could happily have punched.

"*Your son?* I thought he was your husband. No matter. You'll be pleased to know that, for the time being, he has settled your account – by signing his house over to me. That means that this wormhole thing is now mine to do with as I see fit." Herb shook his head. "Did you really think you could keep it quiet? Keep it all to yourselves? You bloody Guardian-reading liberals make me sick! So selfish! This thing belongs to science. *Progress!* You can't stop progress. I'll be making the world a better place, which is a lot more than what you're doing. This planet, whatever it's called, is about to become a nuclear waste dump. You've got ten minutes to clear the area. Consider yourselves warned."

Herb started towards the steps. He had nothing else to say. He'd delivered his warning. Not many people would have bothered. He could have just wiped them out. No one would have known. But that wouldn't have been British. He had principles and he'd stuck to them. That was the difference between him and them. They had no principles at all. They weren't making the world a better place. It was their own stupid fault if they didn't clear out. They could be back on Earth in a matter of seconds if they had any sense.

Agnes stood up to block his path.

"Where do you think you're going? You think you can just swan in here, make your little speech and swan out again? What about my Mary Derek?"

"Yes, I've met your wretched little sprog. I was here when you gave birth on the lawn, remember? I also saw a picture of you on the news today. Taken off the security camera at Central Middlesex Hospital. Seems you're wanted in connection with a stolen baby. So don't get any big ideas of going to the police in a hurry.

"As for you," he went on, shifting his serpent's gaze to Delia, "technically, you still owe Central Electric over thirty-one million quid. That debt is still on the books. I am in a position to see that it's overlooked. But if you make trouble for me, I can certainly make trouble for you. Get the picture? Like I said, you've got ten minutes."

Delia Plant rarely found herself lost for words, but at that moment all she could do was stare hatefully at this loathsome excuse for a human being. She knew she had to come up with something fast but, before she could even imagine what that might be, something caught her eye and she glanced involuntarily over Herb's shoulder towards the edge of the forest.

A near-naked body stumbled into view. They would have been more easily recognizable if the face hadn't been reworked so badly and they hadn't been wearing a sad little rag around their loins.

"Jack!" she shouted.

Everyone turned to see a teenage boy, arms and legs lacerated, feet pulped, face flayed, come staggering across the garden. He got almost as far as the steps, then collapsed in the grass. Gripped by the same impulse that renders some people incapable of driving past a car crash without slowing and staring, Herb made his first fatal pause. . .

"*What happened to you?*" Gran exclaimed, aghast.

Jack squinted up through eyes that were nearly swollen shut. His face looked like it had caught fire and been beaten out with a rake. He shook his head.

"Nasty encounter with a daffodil," he answered cryptically. Peering at the man in the white coat, his first thought was that his science teacher had come to enquire why he hadn't been in class . . . but that couldn't be right.

Who is this guy? Do I know him? What's he . . . oh, I don't care; I'm going to die. There's something wrong with my eyes. I can see a — what? What is that thing? Up there. . .

Jack strained to focus on the top floor window, waving one hand vaguely: "Whatever that thing is, it's going to fall," he said.

Three pair of eyes joined Jack's sight path.

Agnes screamed, "Mary Derek! What do you think you're doing? Get back into bed this instant!"

"Daddy! I heard my daddy's voishe!"

Teetering on the very edge of the windowsill, an enormous baby grinned and pawed at the air with one hand. It was the size of an overweight two-year-old, but with the bald, podgy shape of a baby of two months. Herb gaped upwards. Babies were repellent at the best of times. This one belonged in a horror film.

The situation was rapidly getting out of control. What should have been a clean and calculated move was threatening to embroil him in another idiotic drama. Warning these losers was a mistake. Stuff the principles. He was too soft. He should have flooded the place and wiped them all out in one go; it would have been more humane. They're just muddying up the gene pool. He urgently needed to regain the initiative.

But . . . gazing up at the top windowsill, he felt paralysed by a perverse combination of repugnance and fascination. He could not tear his eyes away from the spectacle of an ugly, bloated infant about to plunge to its death.

Jack got to his poor feet. Delia darted to the lifts and shouted down to Henry.

"Mary Derek, you stay right where you are, you naughty girl!" Agnes wailed. "It's not time to get up yet!"

"*DADDY!*" the horrible thing was calling. "Don't leave me here!"

"You stop that now!" Agnes ordered. "That's not your father, that's the electrical hooligan! Corny's your father."

Jack looked at his aunt, screwed up his pre-distorted face and demanded, "Hang on, Corny's *my* father!"

Henry carried Delia to the top of the tower as fast as he could.

Herb stood, mesmerized by the pink, loathsome splodge shifting ever nearer to the edge, balancing precariously and waving one hand.

Run, he urged himself. *Run before it's too late!* But he stood nailed to the spot, one foot on the lowest step.

Delia stepped lightly from the rope lift into Agnes's room. She started quickly across the floor on tiptoe, desperate not to startle the reckless child. Two floors down, Fiz heard the commotion and stuck her head out of her own window.

"What's all the racket about? Who are you? *Jack!* Why are you wearing a – ?"

Everyone seemed to be staring up at her but no one answered. Her aunt was biting all of her fingernails at once. A fat man in a white coat had gone into a trance. Her brother's face was all beaten up and he was wearing a nappy. Then she realized they were staring at something higher up. She wrenched her neck around to look, just as her grandmother lurched forward to grab the baby —

— and missed.

Mary Derek took one step and dived from the top of the seven-storey tower, trailing a long, blue bungee cord around one ankle.

"*NOOoooo!*" Agnes screamed, hiding her face in both hands.

Like a panicky turtle, Fiz retracted her head just as her new cousin zipped past her window. Jack staggered forward heroically, arms outstretched, ready to at least try and catch it. Herb gaped and did nothing. The baby plummeted down, down, down, directly towards him. . .

"*DA-DEEEeee. . .!*" she wailed, looking more and more like a suicidal Michelin Man with a long blue kite-tail.

In Agnes's room, Delia could see the rope paying out but couldn't see what, if anything, it was attached to. She stomped down hard on the line with her right foot. The rope went taut and stretched. . .

and stretched. . .

and stretched some more —

— just far enough for Mary Derek's over-plump, out-reaching arms to come within stroking distance of Herb's cheek. The baby gurgled and grinned . . . a dollop of drool dripped from its gaping, gummy mouth. Oh-so-slowly it dribbled and, to avoid it splashing in his eye, Herb jerked his head sideways and found his focus falling instead on the plastic hospital nametag that Agnes had yet to remove from the baby's wrist.

And in that snapshot fraction-of-a-second, when his daughter had stopped falling but was yet to *sproing* skyward again, he had just time enough to read what was printed there: *Mother's Name: Anthea Collins.*

It is often said that it's a wise a child who knows its own father. The wisdom of the father in question is less remarked upon. Herb fainted and toppled like a fir tree.

The baby on the bungee cord zinged upward, almost as far as Fiz's window. On the second drop Jack did manage to catch her, although not without being knocked to the ground in the process.

"Again, again!" Mary Derek enthused, clapping her podgy hands. "You musht be Jack. Nice catch! Play much rugby? Love your outfit. Those cotton nappiesh are the besht. Can't shtand disposhables. Elashtics way too tight. And they leak. Know what I mean? We are going to have such a lot to talk about! Have you met my dad? A real go-er with the ladies. Never know it by the look of him, would ya?"

Jack recoiled in horror from the monster talking

baby. It was by far the most frightening thing he'd seen all day. Agnes came to relieve him.

"Poor little diddums!" she cooed, undoing the cord around its ankle. "You were a naughty little diddums, giving Mumsy a fright like that!"

"Jack, you gotta help me — I don't wanna be a girlie!"

Jack got up and stared, dumbstruck. Henry creaked and whistled and, a moment later, Fiz arrived.

"Where did you come from? The father-person just went to look for you. Nice shorts. They suit you. Who's the fat slob?"

"Who are you calling a fat shlob?" Mary Derek piped up.

Jack looked down at Herb. He looked at his sister, whose hair was flat and not green. He didn't dare look back at the infant apparition.

"What, what is that — *that thing?*" he stammered, pointing behind his hand.

"What? Oh, *her*. Aggie stole a baby. What happened to your face?"

The casualness of Fiz's delivery made it seem almost OK. Then Gran came skipping down the steps, pointed at Herb and announced, "Listen, we've got to do something about this ton of lard, and quick!"

"Who is he?" Jack and Fiz asked in stereo.

"He's trouble, that's who he is. Remember the thirty-one million pound electric bill? The one your father signified?"

Fiz blanked. "Yeah. So?"

"Well, in doing so, he lost his house."

"What are you talking about?" Jack wanted to know. "What house? What electric bill? I go out to a party and all hell breaks loose! What is going on?"

Gran smiled sarcastically.

"Oh, don't fret yet, it gets worse: this charming individual now owns 37 Albemarle Gardens and is planning to use the wormhole as a nuclear waste chute! He came to give us ten minutes to clear out."

"But that's terrible!" Fiz gasped. "What about Bweeb? Who's going to warn Bweeb?"

"*Who is Bweeb?!*"

Jack was totally lost. He had to hold his head with both hands to keep from losing it. The fat man started to come around. Groggily he raised himself a few centimetres but Fiz kicked him on the side of the head and he collapsed again.

"OI!" Mary Derek shouted. "Nobody kicksh my old dad around like that!" Wriggling out of Agnes's arms, she started across the grass at an alarming pace. "Dad, wake up!" she cried, kissing him all over his face. "We gotta get outta here – you and me both!"

"Mary Derek, I am warning you for the last time!" Agnes shouted, grabbing her by the ankles. She tried to tear her away, but the baby clung fast around Herb's neck.

"*Da-deee! Da-deee!*" she squealed.

"You let go of that hooligan right now! Do you hear me?" Agnes's voice was sounding more and more strained. The pressures of parenthood were taking their toll. "Let go! Let go right now, I say! I AM WARNING YOU!"

"Agnes, get that baby out of here!" Gran ordered. "Can't you see we're—"

"*Da-deee! Da-deee! Wake up!*"

"She won't let go! Mary Derek, I am your mother and you'll do as I say!"

"No, you're not, you old bat – Anthea Collinsh is. And thish is my dad! I know his voishe from when I was in Mum's tum!"

"Good heavens!" Gran exclaimed. "What if? I mean – *what if he really is the father!*"

Agnes froze. She glared at her mother, furious that she could even suggest such a thing. She fumed and huffed and shook with indignation. Doubts began to creep in . . . her recently acquired maternal instinct was ebbing quickly. She turned back to Mary Derek.

"All right," she barked. "You want him for a father? You can have him, you ungrateful rugrat!

You probably deserve each other! I hope you grow up fat and ugly with a moustache!"

With that, Agnes let go of the baby's feet and plonked her down hard on Herb's chest. Abruptly she turned and marched into the tower.

The scene was now completely out of control and Jack was well beyond any hope of coping with it. His face was burning up from poisonous daffodil pus. His skin had been shredded from hours of crashing through the jungle in the dark. He needed a bath . . . he needed to lie down in a safe place . . . he needed to sleep, sleep, sleep . . . he needed to wake up on some other day, in some other life when this nightmare was well and truly over. He flopped down in the grass. As was so often the case, he turned to the only person he could think of who could possibly deal with it all.

"Has anyone seen Duncan?" he asked.

Fiz turned away and screamed through gritted teeth. She rolled her eyes and banged her forehead with the heel of her hand.

"YOU HAVE THE BRAIN OF A NEMATODE! Bweeb is in the gravest of danger and all my idiot brother can think about is his dog!"

Gran ignored them both. With the giant baby bouncing happily on the fat man's chest, she pounced on the bungee cord and was about to start binding his feet, when – out of nowhere – a sugary voice wafted across the garden:

"*I know where your precious Duncan is.*"

There was a stunned silence. Gran dropped the rope.

"Who is it? Who's there?" she called.

"Mum? Ish that you?"

"It's the DS of UU!" Fiz exclaimed.

Gran glanced at her uncertainly and shrugged. A light breeze stirred the grass and the surrounding trees exploded with a clatter of flapping wings and a rainbow of flying colour.

Jack groaned and fell backwards, shaking his head from side to side. He covered his eyes, moaning, "*No, no, no . . . don't let it be true!*"

Standing in between him and the beached whale behind her, Fiz gazed down at her nappied brother, convinced he had finally lost the plot.

"What are you whimpering about now?"

"It's not the DS of UU," he cried dismally.

As he spoke, a giant soap bubble drifted gently down from the forest canopy. Inside the bubble, a blonde woman wore a spangly blue dress. In one hand she held a golden wand with a star on the end. In her other hand was a white, wire cage. In the cage was an apoplectic miniature poodle. The bubble floated gracefully into the garden and settled on the grass. It burst as soon as it landed. The woman took a few ballerina steps towards them. She stood and beamed a saccharine smile, tilting her head from side to side like a wound-up doll.

"Hello. My name is Glenda. I am the Good Witch of the North. Welcome to Munchkin Land. Now, hand over the boy or I shall turn your poodle into a curry."

At these words, Jack was back on his feet.

"*NO!* Anything but that!" he shouted. "Duncan *hates* curry. He doesn't even like poodles."

He was about to run forward, but Gran grabbed him firmly by one arm. The poodle was going berserk, gnawing and clawing at the bars of the cage. Fiz's eyebrow studs were the only things that kept her eyes from popping out of her head.

"Look, I don't know who you are, but that's not our dog," Gran said. "Our dog is a Jack Russell. Personally, I'm quite fond of poodle curry. Takes me back to when I was in China: garlic, ginger, coriander . . . but you're not having our Jack. No chance."

Glenda smiled even more sweetly. She set down the cage.

"Oh, but I assure you, it *is* your dog. You recognize your dog, don't you Jack?"

Jack turned to his grandmother.

"Gran, it's Duncan. Trust me. I was at her party. She does these weird things with peoples' bodies –

changes them all around. Tried to turn me into Sylvester Stallone . . . you don't want to know. But I'm pretty sure that is actually Duncan!"

Delia looked at the poodle and then back at her grandson for whom she had had such great hopes. *Completely lost the plot,* she sighed to herself.

Meanwhile, the Good Witch of the North transformed effortlessly into Marilyn Monroe, complete with ivory dress permanently billowing up from below. Jack indicated with an upturned palm.

"Get the idea?" he murmured.

Fiz was too stunned to speak. She huddled a little closer to the other two. Gran nodded slowly and bit her lip. She decided to brazen it out.

"Well, I still don't see what you need my grandson for. Just give us our dog back."

Marilyn laughed, taking a few steps nearer. She narrowed her eyes and lowered her voice.

"I need a man, honey. *A real man.* I intend to make him into one if it's the last thing I do."

Gran put a protective arm around Jack's shoulders and snorted, "Ha! You and the rest of the female population. You're looking in the wrong place."

Fiz gave her brother a puzzled look, up and down. *A real man?* All she saw was a skinny teenager with a toilet problem. Meanwhile, Marilyn was leaning to one side, trying to glimpse the strange lab-coated mound lying in the grass behind them.

"Unless, of course," she commented casually, "you know of some other suitable candidate? Human? Male? That's all I ask. . ."

There was the briefest of pauses. Gran looked at Fiz. Fiz looked at Gran. Together they looked down at Herb.

Bang on cue, Herb grunted and opened his eyes. He found he could barely breathe. There was a twenty-kilo baby bouncing on his chest. His eyes opened a little wider and he swallowed hard. Mary Derek clapped her hands with glee.

Oh my God! It's Anthea's brat!

Instantly he rolled the baby off into the grass and got to his feet.

It's still here! Is it? No, it can't be — too ghastly to contemplate. That freak-show is no child of mine. I'm hallucinating, that's what. Seeing things. I'll ignore it. It'll go away. I'll see a doctor as soon as I get back . . . get some tablets. I'm overworked. I'm stressed out. I haven't been eating or sleeping properly. This place is full of freaks . . . enough to make your teeth itch. Excellent site for a nuclear dump. I've got to get out of here. I've got to make the world a better place. A black hole belongs to science. Can't go leaving it to a bunch of flaky, inbred degenerates. I've got principles. I'll wipe them all out! They don't have principles. They don't even deserve a warning.

He badly needed to get a grip. He would steel himself. He would be resolute and unwavering. The entire project could slip through his fingers and he'd lose everything! He picked up his clipboard and straightened his coat. One side of his head was throbbing from where Fiz had kicked him. Out of the corner of one eye, he noticed a giant baby clinging to his leg, but he knew it wasn't real.

"All right, you losers," he barked. "You've had your little warning and I've had enough games for today. I am outta here."

Mary Derek had never been happier in all her short life. She gurgled and waved bye-bye, keeping an iron grip on Herb's leg with her other hand.

He started limping up the steps. He was utterly resolute and unwavering. He didn't look back. Jack and Fiz opened their mouths to speak, but Gran stopped them with a raised finger. By an infallible sixth sense, honed from years of experience with all types of men, she somehow knew that no intervention would be necessary.

Herbert Dribbling was halfway up the steps when a voice appealing directly to his hormones called out, "What's your hurry there, Big Boy?"

His resolute and unwavering step instantly faltered.

I know that voice . . . it sounds like . . . not Anthea, no, it actually sounds like — I don't care. I don't care who it sounds like. I am walking straight through that door and I'm going to flood this place. It's the way of the future! They'll have to be sacrificed — all of them. Science and progress marches on, and I am going with it! I'll see the doc and get this hallucination off my leg. No babe lumbers me with a kid! No way! It actually sounds like —

He knew he must not stop — not for anyone: must not listen, must not turn, must not look left or right. He was a man! *A warrior!* He would gird his loins and march onward, across the room, out through the big black door. A tanker full of fluorescent sludge awaited . . . a fortune was begging to be made. He would make the world a better—

"You wouldn't give a girl the cold shoulder now, would you?"

That voice . . . that deliciously breathy, sexy voice . . . I know it from somewhere. Isn't that . . . I mean, it sounds like — don't be ridiculous! Run! Got to get out. Now!

He dragged his unusually heavy leg two more steps, then he heard another voice.

"Hey, Dad, check thish out! It's Marilyn Monroe! And she's talking to *you*! What are you waiting for, you old dog!"

Herb looked down at his hallucination. Without a doubt, the ugliest baby he had ever seen. He looked up at the big black door. It was precisely three-and-a-half seconds away.

Dear God, give me strength . . . it is her! I knew it! My

hallucination just said so. What is she doing here? Why is she talking to me? Don't make me turn around — not now! But . . . but, how do you say no to Marilyn Monroe? I'd be crazy not to at least get her number. . .

Like so many men before him, Herbert Dribbling could resist anything but temptation. At the top of the broad stone steps, he stopped. And as he stopped, before he turned around, there was the slightest pause while all the cards in the universe were reshuffled. The lines of his palm were redrawn. The hot, dry hurricane of time ravaged all eternity, meticulously erasing every vestige of every future that might have been, that almost was, but would be no longer. . . And in that split nanosecond, he knew he was defeated. He would never make the long walk across the big round room. He would not go into the discount nuclear waste disposal business. He would not get the mountain of cash, the gold-plated front door, the hot and cold running mega-babes. . .

Like a puppet on an invisible string, he turned to face his nemesis. A brassy blonde with more curves than Silverstone racetrack stood on the grass in a provocative, three-quarter pose, one hand resting lightly on her tilted hips, the other pushing up her hair from behind.

"What's the matter, honey? Cat got your tongue?" she purred, flashing him the sauciest, flirtiest smirk in all the history of mammalian courtship.

Herb grinned like a dolt. He needed something to occupy his hands, so he took out his comb and fixed his stringer. Appearance was very important when meeting the ultimate sex kitten of all time.

"Hi. I'm Herb," he managed to say, at last.

"Come on over here and say that."

Marilyn pursed her screaming-red lips and blew him a kiss. Her skirt billowed sensuously about her thighs. Jack, Fiz and Gran all watched silently as he flung his clipboard into the bushes. Peeling off his lab coat, he let it fall on the steps behind him. He stumbled across the lawn like a sleepwalker with a ball and chain.

"Who's your little friend?"

"What? Oh . . . *that*." Herb looked down sheepishly, trying to hide one leg behind the other. "It's sort of a growth. I'll get some tablets. It'll go away."

Marilyn nodded.

The growth waved and chirped: "Derek Wilkinsh, painter and decorator! Besht rugby full-back in all Easht Anglia!"

"Such a modern family. How charming."

Reaching into her handbag, Marilyn produced a tiny perfume bottle and shook a few drops on to the poodle's nose. Duncan exploded into the cage, completely beside himself.

"YOU COME NEAR ME AGAIN AND I'LL TAKE YOUR SCRAWNY LEG OFF, YOU HAIRLESS BIPED! You think you can make a poodle out of me and get away with it? *I am a Jack Rrr-ussell!* DON'T EVER FORGET IT!"

Then sweeping her wand in a wide arch over her head, Marilyn enclosed herself, Herb and Mary Derek in a bubble. It rose gently off the ground then soared quickly up and away above the trees.

Jack shook his head and laughed. "That guy hasn't the faintest idea what he's let himself in for! Not the foggiest!"

CHAPTER thirty-three

Leaning against the front of the lorry, Stretch flicked his cigarette across the street and the lit end spun and glowed like a Catherine Wheel. The street was quiet and grey. Above his head, a faulty sodium light flickered a dull, bloody orange. He checked his watch for the fiftieth time. The geezer in the white coat had been gone for hours. Dolly Parton had played herself out and switched off. Gil was in the cab, snoring.

Stretch swore and kicked the front tyre uselessly. The entire night was shot and they still had to make the long drive back to Cumbria. It would be light soon. He walked up to the house and peered in the doorway. A bare bulb burned in the hall. The hand-written nameplate had fallen down and he bent to pick it up. He stuck it back on the wall. He pressed the doorbell. It rang and rang but there was no response. He swore again and walked back to the lorry, checking over his shoulder for any sign of life. Staring at his pump switches, he pulled at his lower lip. He looked back at the house.

"Damn," he snarled. "I'm not waiting here all bloody night!" and he began detaching the fifteen-centimetre titanium hose that lay coiled under the tanker. He twiddled some rudimentary dials and checked the gauges. After some minor adjustments, he engaged a lever that induced a dull thrubbing from the pump and a nervous twitch to the pressure gauge.

Leaving the pump on standby, he yanked on the free end of the monstrous hose, dragging it behind him like a dead python. He marched into the house, down the hall and out into the garden. He crossed the lawn and pushed back the rhododendron. He stood for a moment, scowling and flaring his nostrils at the hole in the ground, as if trying to intimidate it. Without a second thought, he thrust one end of his flexi-tube into the hole.

Instantly, all of the slack was taken up. The hose sprang taut and out in the street, there was an almighty grinding and squealing, followed by a juddering crunch as the lorry jerked sideways and was hauled up on to the pavement, jamming itself against a low brick wall. Stretch ran out to see Gil, astounded, dazed and horrified in equal measure, climbing down from the cab.

"What the hell was that?! What happened? An earthquake, or what?"

Stretch quickly surveyed the situation and decided it wasn't all that bad.

"Keep your hair on. He said there'd be a tug on the line when they connected us, didn't he? Didn't he say that?"

"*A tug on the line?* He didn't say they were going to drag the whole lorry sideways. Look at it! It's nearly knocked that wall down!"

"Don't be such a wuss. The slightest little thing and you completely lose it. I'm never working with you again as long as I live. Go back to your country music, why don't you."

Stretch rechecked the gauges and brought the pump up to pressure.

"What are you doing?" Gil demanded. "Where's the guv'nor? Did he come back then?"

"Nope."

"*No?* So what are you doing? He said —"

Just below the gauges two buttons nestled in a protective safety housing: a red one for "*Stop*" and a green one for "*Go*". Stretch lifted the cover on the housing.

"I don't care what he said. I haven't slept for three days and I'm not waiting around here all night. I get paid by the delivery, not by the hour. There was a tug on the line. That means we're connected. That means we can unload this mess and go home."

His finger was poised to jab the green button, but Gil grabbed it with one hand and closed the flap with the other.

"You can't do that, you halfwit! You don't know what's going on down there. If the guv'nor's not back, then something's not right. He said he'd be ten minutes."

Stretch jerked his finger away and pointed at Gil across the hose that strained in between them, as taut as piano wire.

"Don't you start, Mr Driver. You don't start telling me my job!" and he slapped him on the side of the head as a diversionary tactic.

Instinctively Gil released the cover plate and Stretch quickly flicked it open again. He went for the "*Go*" button a second time, but the driver snatched his finger just before it made contact and wrenched it around backwards. There was a painful *crrick* as a few knuckles bent the wrong way.

Stretch screamed, pulling his hand free.

"You damn near broke my finger!"

"I said, don't touch it till the guv'nor gets back."

"What were you like at school, for Chrissake?

'*Teacher, teacher! Johnny's pressing the green button again!*' Relax, will you."

"I'll relax all right. You just leave it be."

"OK, chill out." Stretch wiped his mouth with the back of his hand and sniffled. He shook his sprained finger. "We'll wait a bit more then."

"That's right. We'll wait. Just don't touch that button."

"Yeah, yeah. Don't fret."

"All right."

"All right."

Gil turned, took one step towards the cab and immediately Stretch lunged for the safety flap. He just got the thumb of his good hand on the button when the driver whirled around and swung at him in the nick of time. Stretch dodged, grabbed Gil's arm and pulled him forward over the knee-high hose. Sprawling face first, the driver kicked out at his partner's legs, knocking him to the ground as well. Then he jumped on top of him and the two rolled about on the crazy paving, locked in another futile embrace.

They were interrupted by an unmistakably authoritarian voice leaning over the neighbour's wall.

"Evening, gentlemen. This your lorry, is it?"

CHAPTER thirty-four

"I am certain I stipulated that you could go *only* if Fenella went with you."

By following the sound of Duncan's barking, the professor had arrived back at the tower just shortly after Herb, Marilyn and Mary Derek had left. His face was bruised from encounters with various tree trunks. He never did find his glasses. Seated around the dining table were Jack, Fiz and Gran. The inconsolable Agnes had gone back to bed vowing never to get up again. Jack, in jeans and T-shirt with Duncan curled up on his lap, had just finished telling his story.

"Well, actually, that's not quite what you said," he countered. "What you said was, '*You can go if your sister says she'll go with you,*' which is different. My sister did say, '*she'll go with you*'. Didn't you, Fiz?

So I went. It was Duncan's idea. But you should speak more precisely. Say what you mean."

"Oh, it hardly matters now," Gran said, shaking her head. "Not after all we've been through. If it weren't for Marilyn coming to get you, we could all have been doused in radioactive goo. The entire planet would have been poisoned, ruined! Thank God all that business is over. Sounds like the electrical hooligan's going to be busy for a while. You're just lucky the rain came when it did."

"Oh yeah, that was horrible. Too close. The water must have dissolved the daffodil glue and then the rain on my face brought me around. It still burns though. Do you really think it would have eaten me?"

"*Ha!*" Fiz laughed. "That would've been so typical — you getting eaten by a daffodil. Such a mimsy way to go."

With the green dye washed out of her hair and the absence of make-up, Jack barely recognized his sister. He stuck out his tongue and made a face at her but it hurt too much.

Cornelius, lagging several steps behind as usual, remarked, "What I must have said was, '*if your sister says that she'll go with you.*' You obviously misheard me. The indicative pronoun '*that*' is all-important."

"*The indicative pronoun 'that' is all-important,*" Fiz

mocked in a high, spinsterish voice. "You sound like Miss Osgood. Pedantic old fart." She was still angry with her father and glowered malevolently. "I cannot believe this, you know. Jack goes off with a bunch of aliens, turns into a cowboy, gets seduced by Marilyn Monroe, escapes into an underground cave with a glow-worm, runs around naked with some Arcturan girl you've never even met, then winds up being eaten by a daffodil. And what do you do? YOU CORRECT HIS GRAMMAR! He gets away with murder! *But me?* Ha! Different story. I spend one day with Bweeb and immediately it's, *'Fenella, I don't want you seeing this boy.'* You are such a fascist hypocrite."

"Fenella, that really is—"

"Who is this Bweeb character you keep going on about?" Jack interrupted.

Fiz fell suddenly silent. She stared at the table, twiddling her eyebrow stud.

"It seems you're about to meet him," Gran answered, nodding towards the garden.

Fiz looked up and wailed, *"BWEEeeeb!"*

Skidding back her chair, she rushed out of the room with open arms. Jack craned his neck to see a blue floating skittle smothering his sister in kisses.

"Oh . . . *him*. We already met. On the way to the party. They seem happy. How revolting."

The blissed-out couple came inside and Bweeb

went around the table with his usual greeting. He stopped beside the professor's chair.

Clearing his throat, he squeaked melodically, "Plant Professor. Me very news good have."

"Bweeb! Your English has improved! How did you learn that?" Ecstatically Fiz beamed from her gran to her brother to her father. "Did you hear that? He can speak! This is so wonderful! What's the news?"

"Me very news good have!" Bweeb repeated. "Me —"

But just then, he broke off. A puzzled look came over his face and he turned to stare at the big white door. He went pale all over. His expression became increasingly anxious and uncomprehending. Shaking his head in consternation, he drifted over towards the door. . .

CHAPTER thirty-five

Quickly releasing each other like embarrassed lovers, Gil and Stretch both jumped to their feet.

"Er, mine it is, Constable. I mean, I'm the driver. We were just, er, making a delivery. Dribbling Atomic. Nuclear waste, you know. Shouldn't be long now. Just have to, er, pump it out in the garden, *haha*. Underground site, you see. Fish and CHIP, *haha*. We'll be gone in a minute."

Gil Tiplady straightened his shirt and his hair. Stretch straightened his finger. The policeman eyed them each in turn, coldly and professionally. He glanced at the house. He eyed it up and down as well. Slowly and deliberately, he stepped over the low wall from the neighbour's garden. He paced up to the door and examined the handwritten nameplate. He peeled it back to check the sellotape.

Gingerly, he pushed at the open door with one finger and peered into the hall. Nothing escaped his scrutiny. He noted the pink and orange floral carpet and the fresh white paint. He drummed his fingers on the taut hose. Sucking his teeth, he tutted and shook his head. He strolled back to the brawlers who were waiting rather sheepishly. Raising his chin unnecessarily high, the policeman frowned and stroked his stubbled neck with the backs of his knuckles.

"I don't know what you two think you're playing at, but this will never do," he said severely.

Gil looked at the house. Stretch looked at his hose. They didn't look at the policeman. Stretch sniffled and spat.

"That lorry," the policeman went on, wagging his finger, "is very dangerously parked. You have completely blocked pedestrian access to this section of the pavement. What if someone in a wheelchair came along? How would they get by? If it were daytime, I'd have to book you straight off."

Gil and Stretch regarded each other briefly, then they looked away again.

"Still. . ." The constable cleared his throat and squared his shoulders for dramatic effect. "We in the force do understand the needs of business. And we try, when possible, to take a sympathetic view. You've got your jobs to do. I know that. I'm no fool. But I've got mine as well. I want you to put out hazard triangles five metres from either end of that tanker. So people can see it more clearly. And don't leave it there for too long now, will you."

He turned and stepped back over the neighbour's wall, then stopped.

"By the way, are you sure that hose is connected properly? Looks a bit taut to me."

Without waiting for a reply, he went out through the neighbour's gate and strolled on up the street, hands behind his back.

Totally nonplussed, Gil watched him go . . . but only for a moment because Stretch seized the opportunity to deliver a savage left hook to the driver's right temple, sending him sailing over the hose backwards and flat out cold on the concrete.

Standing victorious, lanky legs in heroic pose, he thrust his crooked finger at the vanquished Gil and spat, "You just don't mess with the pump operator! Got it? Now let's get this job done!"

Striding back to his switches, he ripped back the safety flap and punched the green button without a second's hesitation. Leaning on the tank with one hand, he glowered as the hose throbbed and swelled and the tank disgorged its unspeakably poisonous contents. The only thing that Stretch found at all notable was the speed with which the volume gauge keeled over, helped along by the awesome gravitational suction on the other end. In less than three seconds, the hundred thousand litres were drained off and the needle fell to zero.

Stretch tapped the gauge. He banged on the side of the tank with the palm of his hand. A hollow, metallic echo answered back. It was undoubtedly empty. He shrugged and shook his head.

This is like playing the triangle in an orchestra; you wait around for a lifetime, then you do three seconds' work! If I didn't count all the waiting and the faffing about and calculated what I'm gonna get paid for just that bit, my hourly rate would be astronomical! Hmf. If only. . .

Stepping over the hose and Gil's sprawling legs, he swaggered through the house and out into the garden to disconnect his hose, whistling to the Spice Girls in his head. . .

CHAPTER thirty-six

Everyone around the table was staring at Bweeb. Bobbing a little, his head tilted to one side, Bweeb was staring intently at the white door. No one made a sound. Ever alert, Delia rose silently from her chair.

"Bweeb?" Fiz asked uncertainly. "What is it? Why are you – ?"

He didn't answer, but waved to her without turning around. Duncan, who also realized that something was badly wrong, jumped down from Jack's lap and stood growling and barking at the door. Jack ran the tip of his tongue around his teeth, thinking, *Something not nice is about to happen. Something—*

He didn't have time to finish his thought because the white door flew back and an ungodly, vengeful roar flew out: the sound of the universe in agony . . . an explosion of thunderous outrage that such a vile insult, such a hideous crime could be committed against her.

And in the wake of that soul-shivering shriek that seemed to last an eternity but in fact was only a part of a second, a great gushing stream of luminous atomic bile came spurting through the door at head height.

Cornelius dropped his grommet and it bounced and rolled under the table. Jack pushed back his chair and staggered to his feet. Gran held her face with both hands. Fiz screamed, Duncan fled and everyone gaped, wide-eyed in desperate disbelief as —

— Bweeb opened his mouth.

He opened his mouth as if he were about to speak, or shout, or weep, but his mouth opened wider still, until the top of his head flipped all the way back. His body floated up behind him and he became a sort of distended blue sack, yawning wide at one end. The torrent of glowing goo gushed into his cavernous maw.

It has to be said that, in its passage through the black hole, the vile sludge had been greatly condensed, but there was still enough to swell poor Bweeb to many times his normal size, like a balloon filling with water. Having captured every last drop, his head flipped closed again. His now vast, pendulous bottom dropped down underneath him, swinging from side to side. The door zipped shut. He crossed his eyes, swallowed hard and belched. Grinning like a drunkard, he went a sickly green colour, glowing a little. He sank to the ground, bounced, sank again, then keeled over on to his back.

Fiz was the first to his side.

"*Bweeb?!*" she called. "Are you all right? Is he all right? What was that stuff? Was that the — ? No, it can't be. *It can't possibly be!* He's going to be OK, isn't he? He mustn't — I mean, *he has to be OK!*"

Gran helped her to raise the enormous, swollen Bweeb into an upright position. Everyone gathered around. Not even Duncan knew what to do or say. Bweeb's eyes remained closed. His luminous body went cold to the touch. Sobbing uncontrollably, Fiz took his limp hand and raised it to her lips. She cradled his head in her arms, rocking back and forth, whimpering, "He mustn't die . . . *he mustn't die!*"

CHAPTER thirty-seven

In the days that followed, the weather in London took a turn for the worse. Clouds rolled in, covering the sky in shame. The heavens wept, but the temperature plummeted and the rain turned to sleet. For days on end, a freak ice storm whipped the capital, causing havoc on the roads and keeping the emergency wards working overtime. A metallic wind blew in all the way from Greenland, tearing through the heart of England, taking roof slates and fences with it, stealing hats and ravishing umbrellas.

Fighting his way along the slippery city pavement, Jack clutched at his jacket and came to a stop before a massive pair of stone columns. Had he known that winter had arrived so early, he would have worn a thicker coat. He climbed the three steps looking like something dredged out of the

Thames. As he reached the door, a man in a bowler hat and a Burberry topcoat emerged from the double doors. Taking one look at the bedraggled boy, he reached into his pocket and pressed twenty pence into Jack's hand. The man went on his way. From the shelter of the porch, Jack looked at the coin, then back at the man who quickly hailed a cab and disappeared. Jack turned and pushed open the heavy door.

In the marble-floored lobby, which was only half the size of a football pitch, crouched an immense desk with a frosted glass top. On the wall behind it, important black letters proclaimed: BLAND CRAVEN INCHBUTT. At the desk a red-haired woman smiled a professional smile. A bored security guard lurked by the lifts. He gave Jack a disapproving once-over and took a few steps towards him. Jack approached the desk and asked the woman if he could see Caroline Craven.

"Do you have an appointment?" the woman sang.

"She's my mother."

The receptionist hesitated. This statement was not registered in her standard repertoire of questions and answers.

"Do you have an appointment?" she repeated, still smiling.

"No, I don't. My name's Jack. I'm her son. She knows what it's about."

"Please take a seat. I'll try her office for you."

To the left of the glass-topped desk were some leather armchairs and a coffee table. On the coffee table were copies of *Business Week*, *The Economist*, the *Financial Times* and the *Wall Street Journal*. Jack sat down in one of the chairs, trying not to get it wet. The security guard sauntered back to his position between the lifts. The receptionist buzzed a number on her intercom, spoke briefly, then got up and came over to where Jack was sitting.

"I'm very sorry, but Ms Craven is in a meeting. She's going to be about an hour. Would you like to wait, or would you like to make an appointment to come back another time?"

"I'll wait."

"Can I get you anything? Tea or coffee?"

"Tea please. Milk, four sugars."

The woman turned and minced back to her desk. She buzzed another number and ordered tea. Jack picked up a magazine and started leafing through it. Boring pictures of men in suits, shaking hands. Captains of the Universe. Corporate raiders grinning like reptiles. Anonymous, unelected men, carving up the world, doing deals, turning profits out of thin air. What could be more dull, more odious? He tossed the magazine on to the coffee table and leant back. He gazed out of the door at the people scurrying by in the November gloom, grey upon grey. When his tea arrived, he scalded his mouth on the first sip.

After an hour and a half of shivering, his hair was dry but his clothes were still damp. The intercom buzzed and the receptionist announced, "Ms Craven will see you now. Take the lift to the fourteenth floor. Her office is on the—"

"Thank you. I know where her office is."

The security guard pressed the button for him. It was the most taxing thing he'd done all day. He stood aside as the boy got into the lift. At the fourteenth floor, Jack exited and walked down the corridor to his mother's office. He knocked and entered and found her speaking on the telephone. She waved at him to sit down, which he did, studying the expensive-looking art on the walls. She quickly wrapped up the conversation:

"It's not as if we're talking huge sums here . . . if they go to four-and-a-half million then I think we should settle – but not a penny less. Assuming they meet the rest of our terms, of course. And if not, we'll fight it out. Simple as that. Yes, of course they will. They're not stupid. Yes. Good. We'll discuss it on the eleventh. That's right. Fine. Goodbye."

She replaced the handset and changed her expression like someone trying on a new hat.

"Jack!" she exclaimed.

Getting up, she came around from behind her desk with open arms. But before she could get too close, Jack held out his hand. His mother looked down at it, then, realizing it was all she was going to get, decided to shake it.

"This is a nice surprise," she said, sitting down again. "We really must meet up more often. It's terrible of me, I know. *Work!*"

She threw her hands in the air and, with this easy disclaimer out of the way, went on to comment at length on the foul weather until Jack interrupted and got to the point: "So, did you manage to find out anything about the house?"

Two weeks previous, mainly as an excuse to make contact and partly because he knew his father would never get around to it, he had telephoned and told her about the electricity board's attempt to possess the house. He had left out nearly all the details.

"Yes, I did," said his mother. She reached into a drawer and came out with a green folder.

"I spoke to a Mr Drench who sent me this." She riffled the pages of a ten-page document. "It's a total nonsense. You needn't have worried. First of all, they immediately conceded that it's not humanly possible to use thirty-one million poundsworth of electricity in such a short period of time. The meter was obviously faulty. They've admitted that. Secondly. . ."

She flipped to the back page of the possession order and scowled. "You know, this *is* a nonsense, but your father was a fool to have signed it. I can't imagine what he was thinking. Well, actually I probably can. Never mind. Do you know who was supposed to have witnessed it?"

"Auntie Agnes, I think."

"Ah, that would figure. She signed as '*Mrs Santa Claus*'. Obviously smarter than she looks. The whole thing is null and void. They'll be writing to him with a formal apology. Apparently this Dribbling character who instigated it all has vanished without a trace."

"Really? How strange. I wonder what happened to him."

"Strange indeed. Still. It's no concern of ours."

Caroline Craven put the papers back into the folder, placed it on her desk and folded her hands on top of it.

"Now. Tell me. How's Fenella getting on with her new guitar?"

"Oh, she doesn't seem to play it much. I think she's gone off the idea."

"What, *already?*"

"Hmm. She's got other things on her mind just now."

"Like boys, I imagine."

"Something like that."

"And you? What have you been up to?"

"Oh, nothing much. Same old stuff."

"How's school?"

"School's great. Never better."

"Well, that *is* good to hear!"

By this point in the conversation, Jack's mother was already fidgeting with various papers on her desk, making mental notes to ring so and so, fax that to Hong Kong, chase up such and such. . . He found it distressingly easy to keep things secret from her. She simply did not want to know.

"I guess I'd better go then," he said, getting up. "It'll take for ever to get back with all the tube delays."

Why had he come? What had he expected? His father could have sorted out his own house. Or Gran would have done it for him. Or Fiz. She ran up the bill in the first place. Why did he set himself up for these disappointments?

"Well, let me give you a little something before you go," his mother said.

She reached into her drawer and came out with a chequebook. Jack stood looking around the room while she wrote it out. Everything smelled of money. Her fountain pen alone must have been worth the deposit on a small house. She handed him the cheque and he looked down at the amount. A thousand pounds. Just like that. He smiled sadly, but didn't say a word. There might have been a time when he would have been thrilled, but suddenly it seemed so meaningless. This was not what he wanted. This was not what he had come for.

"Perhaps we could do lunch sometime?" she asked.

Jack sighed and grimaced. He looked at the cheque and he looked at his mother. He shrugged and shook his head.

"You know, Mum, you and I really do live on different planets. I don't know why I came. Thanks for sorting out the house, though. You can put this towards your expenses."

He left the cheque on her desk, turned and walked away. It seemed to take for ever to reach the door and his hand was trembling as he turned the knob. His mother didn't speak and Jack didn't look back.

Outside, the sky was falling. He ran through the darkening streets all the way to Bank station. He rode the Central line, crammed in with a thousand other steaming sardines, as far as Bond Street, then changed to the Jubilee which took him north to Neasden. It was a short walk to Albemarle Gardens and an even shorter trip from there to KlΞrM5. He was welcomed by the ever-reliable tropical sun, clean air, the rude jungle bursting with life, colour, mystery. . .

. . .and his father muttering on the garden steps. Jack raced past then stopped, turned and went to sit beside him.

"Hello, father-person," he said.

Cornelius continued to mumble for a few moments, then cleared his throat and looked directly at his son as if trying to remember where they had met.

"How did your lecture go?" Jack asked.

"*Who?* Oh . . . hello. How was London?"

"Icy. In more ways than one. How was your lecture?"

"Lecture? Oh, that . . . I think it went very well. We seem to have solved the problem of television."

"Really? Already? How did you do that?"

Cornelius shrugged modestly and replied, "A grommet is a protective insulator. It occupies and represents a space *in-between*. The Way of the Grommet is the way of inner peace. Peace resides in the space between your thoughts. Or, in their case, the space between television signals. It's simply a matter of finding that space. But they seem to have grasped the technique rather well. Highly-evolved, you know."

Jack gave him a querulous look. He had never known what to make of all this grommet business. Was it possible that his father had actually done something constructive to improve the lives of billions of sentient beings throughout the cosmos, at the same time redeeming the Earth's vicious reputation? All with his little rubber washer thingies? Who'd have thought it?

He laughed and shook his head. He clapped his father on the shoulder and got up. For years he'd felt vaguely ashamed of his dad, and frequently wished that he did something ordinary like drive a bus or work in a factory. A strange new feeling came over him as he realized that his father might well be someone to be enormously proud of. And that was a very nice feeling indeed.

"I think I'll go and get changed," he called out on his way to the lifts. "I'm soaked through."

The professor continued his unblinking gaze into space, then added casually, "Your girlfriend was asking for you."

Jack whirled around and demanded, "What girlfriend? Who was?"

Cornelius got up. He hitched his trousers, straightened his glasses and sauntered over to the dining table. He flipped open a book that was lying there and started flicking through it. A minute crawled by.

"*DAD?!*"

"Hmm? Oh . . . the Arcturan. Zaÿfa. Came up to me after the lecture. Seems a nice girl."

"And she asked after *me*? What did she say? No — what did *you* say?"

Jack felt suddenly alarmed. His father may well have saved the universe, but he knew absolutely nothing about girls.

Cornelius looked at his son.

"She wanted to know if there had been any improvement in your condition. Seemed genuinely concerned."

"My condition?"

"Hmm."

"*What condition?*" There was another worrying pause.

"Oh, you know, the incontinence."

Jack's mouth fell open and a despairing noise escaped. "And you said. . . ?"

"I said that it seemed much better, thank you."

Jack slumped into a chair. He groaned and shook his head.

"You didn't say that! *You wouldn't have.* No, you . . . yes, you did. Well, that's great. That's just perfect." He covered his face with one hand.

"Did you want me to say it had got worse?"

"NO! But you could have said . . . you should have said . . . oh, never mind."

His father sat down as well. He would never understand teenagers. It was impossible to get it right. They had such strange priorities.

Over in the lift shaft, the ropes started moving and they both turned to look. Jack was surprised to see his sister arrive wearing a big smile. Behind her floated a revived Bweeb, which was even more of a surprise.

For nearly three weeks he had lain in a coma. During that time, his colour had gone from pavement grey to white with bursts of luminous green, all of which were very concerning. But the glow slowly faded, and gradually he came back from a washed-out pastel to a deep and healthy azure. His bloated belly shrank back to normal. Fiz and Gran kept a round the clock vigil, mopping his fevered brow and trying to keep him comfortable. There were times when his pulse seemed so weak they thought they had lost him, but Duncan remained confident that he would pull through. He said that he "*smelled of life*".

And he proved to be right.

Jack smiled and waved and said, "So. He's up and floating."

"He's still very weak," Fiz cautioned, "so you'll be spared the usual snog. Just this once."

"That's OK. It's amazing that he survived at all. It's wonderful! I mean, he saved us." Jack turned to his father. "Didn't he, Dad."

"Well, *ahem*. I, er, I guess, in a way, you could say. Yes. In a way."

Jack rolled his eyes at his sister, who by now was looking decidedly nervous. Jack had no idea why that should be. She should have been thrilled. But apparently she had something tricky to say and she stood shifting from one foot to the other, trying to get started.

"Dad?" she said.

Her father was staring into the garden and he looked back with a start.

". . .yes?"

"Remember when Bweeb arrived, the day it all happened? When he swallowed that stuff and risked his life to save us all from an excruciatingly slow and painful death and everything?"

"Well, er . . . yes?"

"And remember how, just before that, he had started to say something? About some good news?"

Cornelius blanked. He didn't remember. He shook his head.

"*DAD!* You do remember! Oh, it doesn't matter. It's just that Bweeb and I have some wonderful news and I just want you to listen. OK? Just listen."

Fiz turned to Bweeb and nudged him gently. "OK. Go on," she said.

There was some momentary shyness, then beaming his big blue smile, he sang, "Me very news good have!"

He paused and Cornelius shifted uneasily in his seat. Jack tried to imagine what was coming, but failed completely.

"Pregnant me! Fiz father will being soon! Soon so!"

If you enjoyed this book, you may email your comments
to: <u>ablackhole@hotmail.com</u>
If you hated it, you may tell your cat.